DEATH ON WARRIORS WAY

DEATH ON WARRIORS WAY

A NOVEL

DAVE PYLE

Death on Warriors Way: A Novel is a work of fiction. Other than historical events, people, and places referred to herein, all names, characters, and incidents are products of the author's imagination. Any resemblance to actual persons, living or dead, is coincidental and unintentional.

Published by Redrocks, Littleton, Colorado

Back cover art by Matthew Pyle
Book design by Second Star Publishing Works

ISBN (paperback): 979-8-9950083-0-9
ISBN (ebook): 979-8-9950083-1-6

Printed in the United States of America

For my sweetheart

PROLOGUE

Early Monday evening, the rain had begun as a whisper, a fine mist brushing against the tall windows of her study. A single lamp cast a pool of amber light across the Persian rug, illuminating the open book in her lap. She lingered on a passage she could not quite absorb, her mind snagging on the restless quiet of the house. Beyond the glass, the pines shivered in the wind, their black silhouettes trembling against the fading sky. The clock ticked, slow and deliberate, each sound louder than it should have been.

As dusk settled over Warriors Way, she could hear through the slightly ajar French door the loud gobbling of the wild turkeys gathering as they prepared to distance themselves from dangerous nighttime predators. She watched, transfixed, as the bulky birds began to lift off one by one, awkwardly at first, wings beating hard, then soaring higher with surprising grace over the roof of her neighbor's house. For a fleeting moment, the scene was otherworldly, like a haunting vision, each bird fluttering aggressively and circling before reaching the upper branches of the tall pines that bordered her property. The trees swayed gently as the flock settled in for the night. For a long moment, she stayed there, the quiet broken only by the whisper of wind and the faint echo of wings, feeling the strange mix of beauty and unease that often came just before nightfall.

She moved to the window, the glass cool beneath her fingertips, and watched as his silhouette appeared on the back deck. The mist softened his outline, but she could still see the faint orange flare of his cigarette each time he drew on it. She hated that glow almost as much as the acrid smell that seeped through the doorframe and clung to everything in the house. He leaned against the railing, unmoving, a phantom in the fog, and she felt the familiar knot of resentment tighten in her chest. He disappeared back into the living room, and now the dreaded sound of a basketball game hummed low and constant through the house: crowd noise, a commentator's voice, the sharp squeak of shoes on polished wood, all of it a reminder of how far apart their lives had drifted.

Back in her chair, she finished the last chapter of her book and closed it with a quiet sigh, the kind that came when a story's spell faded back into real life. The house was still now, until the sudden crack of the front door slamming broke the calm. She sat up, startled, listening as heavy footsteps crossed the front deck, followed by the sharp metallic thud of a car door and the grumble of the SUV coming to life. Headlights swept briefly across the curtains before disappearing down the street. He was heading to the tavern again, leaving behind the faint smell of smoke and the echo of his impatience. He'd forgotten, as always, one of his small promises, this time the simple task of getting the mail.

Moments later, he texted:

I forgot to get the mail, sorry. Got a text, a sensitive computer part for our desktop was delivered and shouldn't sit in a damp mailbox. Please get it as soon as you can.

Through the front door's beveled panes, the wet driveway gleamed like a mirror. She grabbed the mailbag and slipped on her raincoat, the zipper rasping in the silence, and felt the familiar weight of unease settle between her shoulders. The neighborhood, usually dotted with the soft glow of porch lights and the low hum of evening routines, seemed oddly still. Only the faint hiss of rain filled the night air as she stepped outside, the chill soaking through her almost at once.

The walk down her driveway to the street felt longer than it should. Water pooled in a distant gutter, reflecting the stop sign at the corner in a smear of red. She reached the mailboxes, inserted her key, and tugged it open, the metal creak startling in the quiet. For an instant, she thought she heard a soft crunch of gravel behind her, but when she turned, the path was empty. She put the mail into her bag and lifted the small, damp package from the box, heart beating faster now. It seemed as if the night itself had taken notice of her.

She turned into the darkness and began walking up the path toward home when, suddenly, a familiar figure appeared. The sight stopped her mid-step. For a brief second, she thought she could slip back unnoticed, but their gazes locked as her pulse thudded painfully in her throat and fear paralyzed her body. But not for much longer, as this encounter, whether planned or chance, would be a prelude for her last moments.

TUESDAY

CHAPTER ONE

Tuesday, 6:40 a.m.

The mid-March morning began with stillness and steam. James Brookside, a retired Army colonel and former senior intelligence executive, stood at the kitchen window with a hot mug of fresh-brewed coffee in hand. Steam curled into the first sunlight filtering through the glass as he finished a breakfast sandwich. Below, the sweeping view of Deer Park Ridge sparkled beneath a thin coat of frost. At the base of Warriors Way, the red stop sign stood like a lone sentinel.

After more than forty years of sixty-hour work weeks, James relished mornings like this. Retirement meant time to read, hammer out workouts on his Peloton, cycle twenty or thirty miles in the nearby state park, or tackle projects around the house. Still, he found himself bored at times. A friend recently suggested he write a murder mystery, an idea that had crossed his mind more than once.

Marilyn, his wife of more than twenty years and an OB/GYN geneticist at Colorado General Hospital, stepped beside him, already dressed in ski gear. Today was to be extra special; fourteen inches of fresh snow had fallen over the weekend in Breckenridge, and their daughter Robin, a PhD student at CU Boulder, was meeting them there. It would be a chance for her to catch up with Mom and Dad and for Robin and

Marilyn to spend an hour or two on the steepest black runs.

Marilyn leaned against the counter with her coffee and gave James a teasing smile. "So," she began, "do you mind if Robin and I break away for a while today and head over to the black slopes while you cruise the blue groomers? You know, let the experts stretch their legs while you . . . enjoy the scenery."

James raised an eyebrow, setting down his mug. "Enjoy the scenery? That's your delicate way of calling me the old man of the mountain, isn't it? Remember, I have the fastest time down Peak 7 for my age group. At least that's what my fitness app says."

Marilyn laughed, crossing the room to ruffle his thinning hair. "Not old, just . . . wise. Besides, Robin and I can handle the steeps, and you get your fun without feeling like you're about to fall off the planet."

James gave her a mock frown but couldn't hide his grin. "Fine, I'll stick to Peak 7. But don't come crying to me when you two end up waist-deep in moguls with frozen smiles."

She kissed him lightly on the cheek. "We'll survive. Just don't get lost on your easy runs."

As they looked outside, Marilyn frowned. "The turkeys are acting crazy and loud this morning."

James followed her gaze. "They are. Did you see the video of a mountain lion on the side camera last night? It sniffed around the waterfall and kept moving. Happened about 2:30 a.m. I wonder if it killed something in the field, and that's why the turkeys are in a frenzy?"

The broad swath of common ground between the Brooksides' house and Deer Park Ridge Drive rolled gently downhill, a patchwork of mostly brown grasses swaying in the late winter breeze. Rabbitbrush dotted the expanse, its tangled branches a favorite hiding spot for cottontail rabbits and other small creatures. Spiky yucca plants jutted up from the soil like they were reaching for the sky. From a distance, the area looked almost manicured, but up close it was a rugged blend of prairie and foothill scrub—dry, tough, and resilient. Mule deer often wandered through, leaving narrow trails in the grass that only sharp eyes like James's would notice. The open space gave his house a sense of breathing room but also a clear, unobstructed view of any movement between Warriors Way and the main road.

The wild turkeys had gathered near the stop sign to the left of the field, pecking, and fidgeting. Behind them or among them, it was hard to tell, was something oddly shaped. Not moving. Not an animal.

James grabbed his binoculars from the windowsill. Focusing on the area below, he said, "Someone's kneeling . . . or lying down."

Moments later, he made his way briskly down the hill. The air was still sharp with the chilly morning. As he approached the stop sign, the turkeys scattered into the field. And there she was. At first, he didn't recognize her. Then he saw it was Sophie, the neighbor who lived up the street. Her radiant blue eyes, illuminated by the morning sun, looked directly at him. He initially thought she might be alive, but that hope faded quickly.

His mind reeled as he understood the scene before him. Sophie's body was twisted, her head tilted unnaturally and caked with blood and her blond hair was matted with pine needles and gravel. Tracks of blood stained the ground. She was slumped against the stop sign, brutally beaten, violently posed. James immediately assumed she had been murdered.

He froze, throat tightening, the pungent smell of death in the air, the taste of coffee souring in his mouth. His hand trembled as he pulled out his phone.

He dialed 911, then the community manager, then Marilyn. When the 911 operator asked why he was calling, James said, "There's a . . . dead woman here. I think she's been murdered."

James stood a few yards from Sophie's lifeless body, his breath visible in the cold March air as he gripped his phone tightly, waiting for the sheriff to arrive. A heavy knot formed in his stomach, part dread, part disbelief, as he replayed the moment he first saw her slumped against the stop sign. The brutal stillness of the scene pressed on him, and though his Army years had hardened him to violence, this felt different, too close, too personal, a violation of the quiet street he thought he knew. He scanned the empty road, the silence broken only by the wind rustling the rabbitbrush, and James fought the urge to look back at her again. A flicker of anger sparked beneath his shock; whoever did this had not just taken a life but had shattered the fragile sense of safety on Warriors Way.

James paced near the corner to keep warm for what seemed like hours before he saw the black outline of a sheriff's vehicle cresting the hill, causing the wild turkeys to creep cautiously back from the road's edge. He looked at his watch and was surprised to find it had only been fifteen minutes since he made the 911 call. Time seemed to be slowing as his mind raced to better understand his morning discovery.

CHAPTER TWO

Tuesday, Early Morning

The flashing lights of a Spirit County Sheriff's patrol unit cut across the early sun with an emergency vehicle following. The first officer to arrive, Deputy Matt Ryan, quickly used police tape to mark the alleged crime scene boundaries. After he finished, he placed his notebook on the ground, took a knee, and bowed his head in prayer. James could faintly hear him whispering. He admired the touch of humanity in a moment that seemed completely void of it.

Marilyn arrived minutes later, the ski trip forgotten. Her face was composed, but her voice was tight. Her breath was sharp from the brisk walk, and her eyes were wide with disbelief as she took in the terrible scene. She saw James, rigid, haunted, his face pale and his hands clenched into fists at his sides. Without a word, she stepped beside him and placed a hand gently on his back, then slid her arm around him. He didn't look at her, but she felt the tension in his body give way just slightly.

"I'm so sorry," she said quietly, her voice trembling.

James nodded, his eyes still fixed on Sophie's lifeless form. "I found her," he said hoarsely. "I can't unsee this. And I can't just let it go." He turned to her, resolve cutting through the sorrow in his eyes. "I'm going to find out who did this in front of our home. No matter what it takes."

Marilyn, momentarily perplexed, placed her head on his shoulder. "Do you think she could have been hit by a car?"

James shook his head. "The injuries all appear to be to her head and neck. I'm sure she was attacked."

———————

Lieutenant Sam Walker, the incident commander, arrived just as the morning sun began to burn off the chill in the air. He took charge immediately. The forensics team, led by Deputy Chris Michaels, arrived twenty minutes later. Dressed in dark jackets marked "Spirit County Sheriff – Forensics," they moved with quiet precision, their breath visible in the cold as they worked. Yellow evidence markers dotted the area where Sophie's body had been discovered, the once-ordinary corner now a crime scene. A photographer crouched low, capturing the details of the body's position against the post, the blood patterns on the asphalt, and the disturbed gravel nearby. A technician swept the area with a handheld laser scanner, building a 3D model of the scene while analysts collected soil samples, fibers, and anything that could hold trace DNA. Even the wild turkey tracks circling the area were documented; nature's intrusion into a human act of violence.

A smaller team spread out from the epicenter, working methodically up and down Warriors Way to collect potential secondary evidence. They examined tire marks and shoe prints in the once-frozen ground, mapping out paths of travel from the nearby homes. One deputy worked door-to-door, asking residents about any unusual sounds or movement the previous night, while another officer noted exterior security cameras and doorbell devices that might have captured passing cars or figures in the dark. Above them, a drone hovered silently, taking high-resolution aerial photos of the street and surrounding terrain. To the untrained eye, the quiet neighborhood seemed peaceful again, but to the forensics team, it was a fragile canvas, each detail a thread leading to Sophie's killer.

As the pace of activity around Sophie increased, Marilyn withdrew and joined a group of neighbors up the street. James remained, standing silently with his arms crossed. He had seen war zones, led through crises, and sat in briefings with global stakes, but this struck deeper. Sophie had been a mystery to the neighborhood, but she was still a neighbor.

Deputy Ryan, the first officer on the scene, pulled James aside beneath the shade of a ponderosa pine for a first interview. "Can you identify the victim, Mr. Brookside?"

"It's Sophie Delgado," James said, his voice strained. "She lives up the street. Her husband's name is Ricky Delgado. Do you have any idea when this happened?"

Ryan shook his head. "The coroner will have to confirm the time of death, but I'm guessing it was last evening before midnight. Did you see or hear anything unusual Monday night?"

"No. We had a quiet evening. My wife was reviewing patient files so she could take today off for our ski trip. I loaded my Jeep around 11:00 p.m. and then we went to bed. The wild turkeys got our attention this morning. I walked down to the stop sign, saw Sophie, and called 911. That's it."

The deputy jotted notes. "Did Sophie have any enemies on the street?"

James hesitated. "Not that I know of. She didn't really have friends either. She kept to herself. Her husband, Ricky's . . . a bit of a character. Wears a tilted fedora. Dresses like it's 1957. No one knows what he does."

Lieutenant Walker joined James and Deputy Ryan. James gave them Ricky's address and directions so they could inform him of Sophie's death. Before Walker walked away, James asked him if he knew for sure when it happened.

Walker reluctantly answered. "Not a hundred percent. That won't be confirmed until we get the victim back for an autopsy."

Like fingernails on a chalkboard, a familiar voice chimed in. "Hell of a mornin', what happened here? Oh my God, is someone dead?"

It was Kenny Jacobs, a retired investment broker from the next street over, dressed in a yellow safety vest and colorful pajama bottoms. King, his enormous and overly friendly Irish Wolfhound, lumbered beside him and promptly squatted near the tape. James grimaced from the disgusting smell. Kenny, who normally carried an old 4-iron as a walking stick—his defense against the feared mountain lions and bears—wasn't holding it today.

Kenny moved closer to the taped-off area. "Who is it?"

His aggressiveness frustrated James. "Kenny, stay back. It's Sophie Delgado from up the street."

Kenny ignored him. "That's horrible. I saw Todd out walkin' his dogs last night. Around 8, I think. Didn't the deputy just tell you that was about the time this happened? I wonder if he knows anythin'?"

James's jaw tightened. "The deputy didn't give a specific time. And Todd was in Fort Collins yesterday. He didn't get home until almost 11:00 last night. I saw him drive back into the neighborhood."

Kenny shrugged. "Could be. Maybe I'm wrong. Guess that could have been Sunday night. It's just that he's out most nights around 8 to 8:30 with the dogs. You know, us folks from Minnesota are sometimes a little slow. See ya."

Deputy Ryan heard the discussion and asked Kenny for his contact information so he could do a follow-up interview.

Moments later, James saw Lieutenant Walker escorting Ricky to the crime scene. His demeanor was casual, as if he already knew what to expect. Ricky was freshly shaven and smartly dressed wearing a silk shirt, high-waisted pleated pants, a black leather jacket, and, as always, the fedora.

Ricky stopped well short of the stop sign and then slowly moved forward toward Sophie's body with measured steps, his face set and unreadable. He stood for a long moment, eyes fixed on his wife's battered body. The brutality of the attack flickered across his face, his jaw clenched, his breath shallow, and something raw and unguarded appeared to surface. Then it was gone, replaced by a rigid calm that felt practiced, almost rehearsed.

James moved closer to Walker as he conducted a preliminary interview with Ricky. "When did you last see your wife alive?"

"I left the house about 7:30 and went to Red Rocks Tavern and Brew to have drinks with some of the regulars. She was in her study reading."

"What time did you return home?" Walker asked.

Ricky looked more unsettled by the second. "Got back a little after 10:30."

Walker pressed. "And you didn't see Sophie when you got home?"

Ricky responded, "No. We have separate bedrooms. I assumed she'd gone to bed. I didn't check. Look, there's one thing I need to clear up. Sophie and I had a very flexible marriage, more of a living arrangement that worked for us both."

Walker looked at him in a more suspicious light. "You returned at approximately 10:30. Did you see anything unusual as you turned onto Warriors Way? Specifically, your wife's dead body leaning against the stop sign?"

Ricky casually responded, "Nope. Didn't see a thing. Drove to my house, parked, and went to bed."

James, watching and listening, felt a chill. Ricky didn't look sad. He looked . . . inconvenienced. James would later say, "That wasn't the look of a grieving man. That was the look of someone who wants to move on."

To James, Ricky wasn't just strange. He seemed dangerous. And something told him that Ricky and Sophie's past, so carefully buried, was about to surface.

The atmosphere of the scene suddenly changed. With police radios at max volume, a black Chevrolet Tahoe entered Warriors Way and parked on the side of the road twenty yards from the stop sign. The Spirit County Sheriff for ten years, Jason Carson, arrived just as the investigation of the immediate crime scene area was wrapping up, and a wider search was beginning. He delayed exiting the massive vehicle to finish a cell phone call. Still running, the high-performance V-8 motor of the special-edition Tahoe had a distinctive deep-throated growl and rumble that shook the ground beneath James's feet. Carson's driver cut the engine, and out stepped the sheriff, completely dressed in black: cowboy hat, leather jacket and vest, and shiny knee-high boots. He was a character right out of central casting.

Carson was a rare exception in the county, a Black man who was also an elected official. A West Point graduate like James, he had retired from the Army as a lieutenant colonel after serving twenty years with the military police. He was smart, tough, and a no-nonsense kind of guy. The mostly white voters of the county loved his style and appreciated his service in Iraq, which had cost him half of his left foot. He and James had an immediate connection after meeting four years ago. Both men were recruited and played football their first year at the academy, but they were fifteen years apart in age. The rigor of academics and injuries motivated them both to leave their playing days behind sophomore year to focus on the day-to-day grind of making it to graduation.

James and Carson quietly greeted each other, and Carson whispered. "I'm sorry, friend. It's hard to understand how this could happen in front of your own home. Is it true that you found the victim?"

"Yes, it's something I'd like to forget."

Carson nodded. "You know this street and the people who live here. Let one of my deputies know if anything seems out of place or if anyone doesn't fit. The act of murder is surreal for most killers. They often return to the crime scene to confirm what happened. Seeing the aftermath settles it in their minds. Look around, James. He or she could be in that group of neighbors up the street."

James frowned, his gaze following Carson's to the street

and ridge above Warriors Way. "You're saying whoever did this might be watching us now?"

"Wouldn't rule it out. The smart ones stay close, blend into the background, and watch the reaction. If that's true here, James, then we've already been under the murderer's eye."

James took a moment to take in the flurry of activity around the crime scene. "I guess gathering evidence has really gotten complicated?"

Carson stopped and smiled at James. "Yes and no. Most of it is still like folding clothes at Costco, pure grunt work. Don't worry, buddy, we'll figure this out quick."

Their discussion was abruptly interrupted by an older man watching from the adjacent walking trail, speaking loudly on the phone. After a few minutes he moved as close as possible to the crime scene and stared at Sophie until a deputy directed him to step back.

Carson turned and looked back at James. "Do you know that man? Is he a neighbor?"

James nodded. "He lives across the street. Out here most days walking and talking on his phone."

Carson directed his driver to obtain the man's information and conduct a quick interview.

Lieutenant Walker, who had been listening, decided it was time to interrupt. He asked Sheriff Carson if he wanted an update from the forensics team and the coroner. Carson excused himself, and the two men, followed by Dr. Eileen Murphy, the coroner, headed to the crime scene with the now-covered body. Sophie was being prepared for movement.

Deputy Michaels, the forensic team leader, started the update. "No surprises based on our search of the immediate crime area. We haven't found the murder weapon. All evidence has been bagged or assessed and is en route to the lab. I have five deputies walking the base of the foothill behind Warriors Way just to make sure we didn't miss anything."

Then Murphy took over with her report. "The victim was brutally beaten about the head and neck and died from blunt force trauma. The kill shot was a hit next to the left eye. Whoever did this generated a great deal of torque, indicating they used a long-handled weapon, perhaps a hammer or something similar. The actual murder occurred in that marked area, twenty feet from the stop sign. She was dragged and leaned up against the post. The approximate time of death was last night between 7 and 10 p.m. She was wearing a canvas shoulder bag holding mail and advertisements, and she had a small package. Deputy Michaels and I agree that she must have gone out last night, probably early evening, and stopped at the common mailboxes on the other side of the field. For some reason, she walked over fifty yards in the opposite direction of her house and ended up here at the scene of the murder."

Carson eyed the canvas shoulder bag. "What does that bag say?"

Murphy smiled. "It says, 'My Husband Thinks I'm a Lesbian.'"

Carson responded. "Interesting. My wife bought me the same bag for Christmas."

"What do you think your wife was trying to tell you?"

Carson laughed. "I don't know, and she's not saying."

Sheriff Carson thanked the team for their great work and noticed Ricky talking on his cell phone about thirty yards away. Walker asked the sheriff if he wanted to meet him but cautioned that Ricky smelled like he had bathed in Old Spice aftershave.

Carson told Walker, "No worries, Old Spice turns me on."

Walker smiled. "I'm glad you got that going for you. You should know that Ricky mentioned this morning he had a 'flexible living arrangement' with the victim. He didn't explain what that meant. I assume he has someone on the side, and he is just giving us a heads-up."

Carson nodded. "I'll talk to him briefly and direct him to head home for a more detailed interview with you. Make him uncomfortable by suggesting we know more about the murder. If he's not squirming, press harder. Don't let him get a foothold in the conversation. The guy thinks he's a hotshot who should be running with Frank Sinatra and the Rat Pack when, in fact, he's less than one of the disgusting little voles that live in these foothills. Plus, he's the husband and probably should be our number one suspect. Understand?"

Walker got the message loud and clear.

Carson excused himself and walked over to Ricky. The two men spoke quietly. Carson offered his condolences and promised to find the killer. He also told him to head home, and that Lieutenant Walker and another deputy would be there shortly to conduct a more in-depth interview.

Ricky looked extremely uncomfortable.

While Carson was talking to Ricky, Dr. Murphy walked over and introduced herself to James. "I'm the Spirit County Coroner. I just want to verify that you didn't get close to or touch the victim this morning? It's important for us to know so we can better understand potential sources of contamination."

James shook his head. "No, I kept my distance, and no one else was here. Deputy Ryan arrived within fifteen minutes of my call and marked off the area around Sophie."

Dr. Murphy spotted Marilyn standing up the road. "Is that your wife, Dr. Brookside?"

James nodded yes, and Murphy made a beeline for Marilyn and introduced herself.

"Dr. Brookside? I don't mean to intrude at a time like this, but I recognized you. You're the OB/GYN geneticist at Colorado General, aren't you?"

Marilyn blinked, surprised, then gave her a polite nod. "Yes, that's right. But . . . this isn't exactly the best time or place."

Dr. Murphy shifted uneasily, her voice dropping further. "I know, I know, but my daughter has been dealing with a difficult pregnancy. This is my first grandchild. I've been with her for every appointment and now her doctor is saying that a high-risk fetal surgery may be required. I'd really appreciate your opinion on the surgery options. My daughter is so frightened, and this is way out of my practice area."

Stepping away from the crowd, Dr. Murphy explained her concerns in hushed tones and Marilyn thoughtfully answered all her questions.

When they finished, Marilyn touched her arm reassuringly. "I hope I was helpful."

Dr. Murphy exhaled, relief flooding her features. "Yes, thank you. I feel much better."

Marilyn gave her a firm and compassionate hug. "We're both doctors and sometimes we need to lean on each other. I'm sorry I tried to push you away earlier."

Dr. Murphy nodded and returned to the crime scene.

———

After meeting with Ricky, Carson walked back to where Walker was standing. "That guy is hiding something. He just doesn't seem to care that his wife is lying over there with her skull beaten in. How can anyone be that insensitive? And who was that clown in the pajamas when I first got here?"

Walker responded. "Kenny Jacobs, a neighbor from the next street over."

"He looked like a weird dude. Have Ryan interview him ASAP and make sure the forensics team gets doorbell camera footage from his street. Something about the way he hovered and looked at the victim bothered me. I'm not sure if he was just curious or proud of his work. If we find any sign that he may be involved, get a warrant and tear his place apart."

Carson continued. "What about the loud guy on the phone?"

Walker smiled. "He's an 80-year-old neighbor from across the street. One of the original owners and a retired pastor. I guess we missed it, but he was praying for the victim. Nothing there, boss."

Carson walked back over to James. "What do you think the conversation was about between Murphy and Marilyn?"

James looked up at the sky and smiled. "Normally, when

a lady grabs Marilyn like that, it's about a woman's issue. Do you want me to check with Marilyn and give you a report?"

Carson jumped back. "Hell no. Murphy would kick my ass for nosing into her personal business. Don't you dare say anything."

James smiled as he clasped Carson's shoulder and said quietly, "I just want you to know how much I appreciate the way you and your team stepped up this morning. The response means more than you probably realize." He added, "In a moment when everything felt chaotic and wrong, your steadiness and leadership gave the rest of us something solid to hold on to."

Carson nodded, and James finished. "What happened to Sophie matters to me, and it matters to the whole neighborhood. Thank you."

James walked up to where Marilyn was standing. He greeted his neighbors who were watching the morning's events. Marilyn gave him a quick hug. "I'm going home to call Robin and let her know we need to reschedule the ski trip." James nodded, disappointed that they would miss a day on the slopes with their daughter.

———

In stark contrast, the morning took a different turn for Sheriff Carson after he left Deer Park Ridge. His deputy pushed the Tahoe southbound on I-25, the early morning sun streaking across the highway. The murder scene was still fresh in Carson's mind when the radio crackled to life with a report of three motorcycle riders weaving recklessly through traffic at over 100 mph. Before Carson could even comment, the deputy flipped on the lights and siren, and the high-performance SUV surged forward. Carson's blood began to stir. He wasn't one to shy away from action—he still craved it—and there was nothing quite like the roar of a V-8 engine and the scent of burning rubber to get his heart thumping.

As they gained on the riders, the deputy kept the SUV steady at 110 mph, and Carson's radio chirped updates from other units falling into position. The motorcycles darted in and out of lanes like wasps, but the coordination between patrol cars was flawless. Two units leapfrogged ahead, preparing to box the bikes in, while another tailed just behind them. Carson barked quick instructions over the radio, his voice calm but edged with excitement. The thrill of pursuit coursed through him. The familiar rush that reminded him why he'd stayed in law enforcement all these years.

Carson glanced at his driver with a grin, eyes gleaming. "Let's not let these boys think they can outdance Spirit County."

The trap closed fast. Two patrol cars slid ahead, pinching the riders to the shoulder while Carson's Tahoe came up on their tail like a hammer. The motorcycles skidded to a halt, tires squealing, and the riders threw their hands up as deputies leapt out, weapons drawn. Carson stepped from the SUV, boots crunching on the asphalt, adrenaline still surging.

The moment the cuffs clicked shut on the third rider, he couldn't help but chuckle low in his chest. The murder back in Deer Park Ridge was grim and heavy, but this was dangerous and thrilling lawman's work. Carson felt alive again, the chase washing away the darkness that had settled over his morning.

CHAPTER THREE

Tuesday, Midmorning

The forensics team had no luck finding evidence beyond the Warriors Way entrance. Deer Park Ridge was home to over 1,300 families and covered four miles from the front to the back gate. It wasn't just a neighborhood; it had a living presence where silence meant more than speech, and the wind whispered truths the locals had learned to respect. For James and Marilyn, it was a sanctuary from their former chaotic life in the Washington, D.C. area. Now, after Sophie's murder, it was a place shadowed by uncertainty.

Nestled against the foothills of the Rocky Mountains, the community straddled the line between wild and refined. Mule deer and wild turkeys wandered through yards with practiced ease. Bobcats slipped between sandstone boulders at dusk, and bears lumbered wherever they wanted. The towering red rock formations reached toward the sky. At dawn, they burned gold and crimson. At twilight, they flickered with embered light.

James often said the view from their front deck made every day feel like a vacation. Now, even the most familiar ridge lines felt slightly foreign, as though the land were holding its breath. Below their house, the Deer Park Ridge Golf Course carved through the terrain like a sculpted river, its fairways framed by ancient rock monoliths and pines. James had played the course dozens of times but never without pausing to admire a hawk's glide or the glint of sun on stone.

Marilyn, more at home on the nearby trails, often returned from running with dirt on her shoes and peace in her eyes. "The rocks feel like old souls," she told him once. "Not indifferent, just patient."

Before going inside his house, James spotted Manny, his always-friendly, always-helpful neighbor, bent over his gleaming silver 1960 Porsche 356, carefully buffing the fender as if nothing in the world mattered more than the shine.

"Morning, Manny," James said, his voice heavier than usual. "Not the kind of day I ever thought we'd have on Warriors Way. Finding Sophie like that, well, I'll never forget it."

Manny straightened, resting his rag on the windshield frame. His brow furrowed, but he tried for a steady tone. "I heard, man. Word travels quick. I can't even wrap my head around it. She was just … there. And then gone like that? My wife is really upset."

James nodded, folding his arms as his gaze drifted from the polished Porsche to the stop sign in the distance. "The sheriff's office is digging in hard. I mean, look at all the resources they have out here collecting evidence. I have no inside information, but I can't shake the feeling that whoever did this isn't a stranger who wandered through."

Manny ran the rag slowly across the hood, eyes narrowing as he leaned closer to James. "Come on man, you're saying it's someone here? On our street?"

The question hung in the crisp morning air, and James met his neighbor's eyes, choosing his words carefully. "I'm saying we all need to pay closer attention than we ever have before."

———

James cut across Manny's yard back to his house. As he reached the front porch, he turned and looked down at Warriors Way. There was a shift like a tremor just beneath the surface. The murder hadn't just taken a life; it had disrupted the rhythm of the place as the morning progressed. Neighbors who had been watching the police activity looked unsettled as they returned home. Kenny lingered on a far corner with his dog, King, sniffing for friendly neighbors who should be out for their morning walks. James's neighbor John, who normally arrived to "work" on his nearby property by 8:30 a.m., hadn't shown.

James had now been outside for almost two hours, and suddenly he became aware of the cool March air cutting against his cheeks. The image of Sophie's battered body still clung to him like a shadow he couldn't shake. Below, at the entrance of Warriors Way, the sheriff's deputies moved methodically, finishing their investigation, measuring and collecting what little the wind hadn't stolen during the night. Their voices carried faintly up the hill, low and purposeful.

Above him, a red-tailed hawk circled in slow, patient arcs. The bird was almost motionless in the air despite the breeze, its keen eyes fixed on the open ground beyond the pines. James watched it dip lower, tightening its pattern, each pass more deliberate than the last. There was a brutal elegance in its hunt, silent calculation mixed with instinct. He found himself unable to look away, mesmerized by the tension between stillness and sudden violence.

Then he glanced back at the deputies below, and the parallel struck him with unnerving clarity. They, too, were circling, drawing ever-smaller rings around the truth of what had happened to Sophie. Each question, each piece of evidence, each quiet exchange between them was another pass over the field. Somewhere out there, he thought, the murderer they were searching for was still moving freely in the neighborhood's shadows, but he hoped not for long.

James joined Marilyn in the kitchen, where they tried to call their friends Todd and Julia Krantz, who lived at the end of Warriors Way. No answer. Marilyn texted Julia, still nothing. That was surprising. The two couples were very close, having both moved to Deer Park Ridge about five years ago and renovated their homes at the same time.

Todd, an aerospace engineer, had recently retired from a local defense contractor. A leader in emerging engine technology related to the Artemis moon mission, he was burnt out from brutal hours and too much time on the road. Julia, a senior VP at a major IT firm, was still working. She had recently begun drafting a book on corporate culture, using her deep understanding of generational issues from years in leadership positions as the foundation for her narrative. James sometimes teased her about making the book a murder mystery instead. She'd smile and tell him to write his own damn book.

The couples usually had dinner out every weekend and rarely missed trivia night at Red Rocks Tavern. Conversation flowed easily. Correct answers, not so much. But they were all highly educated, politically aware, and family focused. No longer night owls, most evenings out for them ended by eight, followed by TV, books, and early bedtimes.

James and Todd had many common interests. They played in a band that gigged at Red Rocks a couple of times a month, performing '60s and '70s rock with the occasional Sting cover. Other neighborhood musicians sometimes joined in. Julia and Marilyn often accompanied the band as backup singers, and both could play a mean cowbell.

James and Todd were also avid cyclists. The Sunday morning before the murder, when the weather was unusually warm, they clipped into their road bikes and began the steady climb up Deer Creek Canyon, one of their favorite routes for its mix of beauty and challenge. The narrow ribbon of asphalt wound its way through the foothills, flanked by steep rock walls, stands of ponderosa pines, flocks of sheep, and sprawling ranches with weathered split-rail fences. As they pedaled higher, the air cooled, and the scent of sun-warmed sagebrush drifted across the road. An eagle circled lazily overhead, and in the distance, the jagged outline of the Front Range shimmered under a brilliant blue sky. Todd and James took turns pushing a steady cadence.

After the ride, the friends coasted back down the canyon, the cooler air whipping past as they dropped into the valley below. By the time they rolled into the parking lot, their legs were pleasantly spent, and their jerseys streaked with salt. They loaded their bikes and headed to a small brunch spot in Morrison, just a couple of miles from the world-famous Red Rocks Amphitheater. They found a rustic café with a sunlit patio and the smell of fresh coffee drifting from the open windows. Over steaming mugs and plates of huevos rancheros, they recapped the ride and laughed about Todd's near miss with a squirrel darting across the road.

As the conversation drifted, Todd mentioned how quiet Warriors Way had been lately. He hadn't seen any of his neighbors, including Ricky and Sophie. James brushed it off, chalking it up to Sophie's usual reclusiveness, but he caught the edge in Todd's voice, a subtle tension that felt out of place in the Sunday calm.

Now, the silence from Julia and Todd that Tuesday morning felt . . . off.

CHAPTER FOUR

Tuesday, Midmorning

A search warrant for Ricky and Sophie's house was approved at 9:30 a.m. on Tuesday morning. By 9:50, a forensics team arrived at their house in unmarked SUVs and vans, moving silently into the driveway. Deputies secured the perimeter while the white-suited technicians fanned out across the property, carrying cameras, evidence kits, and fingerprint dusting tools. The lead investigator, Deputy Kimmel, a seasoned detective with a measured voice, directed her team to work methodically: one pair photographing the exterior and entry points, another sweeping the porch railing and front door for prints. Unlike most homes in the neighborhood, the outside of the house was a bit shabby and should have been repainted years ago. The front, back, and one side were overgrown with low-quality bushes and shrubs. The front deck had a beautiful view but was in poor shape and probably needed to be replaced.

Inside, the house was eerily quiet. In the kitchen, a half-filled glass of bourbon stood near a bottle on the counter, its rich amber tones catching the light. Upstairs, the primary bedroom showed subtle signs of unfinished chores, with clean folded laundry on the bed, two drawers slightly ajar, and a large, open jewelry box on the dresser with what appeared to be expensive jewelry and a woman's diamond Rolex watch.

During the search that morning, two rooms stopped the deputies in their tracks.

The first was a combination office and library. A hand-painted sign on the door reading "Sophie's Space," with her signature on the bottom, established ownership of the room. Tucked behind a set of double doors off the main hall, it was a striking contrast to the rest of the modestly decorated home. Floor-to-ceiling built-in bookshelves holding hundreds of carefully arranged volumes, their spines a blend of academic texts, best sellers, classic literature, and medical journals. Centered on a middle shelf was a large trophy featuring a tennis player. The inscription read: *Texas State Champion, High School Division 6A, 2002.* Next to it was a picture of a young woman holding the same trophy. It was hard to tell, but the deputies concluded it was a picture of Sophie.

Rich mahogany furniture anchored the room, and a deep brown leather reading chair sat beside a small side table bearing a crystal tumbler and a closed book, as if she had just stepped away. Expensive, abstract artwork adorned the walls, but it was the far side of the room that drew everyone's gaze: a wall of French doors, glass panes shimmering in the morning light, revealing a sleeping garden beyond. Rows of perennials that would certainly be spectacular in springtime, and a variety of rose bushes just waiting to stir back to life. It was a space of elegance, intellect, and solitude: Sophie's private world, hidden in plain sight.

The sheriff's team also opened a heavy, soundproof door at the back of the main hallway and stepped into a surprisingly well-appointed workout room. The space was spotless and professionally equipped, featuring a commercial-grade treadmill, a full rack of free weights, and five high-end workout machines arranged with precision. A mirrored wall reflected the sterile order of the room, while a surround-sound music system was built into the ceiling, controlled by a wall-mounted tablet. The air smelled faintly of eucalyptus, and folded towels were stacked neatly on a chrome shelf in the corner. A whiteboard was mounted on the wall with Sophie's workout schedule and progress. There were no signs of Ricky ever using the equipment. It was another room—a stark contrast to the rest of the modest, dated décor—clean, modern, and obsessively maintained.

Deputy Kimmel texted Lieutenant Walker, "You're going to want to see the gym when you get here. Exactly what you want for your house."

In a chest of drawers in what the deputies concluded was Ricky's bedroom, they found a men's University of Michigan sweatshirt and old pictures from college. More interestingly, investigators found four graduate-level chemistry textbooks arranged on a shelf. They were dense with advanced material related to biochemistry, drug design, pharmacology, and the development of advanced medical therapies, raising questions about why Ricky, a man with no known scientific background, would have them. Some volumes had bookmarks and annotations in the margins, suggesting they had been actively studied rather than collected for show. A ticket stub for the Michigan State vs. Michigan football game on October 21, 2000, was used as a marker in one of the books. To the detectives, the presence of these texts hinted at a hidden side to Ricky's life, one that might connect to the mystery unfolding on Warriors Way.

While the search of his house was underway, Ricky patiently waited in the kitchen for Lieutenant Walker. It was now almost three hours since Sheriff Carson had told him to head home and wait. Walker knocked on the door and let himself inside. Ricky greeted him and offered iced tea or a soda. Walker declined and placed his water bottle on the table.

Since joining the sheriff's department eight years ago, Lieutenant Walker had built a reputation as a dependable, even-keeled officer with exceptional instincts and an unshakable moral compass. He didn't seek attention, but people listened when he spoke, whether on a crime scene, in the community, or at a department briefing. Sheriff Carson often relied on Walker for the most sensitive investigations, and his military background proved especially useful during high-stakes cases. While junior deputies leaned on procedure, Walker brought a deeper sense of perspective and was always willing to go the extra step to understand motive, emotion, and human complexity. His presence on the Sophie Delgado case gave the investigation a steadier hand.

"Shall we begin?" asked Walker.

Ricky nodded.

Walker pressed the start button on his recording machine.

DELGADO INTERVIEW TRANSCRIPT

Walker: This is Lieutenant Walker with Ricky Delgado, husband of the deceased, Sophie Delgado. It is 11:10 a.m. on March 17th. Mr. Delgado, do you understand you're not under arrest and are free to leave at any time?

Delgado: Yeah. Carson said this was routine. I'm not going anywhere.

Walker: How long have you and Sophie been together or married?

Delgado: We met through work in 2009 and married after about a year of dating in 2010.

Walker: When was the last time you saw your wife alive?

Delgado: Last night. A little before … 7:30. She was sitting in her study by the window like she always does.

Walker: What were you doing at that time?

Delgado: I was watching the start of the Nuggets game in the den. Had a whiskey, maybe two.

Walker: Did you and Sophie argue last night?

Delgado: We didn't argue. We … we didn't talk much anymore if that's what you're fishing for.

Walker: Any reason for Sophie to leave the house last night?

Delgado: I . . . I don't think so. She didn't like going out at night. But you know women, sometimes they step out to clear their heads. Also, I forgot to get the mail for the last few days. That didn't have her in the best mood. Maybe she went to the mailboxes to get it.

Walker: Did you leave the house last evening?

Delgado: Yes, I left just after 7:30 and went to Red Rocks Tavern & Brew. The place was pretty quiet, being a Monday night. I was there for a while with the guys and came home at about 10:30.

Walker: When did you realize she was missing?

Delgado: We have separate bedrooms, so not until this morning. I woke up, made coffee, and didn't see her. Walked the house and . . . nothing.

Walker: Why didn't you call anyone?

Delgado: Because she's a grown woman. She sometimes goes for walks, runs, or goes to the store early. I didn't think anything of it.

Walker: Neighbors describe you as private. Some say they've never seen you work a regular job. Can you tell me about your income?

Delgado: That's not your business, is it? Let's just say I made good investments back in the day. We didn't want for anything.

Walker: Did Sophie have any enemies? Anyone who might want to harm her?

Delgado: Sophie wasn't exactly Miss Congeniality, you know? She kept to herself. But enemies? No.

Walker: Let me ask again, where were you between 8 and 10 p.m. last night?

Delgado: I already told you, I was at Red Rocks. Mike the bartender will back my story.

Walker: Can anyone else verify that?

Delgado: People come and go. I was talking to everyone and no one. Mike will probably remember who was there last night.

Walker: You have an interesting collection of advanced chemistry books. Are they yours from college?
Delgado: No. I didn't go to college. I bought them at a garage sale. Thought they might be interesting.

Walker: So, you didn't go to the University of Michigan?
Delgado: No.

Walker: We'll need you to stay in town while we investigate.
Delgado: I'm not going anywhere, Lieutenant. But let me say this, Sophie wasn't easy to live with. But I didn't kill her.

Walker: Good to know that you didn't murder your wife. I just want to ask again about the University of Michigan. We found a men's 'Go Blue' sweatshirt and a ticket stub from the Michigan State vs. Michigan football game in 2000. So, you have no connection to Michigan?
Delgado: No. I liked the team when I was younger.

Walker: We'll keep you informed on the progress of our investigation. Do you have any questions of me?
Delgado: No.

Walker: I have no further questions. It is 11:40 a.m. on March 17th.

END OF TRANSCRIPT

Walker stopped the recording machine. At this point, Ricky was clearly distressed. The smell of his sweat, mixed with Old Spice aftershave, had Walker feeling slightly nauseated.

In the basement, two technicians examined a set of muddy boots by the back door and noted a locked cabinet that seemed out of place. Another began swabbing door handles and light switches for DNA while a colleague set up alternate light sources to search for hidden blood traces. Outside, a pair of investigators sifted through garbage bins, carefully bagging torn envelopes, receipts, and a crumpled-up map of Deer Park Ridge. The air inside the house smelled faintly of fingerprint powder and latex gloves. Every detail, no matter how small, was logged, photographed, and bagged, as the team worked to piece together the final hours before Sophie's life ended so violently.

By the time the forensic team wrapped up their search in the early afternoon, it was clear that nothing overtly incriminating had surfaced. The house, while slightly disordered in places, offered no signs of a violent confrontation: no blood, no weapon tucked away in a closet, and no trace evidence linking the crime to Ricky directly. The fingerprints collected were mostly from the homeowners, and the locked basement cabinet, once opened under a search warrant, revealed nothing more than boxes of old financial documents and a stack of vintage playing cards. Even the muddy boots in the laundry room didn't match the distinctive tread pattern found near Sophie's body. As the team packed up their equipment, a quiet sense of frustration settled over the group. The house seemed almost too ordinary, as if it were designed to keep its secrets buried just out of reach.

Deputy Kimmel let Walker know they were done. Walker gave her a half salute as he thanked Ricky for being forthcoming with his answers. He also informed him that, in addition to the evidence collected, they had taken digital images of fourteen pictures and detailed handwritten notes found in the four textbooks. On behalf of the sheriff's department, he again offered his condolences and assured Ricky they would do all they could to find justice for him and his family. Ricky nodded his head and offered a half smile.

CHAPTER FIVE

Tuesday, Late Morning

While the search of the Delgado house was ongoing, a knock, sharp and deliberate, came at the Brooksides' door just after II a.m. James opened it to find Deputy Ryan on the porch, a notebook in hand and a polite but unreadable expression on his face. Marilyn, now in running gear, joined James and Ryan in the living room; outside, the crime scene vans still dotted Warriors Way, a constant reminder of the brutal discovery.

"Mr. and Dr. Brookside, good to see you again. I just need to clarify a few details about last night and this morning. Is that okay?"

"Of course," James replied evenly as the three sat down. "We want to help however we can."

"Please tell me about last night and this morning in as much detail as possible," Ryan began.

Marilyn spoke first, her voice steady. "I was working in our office last night. At about 8:30, my neighbor Julia Krantz stopped by to drop off a book for our book club. She seemed off, maybe a little nervous. She told me her husband, Todd, hadn't got home from Fort Collins yet, so she had to walk the dogs. They were really being crazy."

"Did the two of you talk?"

"Julia didn't say much other than she hoped I could get through the book by Thursday. I said that I'd probably only be able to give it a quick scan, and she joked that most people do the same. Then she left quickly. This morning, we were looking out the window, saw the turkeys acting agitated by the stop sign, and James went down to look and found Sophie."

"In as much detail as possible, what was Julia wearing?" Ryan asked.

Slightly surprised, Marilyn responded, "She had on blue jeans, a gray top, and a navy-blue rain jacket that zipped down the front. It had a Baylor University logo. I think she was wearing running shoes. She was also carrying their big metal flashlight. A lot of people here carry them at night for protection."

"Excellent," Ryan said. "Thank you. Please tell me what you know about the victim."

As Deputy Ryan flipped through his notepad, Marilyn hesitated, then spoke. "Sophie was not very social. She normally dressed in what I would call casual attire, oversized clothes, rarely any makeup. She was a big runner, always by herself at a punishing pace. I did see and talk to her on occasion."

Marilyn paused. "I was at a medical conference in Denver last summer, a symposium on chronic pain management. Sophie was sitting in the back of a seminar on new non-opioid pain medications. She was professionally dressed, sharp-looking, almost . . . corporate. It caught me off guard. She didn't seem like the woman from down the street. She looked right at me, gave a slight nod, but didn't stop to talk. It was . . . strange."

"Any other significant interactions?"

"About five months ago, I stopped at Safeway, and there she was in the checkout line, again looking like a 5th Avenue model for corporate attire. A stylish dark suit, her hair tastefully done, perfect makeup. A shocking transformation. She was stunning, beautiful and very, very fit. Oh, and I forgot to mention this to James. I talked to her briefly yesterday afternoon at the library. She had a book we had read recently in our book club. I gave her the name of this month's book and suggested she join us. At first, Sophie seemed enthusiastic, and then she told me she might have a conflict."

Ryan pointed his pen at James. "Mr. Brookside, we talked earlier, but please tell me again about last night and this morning."

James sat up straight. "Nothing special was going on last night. We were planning to go skiing today, so I wanted to get everything done. I loaded my Jeep at about 11 p.m. with the garage open. I saw what looked like Todd Krantz's SUV drive up the street. As I was finishing, Todd walked up our driveway with his dogs. He said he had just gotten back from working on his rental property in Fort Collins. As I think about it, he seemed a little shaken and wasn't interested in an extended conversation. That was understandable. The dogs were restless, and it had been a long day for him. We said our goodbyes, and he was off toward his house. The whole thing took a little less than five minutes."

"What about this morning?"

"We heard the wild turkeys. Something near the stop sign didn't seem right. I quickly changed, walked down, and found

Sophie. I didn't touch anything. Just grabbed my phone and called 911, the community manager, and Marilyn. You and I talked shortly after you marked the area with police tape. One thing was odd though, Kenny, the guy with the crazy outfit and big dog, mentioned that he saw Todd out walking his dogs around 8 p.m. When I told him Todd was up in Fort Collins, he quickly backed off the comment. I felt like Kenny had been caught in a lie."

Ryan's expression hardened. "James, you have a direct line of sight to the stop sign from your house. The victim was dead and leaning against the signpost when you were talking to Todd last night. How did you not see her?"

James's face flushed. "It was drizzling and pitch black. This is a dark-sky community, which means we don't have streetlights, and homes are minimally lit. Unless you have a full moon, it's difficult to see distant objects."

Ryan nodded, leaned forward, and spoke in a much more aggressive tone. "Beyond what you've told me, do you have anything else you want to add? Were either of you out on the street or near the stop sign last night? You've told me you first saw her body this morning. Is that true? Again, you didn't see her last night? You didn't get into a confrontation with the victim?"

James and Marilyn were shocked at the deputy's tone. After looking at each other, they both shook their heads.

Deputy Ryan stood. "Thank you both for providing additional information. Just one more question. Have either of you talked to Todd or Julia Krantz since last night?"

James acknowledged that they had tried to call and text earlier, but there had been no response.

Ryan nodded. "I understand. I'm heading to the Krantz house now. Please do not call them or share what we just discussed."

The couple nodded in agreement.

James walked Ryan to the front porch. The deputy stopped, turned sharply, and leaned in close. "Mr. Brookside," he said in a muffled voice, "I spoke with a neighbor this morning. She said you'd been helping the victim with her garden, unloading bags of mulch from the victim's SUV last summer and carrying them to the backyard. She also mentioned seeing you in Mrs. Delgado's yard, talking for quite some time. According to her, Mrs. Delgado often remarked about how helpful you were, even saying she wished she had someone like you instead of her lazy husband. So, are you leaving something out about your relationship with her? Did you spend much time at the Delgado home?"

James froze, caught off guard. It took him a moment to gather himself. "No," he said finally. "I was walking back from Todd Krantz's house when I saw her struggling with the mulch. I helped unload about fifteen large bags, and she showed me her garden. The whole thing took maybe twenty minutes. I told Marilyn about it the same day."

"How convenient that you were the one to find the body," Ryan said, his voice edged with suspicion. "An attractive younger woman, unhappy in her marriage, but maybe interested in you. We'll find out soon enough if you're lying about your relationship with her. Were you involved? Better to tell me now, otherwise, you'll be one of my top suspects."

James stiffened, his patience gone. "I respect your badge, Deputy, but that's a ridiculous accusation. I did nothing more than help a neighbor. That's it. Now go do your job."

Ryan, taller and looming over him, gave a thin smile. "Asking tough questions is my job. I'm satisfied, for now. Thank you, Mr. Brookside."

After Ryan left, James slammed the door and looked at Marilyn. "That bastard implied that I might have been having an affair with Sophie. What the hell?"

Marilyn responded. "I know there's nothing to it. Maybe he was just trying to get a reaction from you."

James was so distraught that he decided he needed professional advice. He called a retired police officer buddy who lived nearby and told him the basics of what happened that morning. They agreed to meet later that afternoon at the Brooksides' home.

———

Deputy Ryan drove to the Krantz house. Julia opened the door as Todd escorted their large, overly playful dogs to the bedroom. Once settled in the living room, Julia mentioned that another deputy had already been by about an hour ago. Ryan had notes from the earlier visit but clarified that he needed to ask follow-up questions.

"So, according to your earlier interview, you did not see or hear anything related to the alleged murder?" Ryan started.

Todd answered first. "No. We live at the end of the street and sit down below the main part of Warriors Way. The stop sign is about a hundred yards away, but we can only see it from our back deck. It being March, nighttime, and with the light rain, we weren't out there. This morning, we could see the flashing lights. Julia and I walked to a point where we could see the police activity but came back. We had nothing to offer, so why interfere?"

Julia looked at Todd and back at Ryan. "I really don't have anything to add. The deputy didn't tell us anything earlier about the victim. Was it someone from our street?"

Ryan looked directly at her. "Her name was Sophie Delgado. I believe she lived five houses from you?"

Julia turned pale. "Sophie? When did this happen?"

"Last evening before midnight, probably between 7 and 10."

Todd jumped in. "The Delgados really keep to themselves. We don't know much about them."

"It's my understanding that you dropped off a book at the Brookside house around 8:15 to 8:30. You apparently were walking two large dogs and carrying a long, heavy-duty metal flashlight. Is that correct?"

Julia nodded. "The book was for our book club meeting this coming Thursday. Todd was late getting back from Fort Collins, so I had to walk the dogs. We carry a flashlight at night for light and protection. We have predators like mountain lions and bobcats that are often out in the evening."

"So, you didn't see anything unusual or cross paths with Sophie Delgado?"

"No. I dropped the book off to Marilyn and walked back home. I didn't see anyone else, although I thought I saw the shadow of a person near a pine tree in the opposite direction I was walking. That's it. I have nothing else to add."

Ryan turned his attention to Todd. "I understand that you were in Fort Collins yesterday and got home somewhere close to 11 p.m. Is that correct?"

"Yes."

"What did you do after you got home?"

Todd hesitated. "The dogs were restless, so I decided to walk them again. James was in his garage loading his Jeep for a ski trip. We talked briefly, and I returned home."

"Did you go near the stop sign or see anything unusual? Did you see anyone else out on the street?"

Todd shook his head.

Ryan looked around the living room and noticed a family picture on the wall. "Does anyone else live with you?"

"No," Julia said. "Our daughter, Faith, graduated from college two years ago and took a job in Dallas. She visits often, but I'm certain she never met the Delgados. We've all seen Sophie running through the neighborhood. Faith just ran her first marathon and wishes she was that fast."

Ryan made a few notes and looked at Todd and Julia. "Do either one of you work?"

"Todd is retired," Julia answered. "I took the day off because the police activity was blocking the Warriors Way entrance."

Ryan looked steadily at Todd. "One last question. When you came home last night, you turned onto Warriors Way within ten feet of the stop sign. Based on the location of the crime scene, it's hard for me to understand how you didn't see the victim's body. Can you explain that to me?"

Todd returned Ryan's gaze. "I don't know, and I can't really explain how I missed her. It was late and dark, and I just wanted to get home after a long day."

Ryan thanked them for being forthcoming and left.

Todd closed the front door, his hands trembling as he turned to Julia. "God, you were too nervous. He could see it, you were practically shaking."

Julia pressed her palms against her temples, pacing across the living room. "Of course I was shaking, Todd. Sophie is dead, and I was out there around the same time! They're going to put this on me."

"Look, I didn't tell you this last night because I was scared, but I did see Sophie's body when I walked the dogs. She was against the post. There was blood everywhere. I know you didn't do this. Okay?"

Julia hesitated and whispered. "Okay."

Todd's voice cracked as he tried to steady her. "We stick to what we told him. You walked the dogs, dropped the book off with Marilyn, and came straight back. That's it. Simple."

Julia nodded. "How long do you think it will take before they realize Sophie Delgado is Kate Jennings and find out that she killed my sister? I'm really scared."

Julia stopped and stared at him; her eyes widened with fear. "What if Marilyn told them I seemed upset or that there was a stain on my jacket? They'll pick that apart."

Todd swallowed hard, his face pale. "Then we hold the line. We don't let them twist it. You didn't kill her, Julia. But if you start cracking, they'll make you their easy answer."

"I can feel it already," Julia whispered. "They're circling me. And I don't know how long I can keep it together. What if the police blame me for her death? My God, what are we going to tell Faith?"

Todd hugged Julia and didn't say anything as he noticed a small scratch on her neck.

Deputy Ryan's next stop was the home of Kenny Jacobs, which was located near Warriors Way. The house sat high on a foothill, and Ryan guessed that it had a commanding view of the community and even downtown Denver. He was surprised to see the covered pool off the front patio; private pools were rare in Colorado.

Kenny answered the door at the first knock. Clearly, he'd been watching and waiting.

Ryan introduced himself and entered the large, impressive home. Kenny had changed out of his yellow vest and pajama bottoms and was now wearing a tasteful cashmere sweater and dress slacks. He was also wearing a Rolex watch and expensive leather shoes. The outfit contrasted with his dog-walking attire. The two sat at a table next to the massive kitchen. The Wolfhound sat between them and seemed to be following the conversation.

Ryan started by asking the typical questions. Kenny had lived in Deer Park Ridge for over ten years. He was a very private person, especially since his wife died from cancer four years ago. He was fully retired. His one vice was golf. In good weather, he played three or four times a week at either Deer Park Ridge or Sparrow Hawk, a private club in an exclusive neighborhood next to Deer Park Ridge.

Ryan asked his next question. "You were walking your dog last night on Warriors Way between 8 and 9, is that correct?"

Kenny's eyes closed and opened. "I walk my dog most nights about that time, but last night I was out early, probably around 7 p.m."

Ryan looked stern. "You told James Brookside you saw Todd Krantz walking his dogs around 8 p.m. We have doorbell camera footage from Warriors Way and your street. Do you want to rethink what you just told me?"

Kenny adjusted in his seat. "It could have been later. I sometimes get my nights mixed up. But regardless, I didn't see anythin' unusual last night. I didn't go near the stop sign or see the victim."

"Did you know Sophie Delgado or ever cross paths with her?"

Kenny's eyes lingered on King. "I sometimes saw her out on the street. Hard to miss or ignore. She was stunnin', an extremely attractive woman, although she dressed down to hide it for some reason."

"A couple of neighbors mentioned that you had a confrontation with Sophie last fall that got a little out of control. Something to do with your dog?"

Kenny turned red. "That's true. My dog, King, slipped his collar and got into her rose bushes. King is big and playful. When Sophie came outside, he jumped at her and tried to lick her hand. Sophie kicked him, which really upset me. After I got his collar back on, I apologized, but she didn't want to hear it. I left after a couple of minutes. She yelled a few choice things at me as I walked away. Not sure what she was sayin'. I assumed Sophie was havin' a difficult day."

"Any other encounters?"

Kenny's breathing was heavy. "No. Again, I felt bad about King goin' on her property. You should know that the Delgados' yard is a mixed bag. It looks horrible from the front, all overgrown and ratty lookin'. On the side, out of view, is a pristine garden area. During the summer months, there are all kinds of flowers arranged in several beds, and of course, the roses—all kinds of roses. I assume that was all Sophie's doin'."

Ryan looked around. "Anyone else live with you?"

"No. As I said, my wife died four years ago. We didn't have any children. I don't socialize much other than with my golf groups."

"I understand you normally carry a golf club when you walk your dog. You didn't have it this morning. Was there a reason?"

"I always carry it at night for protection, but only sometimes during the day."

Ryan started to feel something was off. "You're pretty dressed up now. What's up with the pajamas when you walk the dog?"

Kenny's eyes quickly reddened. "As a joke, my wife bought matching pajamas for me and King the Christmas before she died. The dog went nuts when I tried to put them on for a picture. I started to wear the bottoms just to make her smile. It's been over four years now, and I can't stop. It makes me think of my wife. I know people think I'm crazy, but so what? I don't need to impress anyone in this neighborhood."

"Our team is reviewing all the evidence collected today, including the doorbell cameras. Please call me if you remember anything else or feel that you need to correct any of your statements. It would be a big mistake to provide misleading information in a murder investigation. Also, we'll probably call you in for a more formal interview soon. Do you understand?"

Kenny nodded, and Ryan left.

At exactly noon, Lieutenant Walker stepped up to the portable podium set in front of the Deer Park Ridge Community Center. The media had gathered quickly: local TV crews, a few Denver outlets, and several community bloggers, all eager for answers.

"Good afternoon," Walker began, his face composed but grave as he presented talking points prepared by the department's public affairs officer. "Early this morning, at approximately 6:45 a.m., the body of a female resident was discovered near the entrance to Warriors Way. The victim has been identified as Sophie Delgado. This is an active homicide investigation, and we are treating the crime scene with the highest level of forensic attention. At this time, we believe the incident occurred on Monday evening, and the body remained undiscovered overnight." He paused as camera shutters clicked.

"We are collaborating with the Spirit County Coroner's Office, forensic specialists, and crime scene analysts. We are also seeking any residents who may have seen or heard anything unusual between 7 and 10 p.m. last night."

Hands shot up, and Walker pointed at a reporter from Channel 7. "Lieutenant, were there any signs of forced entry or robbery?" she asked.

"No," Walker replied. "The victim was found in a public location, not in or near a residence. There are no signs of robbery as a motive."

Another reporter from *The Denver Post* followed up: "Are you looking at any persons of interest?"

Walker nodded slightly. "We have begun interviewing neighbors and close contacts. At this point, no one has been detained or charged. We're asking for patience while we verify timelines and collect surveillance footage. And yes," he added, anticipating the next question, "we are analyzing DNA evidence recovered from the scene."

A murmur spread through the crowd.

"We are committed to solving this case swiftly and thoroughly. The safety of this community is our top priority. Thank you."

Walker retreated into the community center and took a couple of deep breaths. Dealing with the press was one of his least favorite parts of the job, but he had done an excellent job of hitting the key talking points. He pulled out his phone and called his wife to let her know the next few days would be long and difficult.

The afternoon brought high tension for Todd and Julia. Immediately after Deputy Ryan left their house, they began destroying evidence. Todd stood over the utility sink, scouring a bloodstain out of Julia's rain jacket for the third time before running it through their washing machine's heavy-duty cycle, while she scrubbed furiously at the laces and treads of her running shoes.

"It's not enough," Julia whispered, her voice shaking. "They'll find something, they always do. Maybe we should throw everything away just to be safe."

"Okay, everything except the rain jacket. It has the Baylor University logo. Ryan will be suspicious if he comes back looking for it and you don't have it. So, the jeans, top, and shoes go in the dumpster when you go to Target. No one will ever check there. And the flashlight, I'll take care of the old one. Buy the same model, pay cash, we'll keep it in the drawer as if nothing happened."

Julia nodded, her eyes hollow. She slipped the clothes and

shoes into a trash bag, and headed out. After tossing them into a grimy dumpster behind Target, she went inside. At the register, Julia laid down wrinkled bills for a brand-new flashlight, forcing a casual smile as though she were just another shopper preparing for a camping trip.

Todd was on a separate mission. He pulled his SUV into one of the many parking areas inside Chatfield State Park. With his hands trembling, he pulled the heavy-duty flashlight from a duffel bag. The metal casing still bore faint dents where Julia had struck Sophie, though he had scrubbed it obsessively.

"No one can ever see this again," he muttered under his breath.

With a pair of heavy-duty tin snips, he sat in his SUV and cut the flashlight into jagged chunks, sweat beading on his forehead despite the cool March air. Each metallic snap echoed in his chest like a gunshot.

Over the next hour, Todd drove slowly through the park, stopping at random trailheads and picnic areas. He moved with calculated calm, dropping two or three pieces of the flashlight into trash cans scattered across miles of wooded land. At one stop, he buried a shard under fast-food wrappers; at another, he slid fragments beneath a bag of dog waste someone had tossed aside. Each deposit felt like he was scattering evidence into the wind, making it impossible to ever piece the weapon back together.

By the time Todd left the park, he forced himself to breathe steadily, knowing that the new flashlight wouldn't provide any incriminating evidence linked to the confrontation between Julia and Sophie.

CHAPTER SIX

Tuesday Afternoon

For over a decade, Ricky and Sophie lived on Warriors Way. Quietly. Reclusively. People said they bought the house with cash. No one ever really knew what they did, although Ricky liked to joke that he "had Vegas money," always delivered with a wink and a laugh that didn't quite reach his eyes. He said he was from Ohio, but even that detail was suspect. Neighbors shared theories: drug money, lottery winners, retired entertainers. But most gave up wondering. The couple didn't cause problems. They didn't attend block parties or HOA board meetings. They were ghosts with an overgrown yard. But ghosts don't get murdered. Ghosts don't die on the side of the road.

In Deer Park Ridge, the cracks in Ricky and Sophie's marriage began to widen, and one of the deepest fault lines was their battle over children. Sophie had always imagined herself as a mother, but Ricky shut down the conversation whenever it came up. He dismissed the idea as impractical, a burden that would tie them down and shatter the carefully constructed lifestyle he enjoyed. For Sophie, his refusal felt like a betrayal of the future she had envisioned, leaving her heart heavy with disappointment. The silence that followed each argument lingered longer than the words themselves, and what had once been an intoxicating partnership began to feel like a cold negotiation with no room for her dreams.

The beauty of the area only seemed to deepen Sophie's despair, which had begun years earlier but now hardened into a quiet, impenetrable wall. She grew more withdrawn with each passing month, clinging only to her solitary morning runs and races. Ricky, restless and increasingly reckless, began disappearing for nights at a time. The neighborhood's isolation, so picturesque from the outside, became a kind of prison, magnifying their distance and amplifying their silence. They lived under the same roof, but the connection that once held them together was gone, replaced by secrets, blame, and long, bitter stretches of silence.

Ricky was a regular fixture at Red Rocks Tavern and Brew, holding down his favorite barstool three or four nights a week with a glass of whiskey or a local IPA in hand. He loved telling stories: wild, meandering tales about his supposed time in Vegas, run-ins with mobsters, and big-money card games. Most of what he said didn't add up, and everyone knew it, but no one really minded. His stories were entertaining, and Ricky had a way of making even the most outrageous lie feel like a half-forgotten truth.

Sophie was rarely seen. On occasion, a neighbor would see her food shopping at the local Safeway. Her hair was always neat, her clothes nondescript, her expressions unreadable. The one exception was her obsessive running. Sophie was known in the neighborhood as "The Panther," often spotted gliding down the paths and streets of Deer Park Ridge with a fierce intensity. Her stride was long and efficient, her pace relentless as she easily hit six-minute miles. Clad in sleek black gear and mirrored sunglasses, she ran with a kind of tunnel vision, utterly absorbed in her rhythm. Neighbors would wave, but Sophie never seemed to notice, her focus unbroken, her mind clearly somewhere else. It was as if she ran not for fitness, but to outrun something only she could see. James waved whenever their paths crossed; she would only nod in return.

On Saturday mornings, Sophie could sometimes be spotted at races held at Chatfield State Park, sponsored by the Deer Park Ridge Running Club. Whether it was a 5K, 10K, or a longer trail run, she consistently posted the fastest time among the women and often beat all but one or two of the men. Her performance was effortless and disciplined, as if she were racing against something internal rather than the other runners. She arrived alone, typically just a minute before the start, gave a curt nod to the race organizer, and stood silently at the front of the pack. As soon as she crossed the finish line, she'd jog straight to her car without saying a word, never staying for water, snacks, or the post-race chatter. To most, she was a mystery with perfect form and a stopwatch for a heart.

The only true bright spot in their marriage was skiing. No matter how strained things felt back home, the moment they drove up to their condo in Vail and stepped into their skis, they put their differences on pause. Both were excellent skiers: fast, graceful, and competitive enough to push each other down the slopes. The crisp mountain air gave them a sense of freedom that didn't exist anywhere else in their lives together. Time in Vail became their unspoken truce, a ritual where they could laugh on the chairlifts and chase each other through powder. There were even nights when romance returned to the marriage. For Sophie, it was a fleeting reminder of the spark they once had; for Ricky, it was simply the one part of their relationship that sometimes still worked.

After the search team left Tuesday afternoon, Ricky sat alone at the kitchen table, the house eerily quiet. A single mug of coffee, long gone cold, sat untouched in front of him. His hands trembled slightly, resting on the wood surface that still bore the faint outlines of fingerprints from the sheriff's crew. For the first time since the whirlwind of sirens and questions began, a heavy stillness settled over him and with it, the crushing weight of grief. Sophie was gone. Brutally taken. And now, the image of her lifeless face haunted him with unbearable clarity. His chest tightened, and tears welled in his eyes, uninvited and unstoppable. He buried his face in his hands and, for the first time, let the sorrow come.

Somewhere along the line, Ricky had made choices: short-cuts, lies, and deals dressed as opportunity that had dragged them into darkness. Ricky and Sophie's promising start had unraveled into a life lived on the edge, full of caution and half-truths, always hiding from the past. Deer Park Ridge had been their retreat, a place to vanish. But even in that quiet cul-de-sac with its perfect views and polite neighbors, the ghosts followed. And now Sophie was dead, and all that remained was the wreckage of what could have been.

Ricky sat with the phone in his trembling hand before finally calling the number, dread coiling in his chest. When Sophie's father answered, his voice was cautious, unfamiliar after years of silence.

With a flat and broken voice, Ricky said the words he could barely understand himself: "I'm sorry to tell you this, Alex. She's dead. Murdered."

There was a quiet whisper on the other end, followed by her mother's scream in the background.

Alex's voice was now weak. "Who could have done this to my sweet Kate?"

Ricky could barely speak. "I don't know. The sheriff's department is investigating."

"How could this happen?" The anguished voice of Sophie's mother blared from the phone. "I bet that miserable bastard did it. He stole her from us and ruined her life."

Years ago, they had admired him, drawn to his intellect, his charm, the way he could talk circles around anyone. But over time, they'd seen through it. He had isolated Sophie, moved her across the country, and quietly severed the ties that had once bound her to them. They hadn't seen her in four years. Now they never would again.

As Ricky sat there, listening to the stunned, grief-stricken silence, he felt the full weight of what he'd taken from them. He wondered why he had grown to hate Sophie so much. She was a beautiful and talented woman, yet in the last years, her presence in his life disgusted him.

CHAPTER SEVEN

Tuesday Afternoon

Marilyn sat at the kitchen table, staring into her untouched glass of water, the questions from Deputy Ryan still echoing in her mind. Though she knew she had nothing to hide, the pointed way he had asked about her movements last night left her unsettled, as if her words had been weighed and measured for cracks she couldn't see. She repeatedly replayed the conversation, wondering if her nervousness had come across as guilt. The thought of being even tangentially linked to such a brutal act made her stomach twist. She glanced out the window toward the stop sign at the entrance to Warriors Way, the image of Sophie's body leaning against it flashing unbidden in her mind, and she shivered despite the warmth of the kitchen.

"James," Marilyn said softly, "I can't stop thinking about Sophie. The violence of it—the sheer cruelty of the beating. Whoever did this must have been filled with hate and wanted her gone. That's what keeps gnawing at me."

She stood and leaned against the counter, arms folded, her eyes fixed on the window overlooking Warriors Way. "Sophie was an interesting person, but different. Personable, but reclusive. What if she was hiding something? Something big?"

James nodded slowly, his fingers drumming on the table. "I

think you might be right. People don't end up like that without some kind of story trailing behind them."

Marilyn turned back to him, her expression sharper now. "Exactly. And think about Ricky, the 1950s look, no clear job, yet they've lived here comfortably for over ten years. It doesn't add up, James . . . it must be more than a domestic dispute or random act of violence."

"I agree," James said, "and there's something else." He paused. "I think we need to be careful. I called Jake and asked him to come over this afternoon. Just a discussion, nothing more. That interview with Deputy Ryan really shook me up. And you know, Jake has done contract work for Sheriff Carson and understands how he operates."

Marilyn nodded and headed to the garage to grab her trail shoes.

James stood staring out at the stop sign where Sophie's body had been found just hours earlier. The quiet of Warriors Way felt unnatural now, its normal rhythm broken by the violence of the night before. He replayed the moment he spotted the wild turkeys, then the figure slumped at the base of the sign, and the sick weight in his stomach as he realized what he was seeing. The memory clung to him like a cold fog: her blue eyes, battered face, the silence of the street, and the sound of his own boots on the pavement. Here, in the place where he and Marilyn had built a peaceful life, the brutality seemed out of place, almost surreal. James couldn't shake the gnawing sense that this wasn't random, that Sophie's death carried shadows reaching further back than anyone on the street realized.

Marilyn's run started just before 1 p.m. The air was still cool and crisp, carrying the earthy scent of pine and sagebrush as she set out from Warriors Way, her stride steady and strong. The familiar hills rolled beneath her feet as she worked her way through the quiet streets and onto the trail leading up to Martin Peak. The incline was demanding, forcing her breath to quicken. Patches of snow and ice made her extra vigilant, but she welcomed the burn in her calves and the deep rhythm of her heartbeat.

When Marilyn reached the top, she paused. Behind her, the sweeping views of the red sandstone formations unfolded, monoliths glowing in the midday sun. To the west, the view of Colorado's towering 14,000-foot peaks was nothing short of majestic.

On the return, Marilyn pushed her pace as she looped down through steep switchback trails. The downhill section gave her a sense of flying as she let gravity carry her forward, her ponytail whipping behind her. Ascending a dirt path, she took the neighborhood south entrance, rejoining the quiet streets and running the final stretch back to Warriors Way. By the time she reached home, her legs ached with the satisfying fatigue of the long run, her lungs full of cool mountain air, and her mind clearer than it had been since breakfast.

———————

While Marilyn was still running, James realized he had time for a workout. He clipped into the Peloton pedals and started a one-hour high-intensity session, selecting a ride led by a former Tour de France cyclist known for his grueling workouts.

But halfway through, James completely lost focus and

slowed his pace. "What was Sophie thinking in those last moments? How could someone have been that ruthless and just left her there to die?"

After fifteen minutes, James refocused on his ride and picked up the pace. He knew he wasn't riding to stay in shape; he was riding to escape the stop sign and the image of Sophie, although he knew there was no outpacing it.

Jake Reston was one of James's best friends. He hadn't changed much since retiring from the Denver Police Department. He had close-cropped hair, a bushy white beard, and steel-blue eyes that missed nothing. James and Jake met while working on a national intelligence task force in McLean, Virginia. James had years of experience with most of the three-letter agencies. Jake was hired for his deep understanding of law enforcement intelligence operations. Together, they were a powerful presence in encouraging the intelligence community and homeland security law enforcement partners to share threat information more effectively after 9/11. They also found they shared a sense of humor, a love of old cars and martinis, and dreams of being in a band.

Now retired, Jake stayed sharp—attending national conferences, consulting quietly on difficult cases, and keeping in close touch with old colleagues. For him, intelligence wasn't about theory. It was about knowing where the fire was going to start and getting there before it burned the house down. Jake moved back to Colorado four years ago and now lived with his wife, Dee, in an upscale over-55 community on a ridge line in Highlands Ranch, about thirty minutes away from James.

The two friends met up often to talk about old times and life in general. Additionally, James would occasionally join Jake at local meetings and provide law enforcement analysts with insight on smart options for improving intelligence sharing with federal partners.

When Jake arrived, James had just finished pushing his classic 1969 Corvette convertible out of the garage to the middle of the driveway. The fully restored car kept its originality except for modern upgrades to the engine, suspension, and brakes. But now it sat motionless, its battery dead. James, used to the automatic headlights on his Jeep, had forgotten to turn them off on Saturday evening.

Jake laughed when he saw James struggling. "Can I help you push it back into the garage?"

James reluctantly asked for a jump. "You know what they say, American steel is the best."

Jake smiled as he looked at his new Ram pickup with a Hemi V-8 engine that was almost quicker than James's old Vette. "I can see that, but your Vette is fiberglass, right? Open the hood and let's get this over with."

James ignored the comment, wondering if he had killed yet another battery.

After successfully starting the car and putting it away, the two friends went inside, and James offered Jake a glass of ice water as they settled at the kitchen table.

"This is murder, Jake. I called you because there's something about it that just doesn't seem right. She was slumped right there," James said quietly as he pointed toward the stop sign.

Jake nodded. "How long between when you saw her and when the sheriff arrived?"

"About fifteen minutes. I didn't touch the body. Just made the calls and stood back. A deputy told me the first report estimated the time of death was last night before midnight. I assume Sheriff Carson will have a better timeline later today."

Jake knew Sheriff Carson well. They had a great deal of respect for each other, and Jake often consulted on cases where organized crime was suspected. He took a slow sip of water. "Tell me everything you remember from last night. Anyone come over, or did you see anyone out on the street?"

James began retelling what had happened last evening and the sequence of events that morning.

Back from her run, Marilyn joined the conversation at the kitchen table.

Jake raised an eyebrow when they told him that Julia and Kenny were out walking their dogs around the time of the murder.

"And what about her husband?"

James answered. "His name is Ricky Delgado. He told the deputy he was bored and headed down to Red Rocks around 7:30 for drinks, didn't get back until 10:30."

Jake shook his head. "You know what they say in homicide work? The spouse is always suspect number one. But I've seen guys who know how to play the long game. Disappear into their own BS story until it becomes the truth. I'll check with the Red Rocks' staff to see if anyone remembers his timelines from last night."

James considered the rumors he'd heard. "Before you go, there's something that might matter. Ricky and Sophie lived here for over ten years; no one ever saw them work. When asked, Ricky would joke that he 'had Vegas money' and that he made some smart investments. Sophie was personable and a good listener, but very guarded when asked questions about their past."

"Odd behavior and murder are often connected. I'm sure I can get current pictures of Ricky from Carson's folks. I'll send them out to a buddy who works in the Vegas law enforcement fusion center to see if he can get any hits. Did the deputy who interviewed you say anything about suspects?"

James looked at Marilyn. "Aside from implying that I was on his short list of suspects, not really. He focused on who was on the street Monday night—Julia, Todd, and Kenny. Carson also mentioned to me that there was a good chance the murderer was watching the police activity this morning to confirm what happened. That's about it."

Jake nodded. "All very interesting. Let me make a few phone calls. I'll get back to you tomorrow."

After Jake left around 3:30, James and Marilyn's heads were spinning. They headed to the community center for an update by the sheriff's department on the Delgado murder. By 4 p.m., the center was packed with neighbors standing shoulder to shoulder, voices rising in nervous chatter that bordered on anger. The air smelled faintly of beer and sweat, but tension dominated everything. Lieutenant Walker stepped up to the microphone in his uniform, the weight of authority evident in his posture. Before he could speak, one of the men near the back, George Reading, a burly resident in a leather vest, called out, "If you folks can't keep us safe, we'll take care of it ourselves!"

Murmurs of agreement followed, and residents turned to see Reading and four drinking buddies, each wearing a visible sidearm and smelling of beer. "You tell 'em, Reading. We're not letting any outsiders come in here and kill our people," another shouted.

Walker raised his hand, his voice calm but firm. "I understand everyone's fear. Mrs. Delgado's death has shaken this community, but let me be absolutely clear, we will solve this case. What we don't need," he said, pausing to sweep the room with his gaze, "are vigilantes making matters worse. The facts are these: Sophie Delgado was killed between 7 and 9 p.m. last night. We have no evidence suggesting this was a random act, nor that anyone from outside the neighborhood was involved. We're following several strong leads, and our investigators are working around the clock."

A few mutters rippled through the crowd, but the men with sidearms shifted uneasily, their bluster losing force.

Walker leaned forward, his tone sharp now. "Let me also make something else clear: anyone interfering with this investigation, anyone threatening people, harassing neighbors, or walking the streets armed to intimidate, will be prosecuted. This is not the Wild West."

The room fell into silence. Even the armed men looked down, their bravado deflating. "We're asking for patience," Walker continued, softening slightly. "I promise you, we'll find who did this. But we'll do it by the book."

A quiet murmur of agreement rose from the back, and the crowd began to settle. By the time the meeting ended, most residents left subdued and shaken, but reassured that someone capable was in charge.

As the crowd dispersed from the tense community meeting, Lieutenant Walker noticed the five armed men lingering near the parking lot, their voices rising above the hum of departing residents. One of them was waving his weapon in the air, slurring his words. "We don't need you people telling us how to protect our homes," he barked, his face red from drink.

Walker motioned for his deputies to fan out, their hands resting calmly on their holsters. "Reading, you and your friends need to holster those weapons now," Walker said evenly. "You've had too much to drink, and this is not the time to play sheriff."

Reading sneered. "You gonna' arrest us for defending our neighborhood?"

"That's exactly what I'm going to do. Put those guns away right now," Walker snapped, his voice cutting through the cold air.

The men muttered curses as one staggered backward, hand on his pistol grip.

"Deputies," Walker ordered, "take their weapons."

The officers moved swiftly, disarming the men as protests erupted.

"This is bullshit!" another shouted, trying to pull free.

"You're all under arrest," Walker said firmly, "for being armed while intoxicated and disturbing the peace."

Flashing red and blue lights washed across the lot as the five men were handcuffed and led to the patrol cars, their anger giving way to sullen silence.

Lieutenant Walker exhaled, eyes scanning the dark ridge beyond the lot. "Last thing this community needs," he muttered, "is a bunch of drunks making things worse."

Just fifteen minutes after getting home from the meeting, James heard a sharp knock echo through the front door. He cautiously opened it to find Dana Kelso of The Denver Sentinel, holding a press badge and a voice recorder. "Mr. Brookside, can you comment on what you saw this morning? Were you the one who discovered the body? Is it true the victim's body was leaning against the stop sign like the murderer posed her?" As she peppered him with rapid-fire questions, she tried to peer past him into the house.

James narrowed his eyes. "Ma'am, this is private property, and a grieving neighborhood. I'm not speaking to the press."

He began to shut the door, but she pressed, "Is there someone on the street you suspect? Did you kill her?"

James stepped forward, blocking her view completely. "I said no comment. And if you keep harassing people on this street, I'll ask the sheriff to escort you out of the neighborhood."

He closed the door firmly, his jaw tight with frustration.

After hearing the encounter, Marilyn thought it would be smart to call her parents who lived nearby. She stepped into the office, closing the door softly behind her before dialing their number. When her dad answered, she spoke gently but firmly. "Please put me on speaker phone so mom can hear the whole conversation. Our neighbor Sophie Delgado was murdered on the street in front of our house last night. James was the one who found her."

There was a sharp intake of breath on the other end, followed quickly by her mother's voice, full of concern. "That's terrible. Are you and James safe? Maybe you two should come stay here until this all settles down."

Marilyn pressed the phone closer. "I know you're worried, and I love you for that. But we're okay. The Sheriff's department is all over this, and James and I feel safe staying here. Leaving would almost feel like running away."

She listened as her parents reluctantly agreed but urged her to call at the first sign of trouble.

"I promise," Marilyn said warmly. "If anything changes, you'll be the first to know. For now, just keep us and Sophie in your prayers."

While Marilyn was on the phone, James poured a glass of red wine and opened a worn, leather-bound journal. He sat down, the soft creak of the leather couch a comforting sound. The cream-colored paper was waiting to hold the words he couldn't yet speak. He took a deep breath, the scent of his wine filling the quiet of the living room and began to write.

March 17: The image of Sophie's body slumped against the stop sign is etched into me like a scar. I keep replaying the scene: her blue eyes, the awkward tilt of her shoulders, the lifeless weight of her head, the streaks of blood darkened by the cold, the smell. The wild turkeys wandering around her made it even more surreal. I've seen death in war, in intelligence work, but never this close to home.

What unsettles me most is how easily violence slipped into our peaceful neighborhood. We wave at each other, and yet one of us may have done this. Marilyn tries to mask her fear, but I can see it. Ricky is still an enigma. Everyone carries secrets, but today they feel sharper, more dangerous. I can't help but think my years of training weren't behind me after all. Instead, they've been preparing me for this moment.

The Brooksides' dinner was a quiet affair of tortellini soup and red wine. They had agreed beforehand not to discuss Sophie. As always, they lit a candle for the kitchen table and said a pre-meal prayer.

James started. "Dear Lord, thank you for this food and our family. And God bless Sophie, her family, and our neighbors on Warriors Way. Please keep us safe."

Marilyn finished with "God bless everyone, no exceptions." They touched glasses and toasted "Salute." It was a wonderful tradition they adopted years ago that brought back warm memories from their three years stationed in Germany and many vacations in Italy.

Before digging in, James smiled at Marilyn. "Thank you, Chef."

Marilyn rolled her eyes. "Thank you, Chef."

James looked out the kitchen window and back at Marilyn. "Have you heard anything from Julia? Todd still hasn't responded to my texts. You know they both seemed a little off last night."

Marilyn shook her head. "I called twice and texted her three times. She hasn't responded. This is so unlike them. Should we walk up to their house and see if they're okay?"

"I don't know. We can if you want, or I can check on them tomorrow."

Marilyn nodded. "Okay, please check tomorrow morning. Maybe they're just laying low today because of what happened to Sophie and all the police activity, but it's so strange they don't want to talk it over with us."

That evening, there was a stillness in Deer Park Ridge that was never meant to be menacing. The landscape hadn't changed, but James had. The red rocks still stood in solemn witness. But what had they seen? Did Sophie ever stop looking at them in wonder? Or had she only seen shadows? Even inside their own home, something had shifted. James could feel it in the pauses between conversations, in the way Marilyn moved more quietly, checking locks twice. She wasn't a fearful person, her work as a doctor and geneticist required sharp thinking and steady hands, but the violence had landed hard. One moment you're talking about fresh powder and ski plans, the next you're staring down at a body.

Marilyn broke the silence. "I think we need to be careful in how we involve ourselves in this tragedy. Is getting Jake involved any further the right thing to do? And the two of you together? I know you've read every Hardy Boys and Nancy Drew book twice and hundreds of murder mystery novels, but what makes you think the two of you can help Jason Carson solve this murder?"

James offered a devious smile. "Well, you know I'm pretty magnificent and have a nose for finding clues. And I only read the Nancy Drew books because I think she's hot and, of course, I like that cool blue roadster she drives."

Marilyn tilted her head. "Actually, you're great at getting things done, but not great at finding clues. You get bored after two minutes of looking for something, and call me in. Oh, and you shouldn't be admiring a teenage girl."

James's smile grew more devilish. "Sweetheart, I just turn

to you so that you feel more loved and needed. Tell me I'm old-fashioned, but it's what caring husbands do. And Nancy would be over a hundred by now, so it's all totally appropriate."

Marilyn shook her head and kissed James. "Just keep making me laugh. It's what I need most."

After cleaning up the dishes, they retired to the living room to watch a couple of mindless TV shows. At exactly 8:15, James excused himself and went outside. He stood at the end of his driveway, taking in the darkness. Just twenty-four hours earlier, Sophie had been murdered less than fifty yards from where he was standing. Tonight, the street was quiet with no movement. He again wondered how such a horrible thing could have happened so close to his home. Just as he turned to go back inside, he saw the outline of a lone figure about forty yards up the street. It was Kenny, walking his large dog, and carrying a golf club.

For an unknown reason, a chill ran through his body. He watched as the figure disappeared, and then he rejoined Marilyn in the living room.

"The street was quiet other than Kenny walking King," he said, "I'm convinced he was out on the street last night at the time of the murder and may know what happened. The bigger question is, could someone as clueless as Kenny be a murderer?"

Marilyn looked at James. "I think Kenny is a sweet guy. Maybe a little odd, but not clueless. And the two of you were golfing buddies for a while until your back started to give you problems. I know you're looking for answers, but please be careful not to suspect or judge others. We need to trust that Carson and his deputies will solve this case."

James nodded, but in his head, he was still suspicious about Kenny.

While watching TV that evening, James took a quick look at Facebook on his phone. Normally, the posts in his feed were harmless—old friends' vacations, classic cars being detailed after 30 years, or funny pet videos. But after Sophie's murder, that all changed.

James clicked on a headline in the Deer Park Ridge Facebook group that made his jaw drop in astonishment:

"THE MURDER ON WARRIORS WAY: TIME TO ADMIT THE TRUTH"

"Our neighborhood is no longer safe. Sophie Delgado wasn't killed by one of us—she was murdered by strangers who invaded our community. They sneak over the foothills at night, intent on taking our homes, our money, and now they've taken a life. Ask yourself, why was her body left at the stop sign? A warning. They want us gone. Wake up, Deer Park Ridge."
—A Concerned Neighbor

The comment section had already exploded. Most of the replies were furious, demanding the post be taken down, calling it paranoid nonsense. The others egged it on, feeding the theory with rumors of "strange cars" and "outsiders" wandering the trails. James read in silence, jaw tight. The post was dangerous, not just false, but corrosive. He'd seen the way unchecked stories spread, first as whispers, then as fact, and finally as a cudgel to divide people.

Marilyn looked at him with a concerned eye. "You're brooding, what are you looking at?" she said softly.

"Not brooding," James muttered. "Reading garbage." He handed her his iPhone.

Marilyn skimmed the post, her face hardening. "This isn't garbage, James. This is poison."

"And poison spreads faster than truth," he replied.

Deer Park Ridge was a close-knit community with a love for nature being the common thread that held residents together. But now, thanks to one post, the neighborhood wasn't just frightened; it was terrified. It was starting to fracture.

James printed the post and tucked it into a folder he had begun keeping—notes, timelines, news clippings, contradictions, and fragments related to Sophie's murder. Fortunately, the post was removed after about an hour with a warning from the community manager. James was greatly relieved when he told Marilyn.

"Thank God," James said. "The post was taken down. We don't need that type of insanity dividing us."

CHAPTER EIGHT

Tuesday Evening

Jake asked his wife, Dee, to meet him for dinner at the Red Rocks Tavern & Brew on Tuesday night. He apologized for the short notice, but he needed to check on an alibi related to the murder near James's house. Dee was reluctant to join him because she would drive past twenty good restaurants on the way, and Red Rocks' food was good, but basic. She acquiesced when Jake mentioned it was trivia night and St. Patrick's Day which would likely mean a lively crowd. They had partnered with James and Marilyn in the past and had a fun time.

The Red Rocks Tavern and Microbrewery, located in the Deer Park Ridge shopping center, had the easy charm of a place that had grown into its own identity over time. Housed in a former pizzeria with exposed beams and Edison bulbs strung low over polished oak tables, it smelled faintly of malt and woodsmoke. Behind the long copper-topped bar, chalkboards listed an ever-changing lineup of craft brews with quirky names—each one brewed in the gleaming steel tanks visible through a glass wall at the back. Regulars occupied the corner booths, their laughter blending with the low hum of blues playing on the sound system. The atmosphere was warm and inviting, equally suited for a quiet pint of beer or a spirited trivia night.

Red Rocks was already busy. Jake and Dee arrived at about the same time, grabbed a high-top table near the bar, and ordered two beers. Their server, Barb, asked if they were ready to order food, but they both decided to wait a bit. Then Jake excused himself and went to talk to the bartender, Mike.

"Well, look who's back. You studying up for trivia night, or just here to drink me out of amber again?" Mike said.

Jake smiled. "I'm still recovering from your 'Birds of Colorado' round last month. You play dirty."

Mike chuckled. "Hey, you held your own. What can I get you? The usual?"

"No. My wife and I ordered at the table. I'm looking into a murder, and the husband's name has come up," Jake said, his tone serious. "I was wondering if you've seen Ricky Delgado here lately. You know, the guy with the fedora."

Mike was mixing drinks at breakneck speed. "Uh-oh. Sounds like Jake's in investigator mode again. I understand the woman killed up in the Ridge was Ricky's wife?"

Jake nodded. "She was supposedly his wife. Look, I'm not trying to put you in a tight spot. Just trying to put a few things together about someone I think you know."

"Ricky? Yeah, I know him. Hard to miss. You're not the first one to ask about him today. Deputy Ryan was here about an hour ago with a bunch of questions."

"So, does Ricky come here often?"

"I guess two to three nights a week and most Tuesday nights for trivia. He came here last night at about 9 p.m. He wanted food, but we'd already closed the kitchen because things really slowed down by 8:30. He seemed really frustrated. He told me he had a little something going on and lost track of time."

"Is he much of a drinker?"

"He loves his booze. Ordered two quick bourbons on the rocks and a 20-ounce beer, gave me a $35 tip, and left just after 10. One other thing, he was chatting it up with his newest lady friend, Donna Grisham. She's divorced. Comes in here when her ex-husband has their two kids for the night. Nice-looking woman, but she seems lonely. Just before Christmas, they got really friendly and left together. I think they're a bit of an item."

Jake leaned on the bar. "Interesting about Donna. Are you sure of the times last night? You folks get busy. Easy to lose track."

"Positive. We cut the cooks loose just before 9, and I always remember someone who gives me generous tips. At least for a day or two. Hey, order a drink and tip me $35. I promise I'll remember you in the morning. I might even call you."

Jake laughed. "Thanks for the info. I'd better get back to my wife. I think she's getting jealous."

Mike smiled again. "You and the wife sticking around for trivia? If you are, I heard there's going to be questions related to St Patrick's Day and the recent Winter Olympics."

Jake smiled and returned to the high top. Dee had ordered the loaded tater tots with extra cheese as an appetizer. They tasted great with the ice-cold beers. Barb, their server, came around and suggested they order dinner before the kitchen got backed up from the large trivia night crowd starting to arrive.

Dee started. "I'll take the Chicken Street Tacos with no sides."

"Philly Steak Sandwich and a side salad with balsamic dressing," Jake said.

Dee smiled. "Since when do you order a side salad and balsamic dressing?"

"Trying to behave myself after eating fifty tater tots covered in melted cheese."

Jake looked at Barb. "Do you know a guy named Ricky Delgado? Wears a fedora hat. Comes in for trivia on Tuesdays."

"I know him. Nice guy. Really smart. Knows almost every answer. The ladies from Bill's Cut and Style across the way love it when he joins them. I'm not sure if he comes here other times. I just work trivia nights to make extra money. I'm a middle school English teacher, and we don't get paid much in Spirit County."

Barb paused, thinking for a moment, then continued. "Another thing about Ricky, I mentioned to him one time that my knee was bothering me, and nothing was working for the pain. He got a little amped up and told me never to try any opioid-based medications. Said they were dangerous and addictive. He was very sincere and caring. Just thought I'd mention that because the 'father act' does not fit his tough guy persona. Hey, I've got to go. We're getting busy."

Jake nodded. "Thanks. That's all interesting."

The food came quickly. Jake ordered another beer. Dee switched to water and said she would drive home, meaning Jake would have to Uber back in the morning to get his truck. He was good with that.

The trivia host, or, as some called him, the quizmaster, asked teams to come up to register and pick up answer sheets. Jake went forward only to be reminded that he needed a team name. He came up with "The Bushy Beards."

Dee asked, "What's the deal again on the game?"

Jake thought for a moment. "Three rounds, each round has two games, and each game has eight questions."

Jake and Dee got all the answers correct in the first game. They only missed one answer in the next game, tying another team for first place. Jake was having a good time, and he asked Barb for another beer. His mood changed when Ricky entered Red Rocks, wearing his signature short-brim fedora, a leather jacket over a bright blue-and-white bowling-style silk shirt, and wide-pleated pants.

Mike saw Ricky first. He gave Jake a look and nodded toward the door. Ricky headed to the bar and sat with a couple of women who worked at Bill's Cut and Style. Within a couple of minutes, he had a bourbon on the rocks and was fully engaged in answering questions.

Jake was not surprised when another woman came in at about 7:45. Mike looked at Jake and mouthed, "Donna." The couple sat close and were constantly touching each other.

By 8:00, Dee was ready to go. Jake had seen enough, too. He got the check and tipped Barb well.

As Dee steered her SUV out of the Red Rocks Tavern parking lot, she leaned back in her seat with a grin. "Well, at least we didn't embarrass ourselves tonight. We were still tied for first place after round two," she said, brushing a strand of hair behind her ear.

Jake chuckled, "Yeah, though I still can't believe you missed the question about Lindsey Vonn."

Dee rolled her eyes and swatted his arm. "I was thinking of Mikaela Shiffrin, thank you very much. Besides, you messed up the one about the three-leaf shamrock and the Holy Trinity. And you're a Catholic." They both laughed, the easy banter a welcome distraction from the grim events of the day.

But as the headlights cut through the dark road toward

Highlands Ranch, Dee's smile faded. "Can you believe Delgado was at the bar with that woman? Of all nights to show up—Tuesday. The same day James found his wife's body."

Jake slapped the dashboard, which startled Dee. "Can't say I like it. Ricky was sitting there, calm as if nothing happened, and Donna was hanging on his every word."

"It felt wrong, Jake. Almost staged."

Jake exhaled, his dry wit slipping back in. "Well, if Ricky thinks playing trivia is a good cover for murder, he picked the wrong night."

About an hour later, Ricky and Donna were standing outside the Red Rocks Tavern, the night air carrying the sharp bite of March cold. Ricky pulled his fedora down tighter as he lit a cigarette.

Donna crossed her arms, watching him with narrowed eyes. "Other than answering trivia questions, you barely said a word in there, Ricky. Sitting all calm like nothing happened. But your wife was found dead this morning and you haven't said one thing about it!"

Ricky blew smoke into the dark sky, his jaw tight. "You don't want to get caught up in the sheriff's gossip mill, believe me."

She frowned, stepping closer. "This isn't gossip. She was your wife. Don't you think you owe me more than shrugs and silence?"

Ricky shifted his weight and looked at her hard, the corners of his mouth twitching into something between a smile and a grimace. "What I owe you, Donna, is keeping us both out of trouble. Questions like that? They only dig holes. And holes, well, they bury people in them."

Donna froze, unsettled by the sharp edge in his tone. "So that's it? Sophie's gone, and you're just going to smoke and walk away from it?"

Ricky flicked his cigarette into the parking lot. "I'm not walking away. I just don't see the point in rehashing what can't be fixed. What I do see is a big, empty house, and I don't plan on spending the night alone."

Donna shifted uncomfortably. "Ricky, I don't think that's a good idea. People are going to be watching you—watching us. If I spend the night, it'll look . . . " Her words trailed off, but Ricky stepped closer, lowering his voice.

"It'll look like I've got company when I need it most. That's all. I can't be by myself tonight, Donna. Not after this morning."

His hand brushed against her arm, lingering just long enough to make her shiver. "Come on," he pressed. "Don't leave me standing in that house with nothing but ghosts."

Donna hesitated, caught between fear and pity, before finally exhaling. "Fine. But this doesn't mean I'm not still asking questions."

Ricky gave a low chuckle, opening the passenger door for her. "Ask all you want, darlin'. Just don't expect answers."

As they drove through the parking lot toward the exit, a black SUV raced past them and slammed on the brakes. Ricky was able to stop just in time. Neither vehicle moved for a moment. Ricky started to back up to go around, but the driver of the black SUV hit the gas and disappeared into the night.

Ricky looked at Donna. "Guy must have had a bad night at trivia." They both laughed.

WEDNESDAY

CHAPTER NINE

Wednesday Morning

Ricky and Donna were up early. Donna was feeling very guilty about spending the night and wanted to be out of the neighborhood before anyone saw her. Ricky promised a great breakfast at his favorite diner before he took her back to get her car in front of Red Rocks Tavern. The black SUV was back again, and on their tail two miles after they left the Deer Park Ridge gate. It changed lanes every time Ricky did, never gaining distance, never falling back.

"You seeing this?" he muttered, keeping his eyes on the rearview mirror.

Donna looked over her shoulder and stiffened. "It looks the same as last night at the shopping center. Same blacked out windows." Ricky exhaled sharply. "Yeah. And they're not even pretending to be subtle."

By the time they pulled into the small diner off Highway 85, the SUV slowed behind them, rolled past, then circled the lot like a wolf checking the fence.

"Ricky, this is bad," Donna whispered as they hurried inside. "Do you think it's connected to . . . everything?"

Ricky held the door for her, jaw tight. "Everything is connected to everything now. Let's sit where we can see the parking lot."

After they ordered breakfast, Ricky tried to keep the mood light, but the two were distracted and struggled to keep a conversation going. When the server returned to refill their coffee, she could sense the tension. "Did one of you just find out you're pregnant?"

The two looked at each other and laughed. Donna quickly added, "No, he's very traditional and wants to wait until we get married."

The server hugged the warm pot of coffee. "Marriage, interesting. I thought he was probably your father."

Ricky sat stone faced, while Donna laughed for five minutes.

When their plates hit the table, Donna devoured her meal while Ricky barely touched his eggs; his eyes locked on the SUV idling across the road behind a row of scrub oak.

Donna leaned in. "Isn't this exactly the kind of thing your police friend warned you about? Will you have to move again?"

Ricky shook his head. "Not yet. I need to know who's in that car before I do anything."

Donna's voice dropped. "What does that mean?"

Ricky ignored her question.

When they left the diner, the SUV reappeared, sliding behind them as they merged back onto the main road.

Donna gripped the handle above her door. "They're closer than before."

Ricky accelerated, trying to get space, but the SUV continued to ride their bumper. "I know," he said, pulse pounding. "They want me to know they're there."

The SUV suddenly surged forward, then dropped back, like a threat without words.

Donna's breath trembled. "Ricky, whatever this is—I'm frightened. I can't have this stuff going on in my life. I have my kids to think about."

Marilyn prepared to leave early for work. She grabbed her things from the kitchen counter and turned back to James, a worried look on her face. "We talked about this last night. I know finding Sophie's body hit you hard, and Deputy Ryan's interview was unsettling, but why are you going to follow up with Jake? How is a former cop going to do anything?"

"I owe it to her, and he knows how to get things done."

"No, you don't owe it to her, that's the police's responsibility. Remember what Walker said yesterday afternoon. Let the sheriff oversee the investigation. There's a murderer out there. Do we really want to put ourselves in the spotlight?"

James didn't answer. Marilyn gave him a stern look and then kissed him goodbye before heading to work.

As Marilyn was getting in her SUV, Julia called and spoke quickly, "Hey, I'm sorry I didn't call back last night. We're fine. We just didn't feel like talking about the murder. It's so horrible and hard to imagine that it happened on our street. I just got to work and need to go. Talk later." She hung up before Marilyn could say anything.

Marilyn was relieved to hear from Julia but still felt unsettled. Something in Julia's voice was not right.

James reflected on Marilyn's questions. He couldn't quite put his finger on the "why," but he knew it was more than just the shock of finding her body. There was a sense of duty gnawing at him, the same instinct that had driven him throughout his years in the Army and later in the intelligence world. He had been the one to spot her first, the one to call the sheriff, and the one to stand guard over Sophie waiting for their arrival. That act alone seemed to tether him to the crime, as though fate had thrust him into the role of a reluctant witness and for making sense of the senseless. He told himself he was only curious, that he was simply trying to understand what had shattered the quiet of Warriors Way, but deep down he felt responsible—not for her death, but for being the quiet custodian of the truth.

A short text from Todd came up assuring him they were fine. James was relieved but had an uneasy feeling. Could Todd and Julia know more?

He prided himself on staying sharp and active, but there were times when even the long bike rides and ski trips left James feeling unanchored, as if he had stepped off the map of the life he'd known. Marilyn still had her work and her purpose at the hospital, and Robin was building a future of her own. James, meanwhile, had gone from briefing senior leaders on global threats to travel and managing yard work. Sophie's murder was a jolt—a grim reminder that darkness still existed even in the quiet, manicured corners of Colorado—and, perhaps shamefully, he felt a spark of energy in trying to pull the pieces together. It made him feel useful again.

James was aware, at least in the quiet corners of his mind, that his digging into Sophie's murder could be seen as overreach. Sheriff Carson hadn't exactly invited him into the investigation, and Jake had warned more than once that stepping in too far could make enemies in law enforcement circles. But James couldn't help himself. It wasn't just the brutal scene he had stumbled onto that gnawed at him; it was something deeper, something tied to old disappointments he had never fully shaken. He thought back even further to his years at West Point, the crisp autumn afternoons on the football field, and the searing moment his back gave way. The memory still carried a sting. And later, after decades of service in the Army, there had been another wound—the quiet realization that the stars of a general would never sit on his shoulders. He had done great work, had the right jobs, knew the right people, forged a career he was proud of, but the final and biggest promotion passed him by, and he had to smile through the polite farewells at his retirement ceremony.

A successful career followed in the intelligence community, but by the time he left his last assignment, James felt like a man the world had already started to look past. His final year of work had been colored by politics and shifting priorities, and he couldn't shake the sense that his decades of service had been quietly undervalued. Now, replaying the events of yesterday, he realized how much of this was about reclaiming something he had lost—not glory, not rank, but significance. He told himself he was helping, watching out for his neighbors, but there was a sharper truth beneath it all: James couldn't abide being a bystander. He wasn't ready to fade into the background of a neighborhood where people waved politely but didn't really see him.

As he often did, James looked out the kitchen window.

He saw a beautiful community he loved, but also the reflection of an aging man growing harder to recognize. Was there more?

Shifting back into gear with a smile and endless optimism, James decided to go for a long bike ride to clear his head. Before he left, Jake called and gave him a rundown on trivia night. James was taken aback by Ricky's behavior but not surprised. They agreed to talk later.

James hoisted his road bike into the back of his Jeep Wrangler. The air was crisp, the sky already glowing with a deep blue as he pulled out of Warriors Way and headed down toward Chatfield State Park. The traffic was light, and he cracked the windows to let in the scent of dew on grass and the faint earthy smell of the foothills. At the park's south entrance, he flashed his annual pass to the ranger and waved, the familiar welcome of the place easing the tension that had clung to him since Sophie's murder. Parking near the marina, James stepped out and stretched, then unloaded his bike and put on his helmet. He swung his leg over the frame, pushed off, and clipped into the pedals. The carbon fiber bike rolled smoothly onto the path and felt like an extension of himself.

He started slowly, letting his legs warm to the rhythm of the pedals as he headed west, then north, skirting the edge of the reservoir. A mist still clung to the water, and geese drifted lazily, their low honks carried across the surface. After three miles, James increased his cadence, the soft whir of tires on asphalt and the gentle rush of air past his ears becoming a soothing soundtrack. He passed dog walkers, a handful of other cyclists, and a runner or two, nodding to each as he worked his way north along the South Platte River Trail. The river's voice was constant, a quiet murmur over rocks and debris. Somewhere around fifteen miles in, he felt the first hint of fatigue in his quads and welcomed it. He rose out of the saddle on a gentle incline, feeling the strength in his legs and the slight burn that reminded him how alive he still felt. With the return loop pulling him back south, James let his mind drift, sorting through fragments of conversations—Marilyn's observations, Jake's dry commentary, and Todd's silent treatment.

At mile twenty-five, as he came off the trail, he veered toward the familiar awning of the Coffee House. He ordered a mango-strawberry smoothie. The first sip was blissfully cold, the tart sweetness sparking his taste buds as he eased into a patio chair. Around him, the world moved at an easy pace—cyclists checking their phones, a young couple walking a golden retriever, an elderly man flipping through a newspaper. James let the tension in his shoulders melt, a river at his side, a smoothie in hand, and his Jeep waiting to carry him home; it wasn't a bad way to spend the day, even in the shadow of what had happened on Warriors Way.

Starting up again, James felt the burn in his quads as he powered toward the last big hill behind the Chatfield dam, standing out of the saddle to keep his momentum steady. Just as he crested the first small rise, he caught and passed a gray-haired woman pedaling a sleek new e-bike, her upright posture and gentle smile contrasting with his labored breathing. For a fleeting moment, he allowed himself a sense of quiet victory—until he heard the faint hum of her motor kick up a level and watched as she effortlessly glided past him on the steeper section, offering a cheerful "Nice work!" over her shoulder.

James chuckled under his breath, shaking his head as he dropped back into the saddle. "So much for bragging rights," he muttered, settling into a steady rhythm for the final push.

At the top of the hill, the woman stopped and waited for James. As he reached her location, she turned and yelled. "A little slow today, buddy."

James was taken aback until he realized it was Dr. Murphy, the coroner from the murder scene yesterday morning.

She laughed. "Beautiful day, isn't it? Oh, please tell your wife thank you again for answering my questions yesterday. It really helped." Then she took off as fast as the e-bike would carry her.

James paused to catch his breath as Murphy disappeared down the hill. He briefly considered chasing her down, but his legs were tired, and what would that really prove? But it did reaffirm his strong dislike for lazy e-bikers who put little effort into their rides and often blocked his precious bike paths. Slightly defeated, he headed to his Jeep at a cooldown pace.

With a mile to go, the sun was casting shadows across the asphalt. He shifted down, savoring the ride's rhythm and already anticipating the cold water waiting in his car. That's when he heard the sudden roar of an engine, far too close. A pickup truck surged up behind him, the wind from its grill rattling his jersey as it skimmed past the white line.

The horn blasted, rattling his nerves, and a voice exploded from the passenger window: "Get out of the way, asshole!" The words were raw, venomous, and far too close to his ear. James steered right, fighting the instinct to swerve into the grass and rocks. His heart hammered as the truck sped past, exhaust fumes mixed with dust in its wake. He slowed his cadence, eyes narrowed on the disappearing tailgate, the shock giving way to anger as sharp as the fear.

He had ridden this route hundreds of times and knew the rules, and yet in a second, it was clear—some people didn't care whether he made it home alive. Or . . . could this have something to do with Sophie's murder? The thought was unlikely, but the recent media attention on him was unsettling. He knew that it was better to be vigilant, given that he was the one who had found her body.

Once back at his Jeep, James sat on his back bumper for a moment to gather himself before heading out. "What the hell just happened?"

James made a quick stop at Safeway on his way home from Chatfield. He spotted Julia loading grocery bags into the back of her SUV, her movements stiff and hurried.

Still in his cycling kit, he walked over and helped her with the last bag. "Julia, how are you guys doing? We were a little worried when we didn't hear from either you or Todd yesterday. The news about Sophie was horrible."

"It was horrible, but we really didn't know the Delgados."

"I don't think anyone really knew them. They kept to themselves. So, on Monday night—you stopped by our house around 8:15 p.m. to give Marilyn a book. Did you see Sophie that night or any strangers on the street?"

Julia froze, then forced a tight smile, shaking her head. "No, James. I didn't see her or anything strange. I dropped off the book and went straight home. That's it."

James studied her and softened his tone. "Sorry, I didn't mean to imply anything, but timelines matter. Sophie was murdered not long after eight. If you were out there, even briefly, you might've seen something—someone lurking, a car, anything."

Julia slammed the SUV hatch shut with more force than necessary, her tone clipped. "I didn't see Sophie, and I don't know what happened to her. You and the sheriff's office are twisting things around, and it's scaring me. You know, that could have been me you found Tuesday morning. Think about it. Now leave me alone." Julia's jaw set as she slid into her car, shutting the door like a barricade between them, and drove away.

James stood in the parking lot for a while trying to understand Julia's reaction to his questions. "Something is not right here," he muttered to himself, "but I don't know what I don't know."

Once home, James showered, had a light lunch, and called Jake. The call went straight to voicemail, leaving James at a loss as to what to do next. Being tired after a long bike ride, his Army training told him that a nap would be a smart idea. And it was.

While James was napping, Jake took an Uber back to the Deer Park Ridge shopping center to get his truck. He decided to take a side trip and visit Bill's Cut and Style. Two of Ricky's trivia partners at Red Rocks last night were working. Jake figured he could use a trim and checked in.

Bill's was a modern barbershop with six chairs. The back

left chair, however, was a massive, gleaming antique with hand-tooled leather and polished chrome arms, commanding the room like a throne. It looked like a portal to another era. The cutting area was surrounded by shelves and walls crowded with memorabilia: old straight razors in wooden boxes, black-and-white photos of barbers from the 1920s, vintage shaving mugs, and framed posters from boxing matches and jazz clubs.

After 15 minutes, a barber named Beth waved Jake over. Jake recognized her from Red Rocks the night before; she had been sitting next to Ricky. Jake gave her instructions on what he wanted and started asking questions.

"Did I see you at trivia last night? I was there with my wife, and we really had a lot of fun."

Beth smiled. "Yes, I go most every week after work with a couple of girls from here. It's always fun. More fun when we have our lucky charm, a guy named Ricky. He knows almost every answer. His only weakness is pop culture from the last ten years. The ladies and I are good at that, so everything balances out."

"How did you guys do?"

"We started slow because Ricky was late. But he was on fire the last round, and we finished second. We won $50 that went toward the bar tab. Ricky was in a great mood and covered the rest. Nice for us. A free night out."

Jake hit Beth with the question about Donna. "I noticed a woman with brown hair came in after Ricky arrived. I think her name is Donna. Does she work here, too?"

"Oh, Donna Grisham. She's a looker. No, she's a nurse at the hospital in Highlands Ranch. Sad, she just went through a tough divorce. Nurses have crazy hours, and her jerk husband decided he needed a new friend to fill the void. Donna and Ricky have gotten close in the last few months."

Jake decided to shake up the conversation. "Do you ladies know that Ricky's wife was murdered on Monday night up in the Ridge?"

Beth responded with a defensive tone. "He had nothing to do with it. Ricky told us that he spent the night with Donna. I heard the police have already cleared him."

Beth finished the haircut and offered to trim Jake's beard. He politely declined.

———

The late-afternoon sun slanted across the red rock walls of Deer Park Ridge as the five men from Tuesday's community meeting—rearmed, half-lit, still led by George Reading—paced up and down the walking path along the main road near Warriors Way. Boots scraping asphalt, handguns on their hips, the smell of whiskey and beer trailing them.

When a woman walking her beagle approached, one of them, a thick-shouldered man named Ron, stepped into her path. "Ma'am, we're checkin' IDs today," he said, his speech slurred.

She blinked at him. "You're doing what? Move aside."

Ron planted a hand on his holster as if that would settle it. "County's got outsiders creepin' around. Need to make sure you're who you say you are."

A second man—Dale, the loudest of the group—leaned in, his vest unzipped and his shirt stained with something dark. "Just show the ID, sweetheart. Don't make this difficult. We have a murderer on the loose."

The woman tightened the leash, her jaw clenched. "I'm not showing you anything. You're drunk, and you're not law enforcement."

Others on the trail began slowing, watching. A jogger approached and tried to slip past, only for Dale to swing an arm out in front of him. "Hey! You too! Stop right there."

The jogger lifted his hands. "Get out of my way, man. What you're doing is illegal." Dale shoved him lightly—more swagger than force, but enough to make the small crowd shift uneasily.

Soon, a small knot of residents had formed, voices rising. "Leave people alone!" someone shouted from down the path.

Ron squared his shoulders, wobbling slightly. "Everybody calm down. We're just protectin' the neighborhood."

The jogger stepped forward again. "By harassing people?"

Ron jabbed a finger toward him. "We're doin' what the sheriff won't!"

"The sheriff won't because it's insane!" the woman with the beagle snapped back. "Now, move!"

When Dale tried to grab the jogger's arm, the jogger shoved him hard in the chest, sending him stumbling backward into the sagebrush. The other armed men rushed forward, shouting threats as residents pulled out their phones, some recording, others already calling 911. The air buzzed with tension—shouting, barking, the metallic clatter of a pistol shifting in a loose holster—as the fragile line between bluster and violence thinned to a thread.

Moments later, the men jumped into a large SUV and sped out of the neighborhood toward the Deer Park Ridge shopping center, only to be pulled over and detained by Spirit County deputies a few miles away.

At 5 p.m., Todd and Julia sat stiffly across from Randell Baker's wide oak desk, the quiet of the lawyer's office pressing in on them.

Baker folded his hands, his voice measured. "Let's start from the beginning, Julia. You told me earlier that Sophie killed your sister in a car accident twenty years ago. Tell me what happened on Monday night that triggered the altercation after all this time."

Julia swallowed hard. "We crossed paths near the mailboxes on Monday night just after 8 p.m. She wanted to talk and tried to apologize for the car accident. We had a short argument and confrontation that turned into . . . I . . . I . . . hit her with the flashlight I was carrying."

Todd shifted in his chair, rubbing his temples. "Randell, I need to be clear about something," he said quietly. "I told Deputy Ryan yesterday morning that I hadn't seen Sophie's body that night. That was a lie."

Julia snapped her head toward him. "Todd!"

"I did see her. She had been badly beaten and was leaning against the stop sign when I walked the dogs after I got home from Fort Collins. I panicked."

Baker's eyes narrowed slightly, his pen frozen above the legal pad. "And the flashlight?" he asked.

"We destroyed it." Todd exhaled slowly. "Julia's jacket had blood on it. Her shoes too. We washed the jacket and dumped the clothes, shoes, and flashlight. I told myself it was to protect her, to protect us."

Julia joined in then, her voice cracking. "I was so confused . . .

I just kept thinking about my sister dead on that highway in Texas."

The lawyer leaned forward, the chair creaking softly, studying Julia with care.

"Julia," Baker said evenly, "I need to ask you a direct question, but you don't have to answer. Did you kill Sophie?"

Julia met his gaze, tears spilling over. "No," she said firmly. "I didn't kill her. I fought with her, yes, and struck her once with my flashlight—but when I left, she was standing there and kept saying she was sorry. Whatever happened after that wasn't my fault, it can't be. Please don't ask me again. I'm not a murderer."

CHAPTER TEN

Wednesday, Late Afternoon

When Jake got home, he called James and gave him a complete update on his visit to the barbershop. Then, in a low and serious voice, he said, "Hey, I just got off the phone with my guy in Vegas. He took one look at the pictures of Ricky I got from a buddy at the sheriff's department and said he's ninety percent sure that's the guy they were tracking back in 2013. Went by the nickname 'The Chemist.' Real smart, degrees in pharmacology, maybe chemistry, no one ever nailed it down."

"Really, so it appears Ricky has advanced science degrees? Interesting. What else?"

"If it was Ricky, he met with known traffickers and tried to set up a black-market distribution ring for opioid pills—high-grade stuff, not junk. He was also pushing Fentanyl as a new and cheaper way to expand the market for legal and illegal painkillers. The guy disappeared off the radar before they could make a case. My friend said the drug enforcement guys were sniffing around, too, but they never got enough to tie him to a specific lab or distribution point. Said he was careful, always one step ahead."

There was a long pause as the implications settled over James. "Jake, maybe you should call Sheriff Carson about this latest news, and we take a big step back. I don't want thugs knocking on my door in the middle of the night."

Jake's voice was grim. "James, they don't knock on doors. They'll just shoot you three or four times. You'll never know what happened."

James felt the air go cold in his lungs. This wasn't a small-town mystery anymore. This was a whole different league. His "semi-professional fact finding effort" was no longer a hobby; it was potentially shaping up to be a deadly game.

Marilyn got home early from work and went for a four-mile run on the trail that parallels Deer Park Ridge Drive, the main road in the Ridge. She avoided blind spots without even realizing it. James watched her return from the kitchen window.

She stood on the driveway taking in the view, searching for something she couldn't name. A kind of control. A reset. As the sun set behind the foothills, she went inside and found James standing in the kitchen.

The silence broke when Marilyn's iPhone pinged with a reminder that she needed to pick up two birthday cakes. "I forgot. I need to go to that bakery up Wadsworth to pick up a birthday cake for our office party tomorrow during lunch."

James's eyes lit up. "Did you order one for Todd and me? You know, one with extra thick buttercream icing?"

Marilyn smiled and shook her head. "Yes. I don't know about you two. I swear, you're worse than a gaggle of six-year-olds."

James laughed. "True. How about if I drive and we go out to dinner as part of the trip?"

"Sounds good to me."

While Marilyn was getting ready, James walked outside to look at a small herd of deer that had gathered across the street. They were peacefully grazing on early spring grass that was already popping up. James spotted Kenny walking on Warriors Way with King on a taut leash.

"Hey, Kenny," James called out as he walked over and reached to pet King. "We need to talk. You told Deputy Ryan that Todd was on the street Monday night, right around the time Sophie was killed. But I know for sure that he didn't get back from Fort Collins until almost 11 p.m. What's the deal?"

Kenny shifted uneasily, his eyes narrowing. "I saw someone. Thought it was Todd. Maybe I was mistaken. People misremember things under stress."

"Right now, it looks like you wanted to put suspicion squarely on Todd."

Kenny's jaw clenched, his hand tightening on the leash. "Oh gosh, no. You don't know what you're talkin' about," he snapped, though his tone cracked just enough to betray him. "I've got nothin' to cover up. I'm just tryin' to live my life here like the rest of you."

James stared at him, reading every twitch, every hesitation, and knew Kenny was sitting on something bigger than a simple mistake. "So why don't you tell me the real story before this gets any worse?"

Kenny stood with his golf club now slung over his right shoulder. "Careful there, James," he said with a mirthless smile. "You better watch who you're accusin' around here. Minnesota folks don't take kindly to bein' called liars."

James stood his ground; his arms folded across his chest. "Just looking for the truth, Kenny."

James reached to pet King again, but Kenny pulled him out of reach.

"I told you and the deputy the truth. Now leave me alone, or I won't let you pet King anymore. You'll have to get your own damn dog. You know, you were more fun when we were golfin' buddies. See ya."

Both men retreated in opposite directions.

James walked back to his garage and started the Corvette. He was pleased that the battery seemed fully charged and that the car was running perfectly. While waiting for Marilyn, he thought about how much he liked dogs, especially King, but confirmed in his mind that caring for a dog would be too much of a commitment, particularly when it snowed, or rained, or at night. And what do you do when you want to go on vacation or ski for the day?

Moments later Marilyn slid into the passenger seat and James guided his 1969 Corvette out of the neighborhood and onto northbound Wadsworth, the headlights throwing long beams into the early evening as he downshifted and pressed the accelerator. The big block roared to life, settling into a deep, throaty purr that rolled through the cabin as they passed the dark outline of the foothills.

Marilyn glanced sideways at him, her hair catching the dashboard lights. "You really think keeping this beast is a wise decision? You could have bought two brand new Corvettes if you took that offer last October," she teased, gripping the door handle as the car surged forward.

James grinned, eyes locked on the road. "Absolutely. It's not just a car—it's history, it's muscle, it's freedom on four wheels."

She shook her head, though her smile betrayed her. "Freedom, huh? More like an excuse to relive your twenty-year-old self." Then she let out a soft laugh, almost a sigh. "But I'll admit something . . . when that engine growls, it does something to me. There's . . . a rush to it."

James raised an eyebrow, amused. "A rush, you say?"

After a quick stop at the bakery, they headed to their favorite pizzeria, a cozy spot tucked into a small cluster of storefronts that always seemed to glow warmly against the twilight. The aroma of wood-fired dough and fresh basil greeted them as they stepped inside and settled into a corner booth. They ordered their usual: two crisp pizza Margheritas, a Caprese salad to share, and a carafe of the house red wine that never failed to surprise them with its depth.

There was little conversation at first, a comfortable silence as they let the tension of the past two days drain away. But as they ate, the calm broke, and Marilyn suddenly launched into an issue at the hospital. "I had to compete with three angry surgeons at a board meeting this afternoon. Trust me—I barely made it out alive."

James sat back. "Sounds brutal. What happened?"

Marilyn took a long sip of the wine he offered. "Remember that equipment issue we flagged two weeks ago? The fetal monitors in L&D? Well, one of them failed this morning. Mid-delivery."

James frowned. "Was anyone hurt?"

"Thankfully, no," Marilyn said, her voice tight with residual anxiety. "The resident on duty caught it in time, switched to manual monitoring, and we delivered a healthy baby girl. But it scared everyone. And the family isn't exactly in a forgiving mood."

She took another sip. "Worse, the CFO doesn't want to sign off on replacements yet—he's talking about 'budget cycles.' Meanwhile, I have nurses threatening to go public if we don't fix it at once. And honestly? I don't blame them."

James nodded, his empathy showing. "Sounds like you're caught in the middle."

"Middle? I'm the bull's-eye. I spent half the day fighting for emergency funds and the other half convincing my staff not to stage a walkout. Tomorrow I'll probably have to go straight to the CEO."

James raised his glass. "To my warrior. If anyone can drag them into the 21st century, it's you."

Marilyn's mood softened, and she leaned back in the booth. "You always make it sound so noble. Really, I just want those monitors fixed before we have a crisis."

They finished their meal, the quiet conversation turning to Robin's latest adventures in her PhD program and ideas for a quick trip to Boulder. They savored the quiet break from their beloved neighborhood and the tragic death of Sophie. A complementary piece of limoncello cake to share was placed on the table with the check, more calories than either of them wanted, but it was delicious.

The Corvette rumbled through Waterton Canyon and back toward Warriors Way, the engine echoing low against the quiet houses under a sky lit by a bright waning gibbous moon. With an assist from two and half glasses of wine, Marilyn was softly singing along to Van Morrison's jazzy classic, *Moondance*.

James loved Marilyn every minute of the day, but there were

those times when the feelings were completely overwhelming. He eased the car into the garage and shut it down, the sudden silence making the night feel even clearer, crisper.

Marilyn stepped out, the cool air brushing her face, and gave him a smile that was both playful and knowing. "You know," she said, her voice low, "the music mixed with the sweet sound of that old engine might've been the best part of the evening."

James chuckled, making sure he turned off the lights, and closed the door with a solid thud. "Better than the bakery? Better than dinner?" he teased.

She walked past him toward the door, glancing over her shoulder with a spark in her eyes. "Oh, much better," she said softly. "You'd be smart to follow me straight into the bedroom right now."

James raised his eyebrows, caught off guard but grinning. "Yes, ma'am," he replied. The Corvette still ticked as the engine cooled behind him, but James hardly noticed—he was already chasing something much warmer.

CHAPTER ELEVEN

Wednesday Evening

While the Brooksides were enjoying dinner, Sheriff Carson hosted an update on the Delgado murder at 6 p.m. with Lieutenant Walker; Deputy Michaels, the forensics team leader; Dr. Murphy, the coroner; and Deputy Ryan, who did most of the on-site interviews. When Carson entered the conference room, he found a team that looked worn out.

"What, do we have a carbon monoxide leak in here? Liven it up, folks."

Everyone smiled and appeared to experience a jolt of energy.

Carson opened by thanking his team, acknowledging that they were staying late so they could move through the most critical points quickly.

Lieutenant Walker, the incident commander, gave a quick overview. "The victim is confirmed to be Sophie Delgado, address 7100 Warriors Way. She lived at this address for over ten years with her husband, Ricky Delgado. We couldn't find any employment information on either the victim or her husband. A summary of all the interviews so far shows that they were very private. And, according to Ricky, they had a flexible relationship. Per my interview with him yesterday morning, he was nervous but answered all my questions. In my opinion, he clearly lied about his timelines and where he spent some or all of Monday night. Ryan has more on that based on his interview with the bartender at Red Rocks."

"Interestingly, we found a University of Michigan sweatshirt in his bedroom and graduate-level chemistry books on a variety of related topics. One was titled "Principles of Medicinal Chemistry." Per the forward, it is a graduate-level textbook covering drug design, interactions in human systems, and advanced medical therapies. Deputy Yang is looking a little deeper and trying to trace the collection of books. Maybe Ricky is smarter than we think."

Carson leaned forward, his expression hardening. "I had a call this afternoon from Jake Reston. He bounced Ricky's picture off a deputy working in the Vegas fusion center. A guy fitting Ricky's description was there 12-13 years ago, trying to push opioid pills into the illegal market. They called him 'The Chemist.' Let's get someone out to Delgado's place right now for those chemistry books. Maybe the connection with Michigan is real."

Deputy Chris Michaels took over. "Overall, the collection of forensic evidence went smoothly. We have videos from all doorbell cameras that had a line of sight to the crime scene area and, per your specific guidance, the four cameras with a line of sight to Kenny Jacobs' home. The footage is being analyzed and pieced together this evening."

Walker nodded at Dr. Murphy, the coroner. "I've confirmed the time of death as being approximately 8:15 on Monday night," she said. "No change to the cause of death, blunt force trauma. We don't have the toxicology report yet. So far, there are no indications of drugs or alcohol in her system. We imaged the marks on the victim's head. To do the damage we found, the murder weapon probably had a long handle and a heavy metal end. Regarding the DNA results from the victim's clothing and body, they will take from a few weeks to several months. As you know, turnaround time at the Colorado Bureau of Investigation's forensic lab is still backed up due to the corruption investigation. With your intervention, we might be able to get the samples found under her fingernails analyzed much quicker."

Carson nodded. "Just tell me who to call and exactly what you want prioritized."

Deputy Ryan went last with updates on key interviews. "I interviewed the neighbors, James and Marilyn Brookside, Julia and Todd Krantz, and Kenny Jacobs. Also, Mike Jones, the bartender at Red Rocks Tavern, and Donna Grisham, the woman seen with Ricky."

Ryan went on to summarize the interviews.

Sheriff Carson interrupted. "So, we have Julia and Kenny on Warriors Way on Monday night sometime after 8 p.m. We have confirmation on Julia based on her own statement and the interview with Marilyn Brookside. Kenny's statement places him out there too. We suspect that Kenny was confused or lying about seeing Todd that night. Is that correct?"

Ryan nodded and continued. "I think Kenny could be confused, but yes, I think it is more likely he lied. I'm not sure why he would do that. He would have been better off not saying anything. Next, Jones, the bartender, told me that Ricky didn't get to the bar until around 9 p.m. on Monday night. He wanted food, but the kitchen was closed. Ricky was frustrated and said he was late because he had to take care of some business. Somewhere between two bourbons on the rocks and a 20-ounce beer, Donna Grisham joined Ricky. They talked and got very friendly. Jones estimated they left together at around 10 p.m. Nothing I found so far confirms Ricky's whereabouts on Monday night other than the one hour he was at Red Rocks."

"I met with Donna Grisham this afternoon. She's an emergency room nurse at the hospital in Highlands Ranch. She left Red Rocks with Ricky at 10 p.m. on Monday night, as said before, but went straight to work for a shift that started at 10:30. I verified that with her nurse manager. She and Ricky left trivia together on Tuesday night at 9:30 p.m. and went back to his house. Donna acknowledged that she spent the night."

Sheriff Carson shook his head. "Is she married?"

"Divorced about a year ago. She has two children who are with her ex-husband this week for spring break, so she has plenty of free time."

Carson leaned back in his chair. "Don't answer, but is it more likely that a murderer or an innocent person would take a lady friend back to his house the night after his wife was violently killed?"

There was no reaction from the group.

Ryan wrapped up his summary with Ricky's trivia playing partners, the two lady barbers from Bill's Cut and Style. "They only know him from trivia night. Apparently, he is very smart and can quickly answer almost all the questions. Their little team finishes first or second every week when he joins them. That's all they had to offer on Ricky. Sophie would go to Bill's for a cut every other month. She wasn't very particular, just a little bit of a trim."

Ryan reluctantly leaned forward. "An interesting point to add. Marilyn Brookside, Kenny Jacobs, and the ladies at Bill's all mentioned the victim's beauty. Marilyn saw her dressed up one time and described her as looking like a 5th Avenue model. Kenny got starry-eyed when he talked about her. The lady barbers often encouraged her to go to a stylist. The hidden American beauty was not the vibe I picked up initially when I canvassed the neighbors."

Carson looked at Walker. "It's interesting that Sophie had this hidden side to her, but I'm not sure why. It's possible someone had been watching her, maybe a stalker. Let's not discount that possibility. Okay, time to go home."

The group stood out of respect as Carson departed the conference room.

Once in his car, Sheriff Carson called Jake and gave him an update. Carson told him he felt there was more to the Ricky and Sophie Delgado story and asked if he had a federal contact who could help with the Vegas connection. Jake agreed to make some calls.

Carson started to chuckle. "Hold on a second. I guess before I ask you to get more involved, I should check; you didn't kill her, did you?"

Jake replied, "Not this time."

After talking to Jake, Carson called James. "Did I catch you at a bad time?" James and Marilyn had been home for about an hour after their dinner and the Corvette ride. They were now lying in bed, talking. Perplexed by the call this late, James responded, "No."

Carson's voice was packed with energy. "Can you reach out to one of your agency friends back in D.C. on the Delgados? I have a feeling about these two that won't go away. Just so you know, we're following a lead on four graduate-level books that we found during the search that we're certain belonged to Ricky. They deal with pharmacology and medicinal chemistry. That's probably a subject we both would have flunked at the Academy. Anyway, for our purposes, it's all about the effects of drugs and chemicals on people. It could be connected to legal or illegal drugs. See what you can find out."

Feeling empowered with a real mission, James responded, "I'll reach out first thing in the morning."

"Oh, before I let you go, did you let my old coroner kick your ass today on a bike ride in Chatfield?

Carson laughed. "None of that is why I really called. Okay . . . I really wanted to ask you if you killed the Delgado woman?"

James now understood the real purpose of the call and responded. "No. I'm pretty sure Jake is the murderer."

Carson laughed. "Damn, that's exactly what I'm thinking. To be safe, I think I'll have you both arrested."

Carson hung up before James could respond. Marilyn was returning to bed from the kitchen after checking to make sure her phone was plugged in to recharge. "Who called this late?"

James smiled. "It was Jason Carson. I think he's planning to arrest everyone living on Warriors Way."

Marilyn rolled her eyes as she turned off the light. "Clever move. Sometimes I wonder how the two of you made it through West Point."

James looked up at the darkened ceiling. "Me too."

James plunged through the night landscape, running along Warriors Way as a dense fog crawled over the pavement. The cold air stung his bare feet and shirtless body. Somewhere ahead, he heard a woman crying—thin, distant, but unmistakable. When he reached the stop sign, the fog tore open like a curtain, revealing Sophie, her face as he had found it that terrible morning.

"James . . . help me," she whispered, her voice scraping like dry leaves.

He tried to speak, but no sound came. The world twisted, and suddenly he was inside his own house, the walls pulsing with a slow, dreadful thrum.

A sharp knocking jolted him. James blinked and found himself standing in the kitchen, the clock on the wall reading 11:30 p.m. The sound came again, three hard raps, insistent. As he stepped closer, he froze.

Through the frosted glass of the kitchen door, a shape leaned toward him. "James . . . let me in," came Sophie's voice, cracked and pleading.

When he flicked on the porch light, her face appeared out of the gloom—blood smeared down her cheek, hair matted, her once-bright blue eyes now dark, hollow voids. "Save me, James . . . please."

He stumbled back, gripping the counter for balance. "No . . . Sophie, go away," he said, voice shaking.

But she latched onto the storm door handle with both hands and pulled. "You have to save me," she begged.

James shook his head, feeling his throat tightening. "It's too late," he whispered. "You're gone. Go away, Sophie. Go away." The lock clicked—impossible, he knew he had locked it—and the door began to pry open.

Sophie pushed it wide, her silhouette filling the frame as she stepped toward him, arm outstretched. "Save me," she hissed, inches from his face.

"James! James!" Marilyn's voice cut through the darkness. He jerked upright in bed, gasping, drenched in cold sweat. Marilyn touched his shoulder, eyes wide. "You were moaning . . . You kept saying 'Go away, Sophie.'"

He laid back against the pillows, chest heaving, the sound of the knocking still echoing in his ears.

"Just a dream," he muttered, though his heart hammered like it was trying to escape his ribs. "God . . . it felt so real."

Marilyn squeezed his hand, but he kept staring at the bedroom doorway, half-expecting to see a bloodied silhouette standing there in the shadows.

THURSDAY

CHAPTER TWELVE

Thursday, Early Morning

Deputy Natalie Yang, the Spirit County Sheriff's Department's point person on human trafficking along the I-25 corridor, was a brilliant intelligence analyst with a knack for distilling complex facts into usable talking points for investigations and trials. A former contract analyst at the military's NORTHCOM, she was hired three years ago by Carson on a recommendation from an Air Force Academy friend. Leaders in the sheriff's department considered her to be one of their best hires in the last decade.

Yang was known for asking tough questions about jurisdictional blind spots and pushing for better information-sharing at interagency meetings. It was at one of these sessions that she first met James Brookside, who was invited as a guest speaker. James had given a frank assessment of the strengths and weaknesses of collaboration between the U.S. intelligence community and law enforcement agencies. James was impressed with her precise, insightful questions and could tell she wasn't just absorbing theory, she was thinking about how to apply it to her work in the I-25 corridor.

Still in her office, it was now 1:15 a.m. Thursday morning, and Yang was making solid progress with her deep dive into the detailed handwritten notes found in the chemistry books.

The titles weren't casual reading—they were dense texts covering advanced organic synthesis, medicinal chemistry, and pharmacokinetics. One volume caught her attention for its focus on manipulating molecular structures to improve therapeutic outcomes. She cross-referenced the books with publication records and discovered that the authors had strong ties to pharmaceutical research and development. It was a strange collection for someone with no known professional background in science, and Natalie couldn't shake the feeling that Ricky's interest in them hinted at more than idle curiosity.

Yang noticed that the books and handwritten annotations in the margins referenced lectures and labs that had direct connections to the University of Michigan's Department of Chemistry. Those links raised new questions: had Ricky studied there, or was he collaborating with someone connected to the university? She emailed the campus police operations officer and reached out to Michigan's chemistry department chair to see whether Ricky's name appeared on any student or research rosters. If there was a tie to cutting-edge drug development, it might explain how a man of mysterious means ended up living quietly in Deer Park Ridge.

The large open area in the sheriff's office was quiet this time of night; the fluorescent lights dimmed to a soft hum. The only other person still working was Deputy Ryan, Yang leaned against the corner of his desk, arms folded, looking at him as he finished typing his report. The only sound was the rhythmic tapping of keys and the faint sound of sleet against the windows.

"Thank you for getting those chemistry books from Ricky Delgado. Did he push back at all? Tell you to contact his lawyer?"

Ryan looked up. "No, not at all. He was home when I called and told me to come over and get them. When I got there, he had them in a shopping bag ready to go. He said he had nothing to hide and to call if I needed anything else."

"Interesting. I'm not sure how to interpret that kind of openness from a suspect," Yang said with a half-smile. "You ever notice how this place feels completely different when everyone's gone?"

Ryan smiled, his blue eyes catching hers. "Yeah," he said softly. "It feels ... honest."

Setting his report aside, he stood and moved close to Yang, the air thick with something unsaid.

Yang laughed nervously, brushing a strand of hair from her face. "We're probably breaking about a dozen rules right now," she whispered.

"Probably. But I'm not leaving until you tell me to."

For a moment, neither moved—then she reached out, her hand brushing his sleeve. The sparks between them were undeniable, steady, and real. When they finally stepped apart, the clock on the wall showed it was almost 2 a.m. The spell broke, but neither could quite meet the other's eyes.

"Guess we should both head home," Yang said quietly, a faint smile tugging at her lips.

Ryan nodded, his pulse still racing.

"Yeah," he murmured. "I can't wait until our date on Friday night." As they walked outside, each felt the same truth settle in, the line between duty and desire had blurred, and neither wanted it to disappear.

Yang sat for a moment in her car, barely able to catch her breath as she watched Ryan's car move through the parking lot. They had only been dating for a month, but she couldn't stop thinking about him. Yang reached into her backpack and pulled out six pieces of chocolate she had snatched from Deputy Michaels' desk on the way out. The sweetness was not what she really wanted, but it would have to do for now. Friday night could not come soon enough.

Yang arrived back at work at 5:45 a.m. after only three hours of sleep with two chocolate croissants and a large coffee. She sat for a moment, staring out the window, and thought about last night's encounter with Ryan. It warmed her spirits more than the croissants or hot coffee, but it was game time, and she was eager to get back to work.

Without warning, a series of five sneezes hit in rapid succession, and she noticed her throat was starting to feel raspy. She whispered, "Please, not today. I can't be getting sick."

Within ten minutes, her inbox pinged with a message from Dr. Emily Travers, now a deputy department head at the University of Michigan's Chemistry Department. Travers mentioned she had been a graduate assistant in the early 2000s and she had access to archival student records and departmental class photos from that period. She'd heard about Yang's inquiry and offered her help in checking names or faces against university files.

Knowing this could be the breakthrough she needed, Yang quickly drafted a reply. She attached a current picture of Ricky and a set of enhanced, digitized images from the photos recovered during the search of Ricky's house, including cropped close-ups of Ricky and others in what appeared to be a lab or seminar setting:

If you recognize anyone in these images or can cross-reference them with departmental records from those years, it could help us prove Mr. Delgado's academic ties or even his true identity. If you have likely matches but are unsure, we have advanced facial recognition programs that can be interactively used.

As she hit send, Yang leaned back in her chair, hoping Travers's insider knowledge would confirm her growing suspicion that Ricky's quiet life in Deer Park Ridge was only the surface of a far more complicated past.

Dr. Travers responded with intriguing results. She wrote that after reviewing the pictures, one face triggered a memory:

There is a strong resemblance between the man identified as Ricky and a former student named Bruce E. Bricklin. Bricklin graduated from Michigan's undergraduate chemistry program in 2003 and completed a master's degree in 2005 before moving on to pursue a PhD at the University of Chicago. Here are scanned copies of departmental records and class photos from those years, highlighting Bricklin's entries and noting the similarity between the images. Bricklin was an exceptionally bright student. He took part in research projects in medicinal chemistry and drug design during his time here. After Michigan, he was accepted into an elite chemistry program at the University of Chicago, focusing on the application of chemistry to medical research.

The email also included a note of concern. Bricklin had fallen off Travers's radar after Chicago, and she hadn't heard his name in professional circles for well over a decade. Deputy Yang felt a cold knot form in her stomach as she read the message. If Ricky was in fact Bruce Bricklin, then his deliberate disappearance from the scientific community and reinvention under a new name suggested there were secrets in his past worth uncovering.

Deputy Yang wasted no time after receiving Dr. Travers's email. The potential identification of Ricky as Bruce Bricklin opened a new investigative path, and she began researching points of contact at the University of Chicago's Department of Chemistry. Yang crafted a detailed email explaining her inquiry and attached the same enhanced photos she had sent to Dr. Travers, along with Michigan's records linking Bricklin to studies in Chicago. She specifically asked for confirmation of Bricklin's enrollment, access to his thesis research if available, and any information about internships or partnerships with pharmaceutical companies during his doctoral program.

Within hours, the program coordinator replied:

Bruce E. Bricklin was enrolled in our chemistry PhD program from 2005 to 2010. His dissertation focused on advanced organic synthesis techniques for the development of small-molecule inhibitors targeting cancer-related enzymes—a field with high-value pharmaceutical applications. Bricklin also completed a two-year internship with a prominent drug company in the Chicago area during his studies, working in their experimental therapeutics division. That internship, paired with his innovative research, would have given him access to proprietary compounds and confidential data.

As Yang read the email, her instincts sharpened—Bricklin's background in chemistry and his exposure to sensitive pharmaceutical work might be the key to understanding why he had disappeared from his professional life and reemerged years later.

After reviewing the University of Chicago's response, Deputy Yang composed a carefully worded follow-up email to the Michigan and Chicago professors. She thanked them for their swift replies and acknowledged the significance of Bricklin's work in cancer-related enzyme inhibitors. Then, Yang pivoted to a more pointed question:

Based on your knowledge of Bricklin's research and internship, were there any signs, direct or indirect, that his work might have overlapped with compounds later diverted into illicit drug production or misused in the development of synthetic opioids or painkillers? FYI, this inquiry isn't academic; it is part of an active investigation involving possible connections between Bricklin's past research and criminal activity years later.

The Chicago professor responded with a cautious but intriguing note:

Bricklin's dissertation had legitimate pharmaceutical applications; the enzyme pathways he worked on were like those targeted in the design of certain synthetic painkillers and, in theory, could be exploited for creating novel opioids. There were concerns, years ago, about proprietary compounds from the Chicago drug company where Bricklin interned leaking into the illegal market, though no wrongdoing was ever publicly tied to the company or to Bricklin himself. If someone were inclined to cross ethical lines, a researcher of his caliber could certainly have applied his knowledge in ways that wouldn't show up in any academic record.

Yang felt a chill as she read the words, realizing she might be dealing with a man whose past in legitimate science had blurred into something far more dangerous.

After almost twenty hours, Deputy Yang's research painted a far more complex picture of Ricky, or Bruce Bricklin, than anyone in Deer Park Ridge could have imagined. The University of Michigan confirmed his strong academic background in chemistry, while the University of Chicago revealed his advanced work in medicinal research and an internship at a major pharmaceutical company. Combined, the information suggested Bricklin had deep expertise in drug design and access to sensitive proprietary data during a critical period in the mid-2000s. The implications were troubling: if Bricklin had stepped outside the bounds of legitimate science, his knowledge could have been used to engineer synthetic opioids or other compounds with high value in legal and illicit markets. For Yang, the pieces hinted at a man who may have walked away from a prestigious career not out of disinterest, but to escape or profit from something buried in his past.

A very tired Deputy Yang and Lieutenant Walker entered Sheriff Carson's office suite. Yang stood at the front of the small briefing room, the faint hum of the projector filling the silence as she clicked to the next slide on her laptop, a photo of Ricky in Deer Park Ridge juxtaposed with a younger Bruce Bricklin from a University of Michigan class roster.

"Sir, Ricky is almost certainly Bruce Bricklin," she began, her voice steady. "He graduated from Michigan with a master's in chemistry in 2005 and earned a PhD at the University of Chicago in 2010. His dissertation and internship work focused on advanced drug design, specifically enzyme inhibitors that overlap with pathways used in synthetic opioids and experimental painkillers."

Sheriff Carson leaned back in his chair, his brow furrowed, while Lieutenant Walker scribbled notes.

Yang continued, but a series of sneezes and a runny nose interrupted her presentation. She took a moment to drink water and grab a tissue. Outside Carson's office, another round of sneezes was heard. This time, it was Ryan as he walked past the office door. Yang, Carson, and Walker smiled. The relationship between the young deputies was the department's worst-kept secret.

Yang gathered herself and continued. "There's no hard evidence tying him to illicit drug activity, but a former professor raised concerns about the potential misuse of his research and mentioned rumors of proprietary compounds from his internship company leaking into the black market around that time."

After dismissing Deputy Yang with a nod of appreciation, Sheriff Carson let the door click shut before turning to Lieutenant Walker, his expression tight with thought.

"Well, this changes the temperature a bit, doesn't it?" he said quietly, rubbing the back of his neck. "If Ricky's, or Bricklin's, background ties into pharmaceuticals or synthetic opioids, and illegal activities, we could be staring at a more complex set of threats."

Walker leaned forward, his voice low. "Or it could be a coincidence. We can't let this run wild without something concrete."

Carson nodded. "Exactly. We need to either connect Sophie's murder to his academic and professional past or decisively disconnect it. Start pulling financials, professional contacts, and anything from his time in Chicago that might suggest he was in over his head. And keep pressure on forensics. I want to know if there's anything at that house tying him to drugs, money, or a lab setup."

He paused, eyes narrowing. "Until then, we keep this circle tight. If Bricklin's running from something big, the last thing we need is him realizing we know who he really is."

———————————

Deputy Ryan shuffled into the break room, clutching a steaming mug of coffee and a box of tissues.

"You look like hell, Ryan," Yang said with a sniffle, slumped at the small table surrounded by case files. Her voice was hoarse, her nose red.

Ryan smirked weakly. "Yeah, well, I think you're the one who gave me this plague. You were sneezing all over me last night."

She rolled her eyes and reached for another tissue. "Excuse me, I wasn't sneezing until after you coughed all over me. You basically weaponized the thing."

Ryan laughed, which turned into a raspy cough. "I was fine until that last kiss."

Yang pointed her pen at him. "Cold or not, I'd kiss you right now if we could get away with it."

He raised an eyebrow.

They both started laughing, then groaned as the laughter triggered another round of coughing.

"We're a mess," Ryan said, wiping his nose.

"Yeah," Yang agreed, sniffling, "and we still need to look professional when the lieutenant drops in. Got any cold meds in your survival kit, partner?"

CHAPTER THIRTEEN

Thursday Morning

Based on Sheriff Carson's request, James was up and on his computer by 6:15 a.m. to contact an old agency friend, Mark Alexander, who was part of an interagency working group in D.C. He was certain Mark had access to the right databases.

James, still unnerved by his dream about Sophie, composed a short email with all the information he had on the Delgados. The request, simple on the surface, was for travel and bank records for Ricky and Sophie. But both he and Mark knew there was nothing casual about it.

Within an hour, he received a quick reply: "Give me some time to check this out."

The speed of the response told James his friend was already intrigued, which was both good and dangerous.

When Alexander's first reply came back, James read it twice before leaning back in his chair:

I found travel logs that showed Ricky and Sophie had been in Washington, D.C. three years ago, on the exact same dates when closed-door congressional hearings were held on pharmaceutical industry corruption. Specifically, those hearings were about the distribution of natural and synthetic opioid pills into black-market channels and the offshore laundering of billions in profits.

The flights and hotel were booked by a government travel agent. Interestingly, another name surfaced during my search with the same travel agent, flights, and hotel: Kenny Jacobs. There's no public record of them attending any official events, but the proximity to those hearings is too close to ignore.

I looked at all their bank records going back to 2010. Ricky's accounts showed unexplained cash deposits from wire transfers routed through shell corporations in the Caribbean—amounts just under federal reporting thresholds.

Sophie's activity was quieter but hinted at accounts in Luxembourg.

Kenny's records were the most aggressive, with high-volume transfers bouncing between three different banks in the D.C. area and one in the Cayman Islands.

I'm still digging, more to follow.

James felt the familiar tightening in his chest. He wasn't looking at just a murder investigation anymore. It was the edge of a much larger, uglier web, one that could pull in people far more dangerous than anyone on Warriors Way.

James decided not to rely solely on his Washington contact. Pulling up the Spirit County Assessor's database, he began combing through property records for Ricky and Sophie Delgado's house, as well as Kenny Jacobs' place. The pattern appeared quickly. Both properties had been bought in 2015, but not directly by Ricky, Sophie, or Kenny. Instead, the first buyer was listed as National Relocation Services LLC, a firm James recognized from his intelligence days as one often contracted by federal agencies to quietly move employees, witnesses, and occasionally undercover operatives. Exactly thirty days after the first purchase, the homes were transferred to their current owners at identical sale price transactions that looked clean on paper but carried the faint odor of a setup.

The timing gnawed at him. 2015 wasn't just any year; it was the period when federal task forces were ramping up investigations into pharmaceutical supply chain corruption, and when the opioid crisis hit the front pages. James knew relocation firms like this one often provided not just housing but a layer of plausible deniability, shielding the identities of the true movers and the reasons for their transfers. The fact that both the Delgados and Kenny Jacobs had entered the neighborhood through this channel suggested coordination, not coincidence. Whatever had brought them to Deer Park Ridge, it wasn't random, and it wasn't about finding a beautiful view of the mountains.

James leaned back in his chair, phone in hand, and called the sheriff's department. When he eventually connected with Yang, her voice was strained. "Deputy Yang, can I help you? Oops, just a second."

He could hear her sneezing and blowing her nose. Without thinking James went to the sink and washed his hands.

"Okay, I'm back."

"Yang, it's James Brookside," he replied. "I've come across something you might want to put on Sheriff Carson's radar. There's chatter—reliable chatter—that Ricky, Sophie, and Kenny Jacobs were back in D.C. three years ago and might have testified in a closed congressional session. The topic? Illegal distribution of opioids by major pharmaceutical companies to the black market."

Yang was silent for a beat. "That's not the kind of thing you just 'come across.' Where did you hear it?"

James spoke softly. "Old contact with access, and a little digging. The point is, if that's true, it could explain a whole lot about the secretive life of Ricky and Sophie and why someone might want them quiet."

Yang's voice sharpened. "You're saying our local murder victim might've been tied to a federal-level investigation? I'll run this through Carson and loop in the state investigators."

"Just be careful who you tell. If the wrong ears hear this, we might all need more than coffee to get through the week." He lowered his voice. "And there's another wrinkle you need to know about. Both the Delgados' place and Kenny Jacobs' house? They were bought through a government relocation company, paperwork buried deep, and then quietly transferred about a month later."

Yang's pen stopped scratching. "You're telling me their homes were basically funneled through a federal front company?"

James exhaled. "That's exactly what I'm telling you. Which means somebody in a government office knew exactly who they were and didn't want that fact sitting in the open records." Now it was James's turn to score some information. "Sheriff Carson told me you're researching the chemistry books from the Delgados' house. Do you have anything for me?"

After a long delay, Yang responded. "Not yet. I'll let Sheriff Carson know about this new information immediately. Thanks for all your help."

James was surprised and felt he had been snubbed after providing important information. The professional courtesy he expected had shifted, a subtle but significant signal of the divide between his professional past and the new reality of being almost irrelevant.

Meanwhile, Jake took a call from Lieutenant Walker.

"Jake, I'm going to be blunt," Walker said. "You've overstepped. I've had potential witnesses tell me you've been poking around, asking questions like you're still wearing a badge. You're not law enforcement anymore."

Jake smirked, his dry humor barely concealing his irritation. "Man, I'm not trying to steal your job. People talk to me because they don't feel threatened. Do you think these folks are going to fully open up to a deputy in uniform?"

"If you muddy the water with your little back-porch interviews, you're making my job harder. This is a homicide, Jake, not one of your old intelligence games. So, I'll say this once, you've been helpful with the bigger picture, but I need you to stay in your lane."

Jake's smile faded, and his voice dropped. "And I'll say this once—if staying in my lane means letting a murderer walk free because you won't listen to the people who actually know this street, then I'll take the risk. You can be as pissed as you want, but I'm not backing off." Jake hung up before Walker could respond.

Still frustrated from his call with Yang, James captured his thoughts for the day in a journal entry.

March 19: The puzzle pieces are finally shifting into place, though the picture they form is darker than I could have imagined. I can't shake the revelation that Ricky, Sophie, and

Kenny were potentially flown back to Washington at government expense—quietly, discreetly—to sit behind closed doors and testify about opioid trafficking. Not the street-level garbage, but shipments funneled straight out of the boardrooms and warehouses of so-called legitimate pharmaceutical companies.

I've seen enough during my years in intelligence to know how deep that rot runs. But to think Ricky and Sophie were in the middle of it, living six doors away, presenting themselves as reclusive, odd neighbors while quietly holding explosive information . . . it unsettles me more than Sophie's death itself.

What gnaws at me is motive. If they were government witnesses, Sophie's murder may not have been a neighborhood quarrel or random act of violence—it could have been a silencing, a message, or the unraveling of a deal gone bad. It means the web stretches far beyond Warriors Way. And yet, why plant themselves here in Deer Park Ridge? Was it just a cover, or did they really think they'd blend in among retirees and dog walkers?

James thought again about something Jake had said. "Secrets always bleed through the walls."

He wondered whose walls on this street were hiding the biggest secrets of all.

CHAPTER FOURTEEN

Thursday Morning

While Yang was doing her research and James was reaching out to his old contacts, Marilyn was in a good mood, heading to work. The morning offered brilliant sunshine that illuminated the red rocks of Deer Park Ridge, casting a rust color glow. But by the time she merged her red Alfa Romeo SUV into Denver's morning traffic on C-470, the glow was behind her, both literally and emotionally. Her drive to Colorado General Hospital was a familiar and focused passage between worlds. The cliffs and canyons faded in the rearview mirror; ahead lay fluorescent lights and challenging decisions. After Marilyn parked in her normal spot, she looked back at the shiny new Alfa. It wasn't an overly expensive vehicle, but she loved the sporty feel, the look, and the cool wheels—she loved those wheels.

The morning began with a difficult consult for a 28-year-old patient and her husband. Genetic testing had revealed concerning news about the health of their baby. The woman covered her mouth, eyes filling. Her husband sat frozen, jaw clenched. Marilyn let the silence do what it needed to before she began the process of answering their questions.

At 10 a.m., she received a call from the CFO's office about the faulty fetal monitor problem. Hospital leadership had intervened. A new monitor was already on order, and the others would be fully checked for serviceability.

Marilyn danced once around the desk and texted James. "I won. New monitor ordered. Yay for me."

Then it was back to work. Later, she performed a C-section: twins, one breech, both healthy. The air buzzed with laughter and adrenaline. The contrast from the morning was jarring but familiar. Life and loss stacked side by side. She moved through the hospital like a current—quiet, strong, constant.

———————

After hosting an office birthday party, Marilyn received a surprise phone call. She now sat rigidly in the chair across from Janet Wood, the hospital's Vice President for Human Resources. The polished walnut desk between them felt like a barrier she hadn't expected to confront today. Janet folded her hands, her expression gentle yet formal.

"Marilyn, thank you for coming in on such short notice," she began softly. "I know you've had a busy day, but the board has asked me to speak with you directly."

Marilyn frowned, caught off guard. "The board? About what?"

Janet took a slow breath. "They've been following the news reports and social media about your husband finding the woman's body near your home . . . and your name has come up too, along with your position here." She paused, searching Marilyn's face. "They want to be sure you're okay. And . . . they've suggested it might be smart for you to take a little time off."

Marilyn's eyes widened as disbelief flooded her. "Time off? Janet, I'm fine. I'm completely fine. This is absurd."

"I understand," Janet said, leaning forward slightly, her voice quieter now. "And I told them as much. But they're looking at the optics, the sensitivity of your role, especially with everything happening around the investigation."

"My work hasn't suffered. I'm here, I'm focused, and I'm doing my job. The fact that James found the body doesn't change my ability to function as a physician." Her voice trembled with a mix of anger and hurt.

"I know. Truly, I do. And the board loves you, Marilyn—they made me repeat that word for word. This is only a suggestion at this point. They're trying to be proactive, not punitive." She offered a small, reassuring smile. "But I need to be honest with you, they may push harder if the media attention keeps growing. Remember, our patients are seeing the same articles."

Marilyn exhaled slowly, her shock giving way to a cold, steely resolve. "Well, then the board can talk to me directly," she said. "Because I'm not stepping away from my work."

Janet sighed but nodded, knowing better than to argue with Marilyn when she'd set her stance.

***

After the meeting, Marilyn stepped out of the hospital's side entrance and dialed James, her breath still tight with anger. "You are not going to believe what just happened," she said the moment he answered.

James's voice came through steady and calm. "What now? You sound furious."

Marilyn paced along the sidewalk. "Janet just told me the board is 'concerned' about me because of the press and social media stories—because your name and mine keep coming up. They suggested I take time off. Can you believe that? As if I can't do my job because of what happened on our street."

James sighed. "Are you okay? Do you need to come home?"

Marilyn stopped pacing. "No, I'm not coming home. I told Janet I'm fine, and I meant it. I am not taking time off, and I'm not going to be pushed into anything because the board gets nervous about optics." Her voice sharpened with conviction. "I've worked too hard for this. I'm not stepping aside because people are whispering."

James paused, then said quietly, "I know. And I've got your back, whatever you decide."

Marilyn exhaled, the edge of her frustration softening just a little. "Good," she said, "because I'm not backing down."

Marilyn returned to her office and froze. The hospital's Chief Medical Officer, Greg Litton, was standing by the window, arms folded, his expression unreadable. "Greg? What on earth!" she began, setting her bag down slowly.

"Close the door, Marilyn," he said gently. "We need to talk." She obeyed, tension rising.

Greg took a step towards her. "I just spoke with Janet. And I'm going to be direct: I'm ordering you to take one week off. Starting tomorrow."

Marilyn stiffened. "Greg, no. I already told Janet I'm not taking time off. I'm fine. Damn it, I dealt with a patient issue for a fellow doctor at the scene of the murder on Tuesday morning with the victim right in front of me. These kinds of things don't bother me."

"You're not fine," Greg replied softly, but firmly. "You're functioning, yes. But I know the look. I've seen it more times than I ever wanted." He exhaled wearily. "During my deployments in Iraq and Afghanistan, I treated soldiers and civilians who came in torn apart by blasts, by gunfire . . . and sometimes worse. I thought I was managing it. Thought I was tough enough. But trauma isn't loud, Marilyn. It seeps in. You don't feel it until it's already taken hold."

She swallowed, her voice tighter. "Greg, I didn't see the attack. I just—"

"You found the aftermath in front of your home," he cut in gently. "And that can be just as damaging."

He stepped aside so she could sit, though she stayed standing. "You are one of the most valuable physicians in this hospital," he said. "You save babies and mothers every week. You guide research teams. You mentor residents. And right now, you carry a burden inside you whether you admit it or not."

Marilyn's jaw clenched, her eyes stinging. "Taking time off feels like quitting," she whispered.

Greg shook his head. "It's strength. It's stewardship. It's making sure you and James have room to breathe after witnessing something horrific. You get one week. That's an order from your CMO . . . and from someone who has learned the hard way what happens when you don't stop. Marilyn, the trauma from my deployments almost cost me my family and my life."

Marilyn took a deep breath and nodded.

After Greg left, she took time to clear her calendar with her admin assistant and headed for the garage. Once in her Alfa and on the road, she called James for a quick update. Marilyn could hear the relief in his voice, which offered confirmation as she whispered to herself, "Maybe Greg is right."

The city fell away as she climbed into the foothills to Deer Park Ridge. A mule deer crossed ahead, its pace regal and unhurried. The air cooled. Her shoulders loosened. But the silence felt like a warning that the residents living on Warriors Way were still not safe.

———

While waiting for Marilyn to get home, James sat at the kitchen table with his hands wrapped around a can of soda that had long since gone flat. He kept replaying the dream from last night, each detail arriving with a clarity that unsettled him—being out on the street, the dull pounding on the door, Sophie's hollow eyes, the way her voice had cracked as she begged him to save her. It hadn't felt like a dream at all; it felt like a visitation. He rubbed his temples and tried to anchor himself in the rational explanations he'd leaned on his whole life—stress, trauma, exhaustion—but none of them explained why he'd heard her voice so distinctly, or why it lingered in his mind now like an echo trapped in the walls.

As he stared out the window toward the stop sign where her body had been found, a more provocative question crept in: What if she really had called out to him? He didn't believe in ghosts, or messages from the dead—but he also couldn't shake the sickening weight of guilt pressing on his chest. If Sophie had reached out, in a dream or something darker, was she begging him to see what he had missed? Was she looking at the lights in his kitchen window during her final moment?

James set the can of soda down and forced himself to breathe, but the thought stayed with him, curling tight around his conscience like a hand he couldn't pry loose.

James and Marilyn had a brief discussion after she arrived home. With 45 minutes of light left, she just wanted to go for a walk to clear her head.

Jake arrived at the Brooksides' house as Marilyn was returning home.

She reminded James, "I've got to hurry. Book club tonight at Julia's house. There's a container of chicken salad in the refrigerator, and we have everything bagels and red grapes. There's plenty of food for you, too, Jake."

"Thank you," said Jake. "But I'm meeting an old law enforcement friend in Parker. He owes me an expensive dinner and a bottomless glass of wine."

Shaking her head with a look of amused disapproval, Marilyn rolled her eyes.

On the slightly chilly late afternoon, James and Jake moved to the deck, beers in hand, watching the sun settle over Warriors Way. James took a deep breath and carefully outlined his research related to the deception around the purchases of the Delgados' and Jacob's homes, and Mark Alexander's information on the trips back to D.C.

Jake looked completely dumbfounded. "You've got to be shitting me?"

James shook his head.

Jake rubbed the back of his neck. "Well, Walker and I had ourselves a little dust-up today," he said, half-grinning. "He doesn't appreciate me talking to potential witnesses. Says I'm muddying his investigation."

James raised an eyebrow. "And you told him what?"

Jake chuckled. "That he could be as mad as he wanted, but I wasn't about to stop asking questions. Don't worry, all's fine. He just needed to puff his chest a bit."

"You're sure this won't blow back on us?"

"Nah. Walker will stew, but he knows I'm right. What matters now isn't trading jabs with him—it's pulling from the networks we still have. You've got your old intel contacts, and I've got people in law enforcement who owe me a favor or two. Between us, we can dig up what the sheriff's office can't or won't. That's where the real answers will come from."

Jake nodded toward the next house. "That guy next door. What's his deal?"

"It's supposedly an investment property John is hoping to flip. He shows up daily like clockwork. Never brings tools. Claims he's doing high-end woodwork throughout the place. Looks more like he's hiding in it."

Jake grunted. "You don't hide in plain sight unless you've got a reason."

Before James could reply, the doorbell rang. Todd stood there, holding a plate. "Julia made these for you and Marilyn. Chicken burgers. She made too many for book club tonight, so lucky you."

James took it with a nod. "Thank you. You look wiped out. Everything okay?"

"Didn't sleep," Todd said. "Too much on my mind."

Jake stepped forward, his tone light but eyes sharp. "Todd, what's going on? Kenny said he saw you out on Warriors Way

Monday night around the time of the murder. I know that the sheriff's office is already digging into the conflicting statements. It is better to correct it now than to let them figure it out. So, what is the real deal?"

Todd blinked. "I told James. Fort Collins. Didn't get home until almost eleven."

"You sure about that?" Jake asked sharply.

Todd hesitated just a fraction of a second, then nodded. "Positive."

Todd turned to leave, but James stopped him and went to get two large pieces of birthday cake. "Thought you might need a sugar rush to help with that sleep problem." Both laughed, and Todd headed home.

After he left, James snapped at Jake. "He's my friend. You need to tread more carefully."

"Buddy, you have to ask hard questions if you want to solve this murder. Toughen up, man. You're being too sensitive."

––––––––––––

Fifteen miles away, two old friends were meeting in a strip mall lot. Ricky arrived first and was leaning against his SUV, fedora tilted low. Kenny pulled into the adjacent spot and climbed out, eyes darting around.

They hugged, and Kenny spoke first, his voice low and careful. "Ricky . . . man, I'm sorry about Sophie. I can't believe it."

Ricky didn't lift his head, just let out a slow sigh. "Yeah. It feels like the whole world came crashing down overnight. She didn't deserve to go like that."

Kenny nodded, his hand in his right jacket pocket, uneasy. "You look pretty calm."

Ricky smirked, pulling a cigarette from his pocket. "I'm not calm, man. This is a nightmare. If the sheriff and those idiot reporters keep sniffing around, they'll find holes in our stories. I'm already the number one suspect because I'm the husband. You're going to look dirty, too, my friend. You had the head-knocking session with Sophie last fall over your dog and her precious rose bushes." He lit his cigarette, the flame briefly reflecting in his eyes.

"You got any idea who could've done it? Anybody holdin' a grudge?"

Ricky looked around, his eyes red-rimmed but sharp, studying Kenny. "Grudges? Are you kidding? We had more than our share. But none of them should've followed us here." His voice dropped, almost a whisper. "This was supposed to be the safe place, the quiet life. And now she's gone."

Kenny searched his friend's face. "So, you think this wasn't random?"

"Nothing in my life has ever been random. You know that better than most."

"That's exactly the point. You create your own chaos. I handed you the golden ticket, Ricky," Kenny growled, stabbing a finger against Ricky's chest.

"That's bullshit, man. And don't touch me again."

Kenny looked Ricky squarely in the eye. "We had a clean setup with D.J. Singer, skimming from company profits, and nobody paying attention. I was makin' us rich right under their noses. That was our play, our future. But you couldn't resist runnin' your own little side hustle in Vegas by reroutin' those damn pill shipments from Singer so you could chase quick cash with those street-level gangsters. You were the selfish asshole who blew the arrangement we worked years to build."

Ricky's jaw tightened, his fedora shadowing his eyes. "Don't pin this all on me, Kenny," he said, his voice low and sharp. "You knew the kind of money moving through the Strip—fast, untraceable, and ten times what your 'clean setup' promised. I was thinking bigger. You acted like you were the mastermind, but you were afraid of risk."

Kenny slammed his hand down hard on the hood of the car. "Real money?" he barked. "You risked puttin' us in the crosshairs of the company and the Vegas thugs. And you got one of my friends killed and the Feds breathin' down our necks."

Ricky took a long drag on his cigarette. "Calm down, man. We both knew the deal. We were working for a corrupt company. And we certainly weren't the only ones working backroom deals. Now we are where we are. Going forward, the witness protection program doesn't mean a thing if either of us screws up the cover. Sophie's gone, and that just puts more heat on us. So, here's the rule: we stick to the script, word for word. You start freelancing, we both go down."

Kenny grew more agitated. "So, you think this will go away if we stick to the script? I've had a goddamned black SUV parked on my street at least five times over the last couple weeks. One night, the driver almost ran me over when I got too close walkin' King. Somebody is watchin'."

Ricky thought it was best not to tell Kenny about the black SUV that followed him and Donna to breakfast on Wednesday morning.

Kenny stepped closer, voice dropping. "Look, I'll play my

part, but you better remember—if I even smell you settin' me up, I'll burn your whole story down before I let you take me with you."

Ricky stomped out his cigarette. "Then I guess we both better play nice before we end up lying next to Sophie in the morgue."

CHAPTER FIFTEEN

As the sun set, Jake slid into the leather booth across from Gary Stivers at a steakhouse in Parker. The two men shook hands firmly, old colleagues whose bond had been forged in countless tense national law enforcement meetings. Gary had retired in Colorado a few years earlier. Jake was glad to see his old friend looking so fit and happy in a tailored sport coat, a martini in hand. They clinked glasses, trading laughs before the conversation shifted, as it always did with them, toward serious business.

"Gary, I've got something strange brewing up in Deer Park Ridge. A woman named Sophie Delgado was murdered Monday night. Brutal scene."

As their New York strip steaks arrived, sizzling on heavy plates, Jake laid out the entire story, from James discovering the body to the sheriff's initial investigation. He didn't just report the facts; he described the feeling, the uneasy calm, the odd silences, and the subtle, jarring inconsistencies.

"It doesn't make sense," Jake continued, swirling a glass of red wine. "They've lived there for over ten years. No jobs. No close friends on the street. And Ricky . . . he's got this old Vegas vibe—fedoras, tailored suits, slick talk. But I can tell there's more to him than that. He's too smart to be doing nothing for a decade."

Gary set his fork down. "Hold up, Jake. Vegas vibe? You're saying he looks and acts like an old-school gambler?"

"Yeah," Jake said, nodding. "But not the washed-up kind. There's a sharpness about him. I've met guys like him—calculated, observant, the type who plays the fool but has a mind like a steel trap. The neighbors don't know what he does. They don't even know where his money comes from."

Gary raised his glass and smirked. "So, what's your gut say? Mobbed up? Federal asset gone dark? Or just a rich guy who doesn't like people?"

"I thought about all of those possibilities," Jake admitted. "But here's the thing . . . I reached out to Vegas intel, they're pretty sure our guy Ricky was being tracked by the federal drug and local law enforcement about a decade ago. They called him 'The Chemist.' He was trying to push high-grade opioid pills and Fentanyl onto the black market." Jake whispered. "The trail went cold before they could make a case, and then he disappeared."

Gary's eyes narrowed. "A chemist pushing opioids. You're saying a guy with that skillset and history shows up in a quiet neighborhood, and a decade later, his wife is dead. That's concerning."

"Exactly," Jake said, taking a long sip of his wine. "And it gets crazier. My buddy has a D.C. contact who confirmed that Ricky, Sophie, and their neighbor, Kenny Jacobs, were all flown to D.C. three years ago by a government travel agent. They were there during closed-door congressional hearings about pharmaceutical industry corruption and opioid trafficking."

Gary was quiet for a long moment, the restaurant's background chatter fading. "Spillover," he said finally, his tone serious. "Follow the facts, man. These guys aren't just hiding. They're most likely in a witness protection or similar program. I'll bet the victim crossed someone big and the murder was payback."

They talked for another hour, the wine bottle emptying slowly between them.

Gary tapped a finger on the table, his old investigator's instincts fully engaged now. "If Ricky is as sharp as you say, he's not going to slip up easily," Gary mused. "But people like that, they've always got a history somewhere. Dig deep enough, and you'll find it. Now that you suspect the federal angle, you should get back in touch with your contact in Vegas and see if you can tie their investigation to the congressional hearings in D.C. They may not know it, but the two events could be connected."

"That's the plan," Jake said with a smile as the server delivered two espressos and the check. Jake raised his tiny coffee cup in a toast. "I may need to lean on you, old friend."

Gary reached for the check, but Jake grabbed it first. "I owe you for the insightful conversation."

His friend chuckled. "For a steak and a martini, you can call me anytime."

CHAPTER SIXTEEN

Thursday Evening

When Julia and Todd moved to Warriors Way, it was one of her happiest moments. Julia had vacationed in Colorado as a child and dreamed of escaping the heat and dreariness of Texas for that beautiful state. That joy faded fast two years ago, when a friend of hers recognized Kate Jennings, now Sophie Delgado. The same woman. The same voice. The beautiful profile etched in her memory. Kate, living a few doors away, was inconceivable. The name change was even harder to understand.

Julia stared out the kitchen window, her gaze fixed on the quiet street, but she didn't see the view. She saw what Todd had described: Sophie, her body limp and crumpled at the base of the stop sign on Monday night. Could she be responsible for Sophie's death? Was she a murderer? Was it even fair for her own lawyer to ask that question? It all happened so fast. Julia had caught a glimpse of Sophie walking near the mailboxes minutes earlier. A woman she had avoided for two years. Then she saw her again, appearing from the darkness under the dim glow of distant porch lights.

The argument had been quick. Sophie asked for forgiveness and wanted to come to book club. The rage Julia thought she could control flashed through her body. She hadn't meant to hit her that hard with the heavy metal flashlight she always carried on her walks. The sickening clang of the impact. Sophie stumbled and fell hard but got back to her feet almost at once. At least, that's what Julia told herself.

She flashed back to the courtroom in Texas, the judge's gavel falling, the sentence so light it felt like a joke. The beautiful Kate (or Sophie) walked free while Angela, Julia's beloved younger sister, was buried before the New Year. The memory of that injustice was a raw wound, and for the last two years she had felt a rage building in her that she could no longer contain.

When Todd got home Monday night, Julia told him what happened. How she and Sophie had exchanged words, and the surreal moment she struck her with the flashlight. No one else was around, but she had a feeling that someone was watching. Todd was in disbelief and fearful that their wonderful Colorado life was at risk.

Julia composed herself and finished preparing for book club. Marilyn was the first to arrive for the gathering. When Julia opened the door, though her face was pale and her eyes red, she forced a small smile to greet her first guest.

"I brought food," Marilyn said gently.

"Did you make it?" Julia asked, with a skeptical look.

"Hey, I actually followed the recipe this time."

Julia rolled her eyes and barely responded. The other ladies arrived within the next ten minutes or so, and the social part of the meeting started with food, wine, and chatter about the murder.

Julia filled wine glasses as Marilyn settled into the corner of the sofa, the low hum of conversation bouncing around the living room.

"Okay," Julia said, lifting her copy of the novel, "can we please stay focused on the book for at least ten minutes?"

Kim snorted. "Not a chance. Not when a woman was murdered one hundred yards from here."

Julia sighed, but her eyes flicked toward Marilyn. "I know, I know. It's just . . . I need one normal night."

Marilyn reached over and squeezed her hand. "We all do. But people are scared, Jules. And confused."

Across the room, Karey whispered, "My partner says the sheriff's office is way too quiet about it. Like they know more than they're saying."

Julia kept her tone even. "They always hold things back during an active investigation. That doesn't mean there's a conspiracy."

"Still," Marilyn added, swirling her wine, "someone was out on these streets Monday night, and Sophie ended up dead. People want to know who."

A heavy silence fell until Amy blurted, "Did you hear about the turkeys? That poor woman . . . the whole thing is horrible."

Julia shut her eyes for a moment before replying, "Can we please not relive that part?"

"Then let's talk about what we can control," Marilyn suggested. "Watching out for each other. Paying attention." She hesitated. "But there's something else I've only told James and the sheriff's department. I saw Sophie at the library on Monday."

A hush settled over the room.

"We chatted for a few minutes, nothing heavy. I mentioned our book club, and she said, 'Oh, I'm a big reader, I always have been.'" Marilyn paused, her voice tightening. "She seemed kind of pleased that someone noticed her. And I told her she should come on Thursday night, that we were meeting at Julia's house. I gave her the details—the time, and the book we were reading. She said, 'That sounds wonderful. I would love to come but I might have a conflict.'"

Julia turned pale. "You invited her here the day she was murdered?"

Marilyn nodded. "She was very interested in attending. Honestly, I think Sophie was very lonely and eager to meet our group."

Julia remained silent thinking back to how Sophie had mentioned book club during their confrontation on Monday night. She hadn't understood at the time but now it made sense. The other women commiserated with Marilyn for a while as Julia sat still, mulling over this new information.

The conversation fizzled shortly after, and the women headed home.

———————

Marilyn stayed to rinse her casserole dish with concern weighing heavily on her mind. The two women had been fast friends, and talk always came easy, so Julia's cool behavior didn't sit right with her. They stood at the kitchen island, the silence between them both uncomfortable and loaded.

"This whole thing's rattled all of us," Marilyn said after a moment. "But you've been off since that night. And I know it's not just the shock."

Julia stared at her hands clasped tightly in front of her. Her shoulders tensed as if bracing against something unsaid.

"It's not just about Sophie's death, is it?" Marilyn asked. "I hope you weren't upset I invited her to book club."

Julia didn't answer.

"I'm not here to interrogate you. I'm here as your friend. If something's wrong . . . if there's something you need to talk about, I'm here."

Julia's eyes welled, and for the first time, she looked like she might finally let something go, but not tonight.

Marilyn gave Julia a hug. "I'd better go; you look tired. Thanks for hosting."

"You're welcome. It was good to see everyone."

While Marilyn was at book club, James saw Todd walking the dogs by the light of his big flashlight. He grabbed a couple of beers and met him halfway between their respective houses. The mountain air was cool, but their conversation felt strangely heated. James apologized for Jake's pointed questions earlier. Todd quickly brushed it off and redirected the conversation to home projects and the weather. James felt uncomfortable and couldn't shake his gnawing suspicion.

"You ever think about how strange it is," James said quietly, "that we can live a few doors down from someone for years and not really know them at all?"

Unable to resist, James aggressively petted both of Todd's dogs. They danced around his feet, competing for attention and leaving copious amounts of dog hair on the legs of his jeans.

Todd shrugged, keeping his eyes on the darkening street. "Yeah, well, this kind of thing makes you think twice about everyone."

"Including us?"

Todd's eyes flicked to him, just for a moment. "Are you asking me something, James?" The tension in his tone was subtle, but unmistakable.

"Just trying to make sense of it all. On Monday night, Julia gave Marilyn a book a little after 8:15, and Kenny says he saw you walking the dogs around the same time. I saw you drive back in the neighborhood just before 11 pm. You didn't come home early and go back out again, did you?"

Todd took a slow sip from his bottle. "No, I did not come home early. You think Julia or I had something to do with it?"

James held his gaze. "I think people are confused and scared. Including me."

For a few seconds, neither man spoke. Then Todd let out a short, humorless laugh. "Be careful, James. Once you start pulling at threads, sometimes the whole thing unravels."

Marilyn left Julia's house after book club, clutching her jacket tight as she stepped out into the frosty night. The porch light behind her faded, and the familiar curve of Warriors Way lay ahead in shadow. The pines loomed like menacing creatures, and every rustle of wind made her heart stutter. It's just a hundred yards, she told herself, but the image of Sophie's lifeless face, pale and rigid under the stop sign, flashed before her eyes.

Then, in a sickening twist, the face changed. It was Robin. Her daughter's familiar features lay pale and still, twisted into the same vacant finality, and fear gripped Marilyn so hard she had to stop walking. The thought of Robin meeting such a violent end was impossible to hold, too monstrous to allow. Her breath came fast and shallow until she forced herself to pause, pressing a hand to her chest, inhaling deeply, then again, and again, until the night air cooled her panic and the image finally loosened its hold.

She turned around and walked back to the top of Julia's driveway and fumbled for her phone, whispering, "James, can you come outside? Please. I'm walking home now, and I feel overwhelmed!"

She used the flashlight on her phone to light the way home. After a few steps she could see James waiting, his figure framed in the soft amber of the porch light. When she reached their driveway, her fear broke, and she fell into James's arms. He held her tightly, feeling the tremor in her shoulders.

"It hit me all at once," she murmured against his chest. "The darkness, the silence—it was like she was still out there. I looked down the street and saw that stop sign and Sophie's face again. The way her eyes . . . didn't see anything anymore. Then I thought about our Robin. She thinks she's invincible, but it only takes a moment of being in the wrong place. I know it's crazy, but I suddenly felt so scared."

James took her hand. "Let's go inside." But even as he spoke, they both knew the fear on Warriors Way hadn't vanished; it was still out there, somewhere in the dark.

Todd watched from the shadows as Marilyn and James disappeared into their house. He was free to move forward with his two dogs. The cold March wind cut through his jacket as it swept down Warriors Way. He now saw Kenny with King approaching from the opposite direction, a leash in one hand and a golf club in the other. The dogs barked before either man spoke.

Todd stopped in the middle of the street. "You really told the deputy you saw me out here Monday night?" he snapped.

Kenny shifted his weight, the leash taut in his hand. "I told him what I saw, a man about your size walkin' two dogs near the stop sign. That's all. I didn't say you killed anybody."

"You might as well have! You've put me right in the middle of this mess for no damn reason."

"You're actin' awfully defensive for a guy who says he wasn't even home." Kenny took a step closer, his tone cutting. "Maybe you forgot somethin' that night. Maybe Julia did too."

Todd's face flushed red. "Don't talk about my wife, Kenny. You don't know what you're saying."

The dogs tugged nervously at their leashes as the tension thickened.

Kenny's voice dropped to a snarl. "I know what I saw. But the sheriff's gonna' figure it out, one way or another."

Todd stared him down for a long moment before turning away, his dogs pulling him down the street.

Later that evening, Jake met with a friend who worked at the Spirit County Sheriff's digital archives room. His fingers flew across the keys, toggling through previously sealed court files, old witness protection logs, and real estate transactions buried under aliases. At 11:15 p.m., they struck gold.

The deputy pulled up a file and press reporting. "The Chemist," he muttered, reading from the screen. "A part of the information was sealed testimony, but I'm certain it's our Ricky Delgado. He testified against one of the crime families in Vegas. Disappeared into some type of witness protection program. Looks like he got a new name, new life."

Jake looked over his friend's shoulder. "And he picked Deer Park Ridge?"

But there was more. The deputy found a link in Ricky's Vegas information that took him to a police file from Dallas. "Kate Jennings, arrested for vehicular manslaughter. The date was just before Christmas, over twenty years ago. The victim was a college student. The charges were reduced, and parts of the case were sealed."

The deputy scrolled down, his finger tracing the lines on the screen. "The victim's name was Angela Fielding."

Jake looked at the screen. "Hmm, it says here that Angela had an older sister named Julia Fielding. Julia … I wonder … "

The deputy pulled up the coroner's report on Sophie Delgado. "There's more. The birth dates for Sophie and Kate Jennings are the same."

Jake did a quick search on his phone and found an old marriage announcement. He sat back in his chair, a silent, chilling horror settling over him. "Julia Fielding is Julia Krantz?"

All the pieces fell into place. He looked at his friend, his voice barely a whisper. "Julia knew her."

FRIDAY

CHAPTER SEVENTEEN

Friday Morning

Deputy Yang arrived back at her desk at 5:30 a.m. She felt a little better, but the runny nose and sneezes were still fogging her brain. Plus, she had been awake for much of the night thinking about Ricky, now known as Bruce, and something Sheriff Carson had said about Kenny Jacobs, the man in the pajamas. "If he lied about Todd Krantz being on Warriors Way around 8 Monday night, he's probably lying about other things." Yang took this as a call to action.

She sat staring at her computer screen, the images of Ricky (Bruce Bricklin) and other students side by side. Kenny's name had come up tangentially during early interviews as someone Sophie and Ricky might have known from years back, but no one had been able to place the relationship. Yang couldn't shake the feeling that there was more to it. If Kenny and Ricky's paths had crossed before Deer Park Ridge, maybe the key to Sophie's murder lay in a shared history neither man wanted exposed. Acting on impulse, she sent another email to Dr. Travers at the University of Michigan, this time attaching a cropped photo of Kenny and asking if he looked familiar from Ricky's time there.

The response came quicker than Yang expected. Dr. Travers confirmed that Kenny Jacobs bore a strong resemblance to one of Ricky's roommates from the early 2000s:

After digging through old housing and university archives, I found the answer. His real name wasn't Kenny Jacobs, it was Fredrick R. Lee. Lee completed an undergraduate degree at Michigan in finance and investments, then stayed on, attending Michigan Law School, graduating in 2006. I've attached a scanned housing roster listing both Bruce E. Bricklin and Fredrick R. Lee at the same Ann Arbor address. Both men were outstanding lacrosse players who chose the club team over varsity, a sign of their shared discipline and long-term focus.

Deputy Yang felt a surge of adrenaline as she reread the message. A chemistry prodigy and a law student, both living under new names. A roommate, now connected to Ricky and Sophie in a small mountain community. It was a disquieting discovery. Had Lee followed Ricky to Deer Park Ridge for reasons that had finally boiled over, or was Sophie's murder a loose end someone else decided to tie up?

By 8 a.m., Deputy Yang and Lieutenant Walker were back in Sheriff Carson's office, her voice steady but her mind racing as she laid out the newest pieces of the puzzle. Kenny Jacobs was Fredrick R. Lee, Bruce Bricklin's roommate at the University of Michigan. "So now we've got two men from the same place, both using different names, both living quiet lives in Deer Park Ridge, and one of them has a dead wife and the other was probably out on the street at the time of the murder."

She paused to let the weight of it settle. "This isn't a coincidence. Their connection feels bigger, like something tied to Bricklin's research and possibly corporate corruption. What if they were involved in something during or after their time at Michigan that got out of hand?"

Sheriff Carson leaned back in his chair, arms crossed, while Lieutenant Walker tapped his pen against a notepad.

Finally, Carson spoke, "Well done. No doubt this new information gives us a starting point for Ricky and Kenny's relationship. If Bricklin's research overlapped with pharmaceuticals, and Lee had a law and finance background, it's not hard to imagine they could've gotten caught up in something—illicit patents, insider trading, maybe even black-market drug development. It also links nicely with yesterday's report from James Brookside about the Delgados' and Jacob's trip back to D.C."

Walker looked up from his notepad. "I finally feel like we're getting to some of the deeper truths related to this investigation."

Carson nodded and exhaled sharply. "Keep digging, Natalie. Focus on Bricklin's research, Lee's law connections, and companies where they might have crossed paths. If you can find the connective tissue, we might better understand who else might have skin in this game."

Deputy Yang returned to her desk and settled back into her chair, staring at the growing web of names and dates pinned across the team case board. She tapped her pen against her desk, thinking through Carson's guidance.

She whispered to herself. "Well, this sucks. There's not going to be an easy or direct path to the information I need to support this investigation. Guess I have to dig into a mountain of corporate records, lawsuits, and financial filings. At least I have job security. Lucky me."

Yang sneezed six times before she dove for a box of tissues.

———

The Brooksides awoke to a thin layer of snow covering Deer Park Ridge. Mule deer walked along the fairways of the golf course, their tracks leaving dark imprints on the fresh white powder. The red rock formations glistened as if someone had shaken a snow globe and allowed the scene to settle. With the sun breaking through the clouds, it would all be gone in a couple of hours. James was sitting at the kitchen table with a fresh mug of coffee when Jake called. Marilyn stood nearby, arms folded, listening.

"Hope you're both sitting down," Jake said. "It appears Ricky testified in a big case in Vegas, and we think he's in some type of witness protection program. That would explain why they're not working and their secluded lifestyle."

Marilyn and James exchanged surprised looks.

"There's more," Jake continued, his tone turning serious. "Julia's younger sister, Angela Fielding, was killed in a car accident about twenty years ago by a woman named Kate Jennings. We're pretty sure that Jennings was Sophie Delgado."

"What? How the hell can you make that assumption?" James rubbed his temples. "If that's true, you're saying Julia knew Sophie from before . . . that there's a potential connection from over two decades ago?"

Jake's voice was strained. "I'm saying we don't know for sure what we're looking at yet. But our neighborhood murder may have taken a very strange turn. One thing's for sure, James, it's getting complicated."

Marilyn took a deep breath. "I can't believe this is happening. Julia would never hurt anyone."

James was momentarily at a loss for words. "Jake, I need your help to better understand the background and timing of the Vegas storyline, the court cases, and whether any of it could have been a factor in Sophie's murder."

Later Friday morning, James heard the wail of sirens and the heavy rumble of police vehicles. Red and blue strobes danced on the ceiling of his living room. He bolted out of his chair and raced to the kitchen window. The scene was overwhelming. Multiple sheriff's units were parked in front of Todd and Julia's house.

James called Jake and headed up the street.

"A neighbor called it in," a deputy explained to James. "Heard the dogs barking and saw them running around the driveway and mailbox area. Someone forgot to close the garage door. Inside the house, office drawers were flung open, and paper files were scattered. Other than that, we checked the place from top to bottom, no one's home, both cars are gone, and it's just the office area that's a mess. We also found a flash drive on the kitchen counter addressed to Carson."

James felt lost. "Where are they?"

A moment later, James got a call from Todd. "I'm heading home from the airport after picking up Faith. Julia's not answering her phone, and the security system is going off. Can you please check the house for me?"

James told him about the police activity and the dogs. Todd, in a sickened voice, said, "I didn't know what to do. Julia was so distraught after book club last night. I decided to fly Faith home to help. When I left for the airport, Julia was pulling folders out of her office desk and tossing them on the floor. If she's not home, I don't know where she's gone."

Todd arrived with Faith about twenty minutes later. They parked across the street and walked over to James. Poor Faith looked horrified. Todd stood silent.

James greeted Faith and put a hand on Todd's shoulder. "Sorry, buddy. I don't know what's going on."

Jake arrived shortly after Todd and stood close to James. "Hard for a kid to see their parents in this situation," he whispered. "I wonder what Julia was thinking. I mean, do we really have a potential suspect on the run?"

Deputy Ryan approached the group and asked Todd for a moment. Todd nodded, and they found a quiet spot to talk. He told the deputy about Julia's behavior last night and about leaving early for the airport to pick up Faith. He didn't know anything else about the house being left open or Julia's whereabouts. Shortly after Todd's meeting with Ryan, he and Faith were allowed back into their house. James and Jake offered to help, but Todd said they would be fine. Feeling dismissed, Jake headed out to meet a friend and James walked back to his house.

———

James tried to piece together what happened that morning but could make no sense of it. Marilyn had gone to her parents' house early to help with some paperwork. He decided to give her a quick call.

Marilyn picked up on the second ring, her voice calm but distracted. "Hey, I'm helping my mom. Everything okay?"

James lowered his voice, glancing out at the street. "Not really. The sheriff's office just showed up at Todd and Julia's place this morning. A couple of neighbors called in after they saw the garage door wide open and the dogs running loose in the driveway."

"What? Where are Todd and Julia?"

"That's the thing, Todd left early for the airport to pick up Faith. They're home now, but Julia is missing."

Marilyn let out a quiet curse under her breath. "This doesn't sound good, James. Not at all."

After finishing his call with Marilyn, James was sitting at his desk when his phone lit up with a call from his agency friend, Mark Alexander. "James, I've got more information. This is bigger than I thought, and this stays verbal—no emails, no texts," Mark said without preamble.

"Go ahead."

"The Delgados and Kenny Jacobs went back to D.C. not once, but thirteen times between 2016 and 2023. All of them were billed to the government and arranged through an official travel agency. Flights, hotels, per diem—the whole package."

"Thirteen trips? That's not casual travel, Mark. Any idea what they were meeting about?"

Mark hesitated. "Not yet. But someone with serious pull signed off on every trip. That's what interests me." He paused, then added, "And here's the kicker—two more trips in February, but just the Delgados. Kenny wasn't on either manifest."

James raised an eyebrow. "This year? Just before Sophie's death?"

"Exactly. Both trips were in the past five weeks. Same D.C. hotel, same government billing codes, same travel arranger. Whoever's behind this is still moving pieces on the board."

"I understand Mark, thanks for your help."

James called Jake and told him about Mark's call. Jake delayed responding for a minute or two. "Opioids, Vegas, a car accident, a murder on your street, a woman who is missing, a grieving husband who is not grieving, and a shady neighbor. We need to figure out how it's all connected."

CHAPTER EIGHTEEN

Friday Morning

For ten years, Sophie Delgado was an unassuming presence on Warriors Way. The discovery of her dead body on Tuesday morning by James changed that in an instant. Now it was time for her to go home.

On Friday morning, just after sunrise, the coroner's office released Sophie's body, and by late morning, Ricky found himself sitting stiffly across from the funeral director in a quiet office in the city of Centennial. The room smelled faintly of lilies and old wood polish, and the director spoke with practiced softness as Ricky signed the necessary forms, requesting a direct cremation. He kept his answers short, avoiding eye contact, his voice hollow. He told them her parents would be coming from Texas to collect the remains on Monday morning and asked that everything be ready by then. What he didn't—and couldn't—mention was that a packet of documents was set to arrive at the funeral home the next day, officially changing Sophie's legal name on the death certificate back to Katherine L. Jennings. It was a final act of secrecy, one more layer to the life they'd built from half-truths and buried identities. Even in death, Ricky clung to the belief that erasing the past might somehow protect him from it.

Lost in thought, Ricky reflected on memories and family

stories that had been locked away for years. Kate Jennings was the golden girl of Highland Park, Texas—graceful, brilliant, and destined for a charmed life. Born into a wealthy Dallas family with oil and banking ties, she grew up in a world of cotillions, country clubs, and private schools. At Hockaday, she was a standout both in the classroom and on the tennis court, ranking among the top high school players in Texas. But behind her poised smile and polished manners was a fiercely competitive spirit—one that drove her to win, to excel, and to keep control in a world where appearances meant everything.

As she moved into adulthood, Kate's beauty and sharp intellect made her a fixture at charity galas and private club dinners. Friends from that era recalled her as magnetic yet guarded, the kind of woman who could charm a room and disappear before anyone got too close. There were whispers even then about her disinterest in convention and a deep ambition that didn't quite align with the carefully choreographed life she was expected to lead. Kate wanted a challenging career away from her controlling parents and their plans for marriage and children, something that would have to wait. She eventually left Dallas behind, but traces of that early life never quite left her: the way she carried herself, the layers of refinement and restraint, and the secrets she seemed to keep just beneath the surface.

It was just three days before Christmas during her junior year at the University of Texas at Austin when Kate attended her parents' annual holiday party—an opulent, boozy affair held at their estate in Highland Park. Guests flowed in from across the city's old-money circles, and the laughter was loud. The drinks were strong, but Kate, not yet twenty-one, had been cautious. Then her father's closest friend, a man she'd known since childhood, began refilling her glass with what she thought was harmless punch. What she didn't know was that he'd laced it with vodka, laughing off her protests with an easy charm and flirtatious wink. By the time she left the party just after midnight, she felt lightheaded but didn't recognize how impaired she truly was.

Driving back to Austin along the dark stretch of I-35, Kate lost control of her BMW just outside Waco. Her car crossed the median and slammed into a small sedan carrying two Baylor students driving home for the holidays. Julia's younger sister, Angela, died on impact. The girl in the passenger seat survived but was never the same. Kate was hospitalized and later claimed to have no memory of the crash. Her family's lawyers acted swiftly, ensuring that blood alcohol reports were delayed and quietly disputed. The charges were reduced from felony vehicular manslaughter to reckless driving, and she was given two years' probation. Her father's connections kept her name out of the headlines, but the incident became a whispered scandal among those who knew the truth. For Kate, it marked the unraveling of everything she had built— her confidence, her place in society, and the beginning of a guilt she would carry in silence for decades.

After the accident and trial, Kate returned to college and enrolled in an accelerated, dual undergraduate and master's program. The once-vibrant, charming young woman who lit up every room was gone, replaced by someone quieter, more guarded, disciplined, and distant. She kept her head down, avoided social gatherings, and poured herself into her studies with an intensity that surprised her professors.

With advanced degrees in both marketing and chemistry, an unusual but powerful combination, Kate accepted a position in sales with a major pharmaceutical company based in Dallas. Her scientific background gave her credibility with doctors and pharmacists, while her marketing training made her a persuasive and strategic communicator. She quickly rose through the ranks, praised for her ability to translate complex product details into compelling sales pitches. But beneath her polished professionalism was a woman still running from the past, burying guilt and grief beneath layers of corporate success. The accident that killed Julia's sister had never truly left her, and worse still was the shame of her professional life. She had been a part of the early rollout team for a drug that had fueled a national opioid epidemic, coordinating presentations that downplayed the drug's addictive potential. To her colleagues, she was ambitious and sharp; to herself, she was a person simply trying to stay ahead of a past that was always threatening to catch up.

Bruce Bricklin and Kate first met in 2009 at a pharmaceutical industry work conference. Both were sharp, ambitious, and quick to notice the other's mix of confidence and charm. She was just finishing a presentation on marketing strategies for prescription drugs when he wandered into her breakout session.

He approached Kate with a grin and said, "Guess I'm lost, but if getting lost means I end up in the right room with you, I might just make it a habit."

Kate laughed, intrigued by his easy charm and the glint in his eye. "That's a pickup line if I ever heard one."

They talked for an hour, both pretending they didn't have

somewhere else to be. As they parted, Bruce boldly kissed her on the cheek. "How about a real conversation? There's a Halloween party tomorrow night. Come with me."

Their first date was a blur of music, laughter, and sex. Kate wore a sultry white tennis dress and matching visor, teasing him, "I forgot my racket, tough guy."

Bruce was in a sleek pinstriped suit and his signature fedora, looking like Sinatra's younger brother. He smiled broadly and touched her arm. "I'm more of a lover than a tough guy."

Kate smiled and flashed her beautiful blue eyes. "You should know that I'm from Dallas, Texas. Our men wear real hats, like a Stetson. You know, a cowboy hat. As I recall, little boys wear those fedora things to church on Easter."

Bruce was momentarily offended but laughed it off.

As Bruce spun Kate around on the dance floor, happiness overwhelmed her mind and body. She momentarily feared this could be trouble, a good kind of trouble she hoped. Their conversation that night flowed effortlessly, the chemistry undeniable. As the evening wore on, they discovered that their attraction wasn't just about appearances; it was the beginning of something that would hold them together for years to come.

Eventually, Kate took the fedora and wore it for the rest of the night, including the three hours she spent in Bruce's hotel room.

During her years in Deer Park Ridge, Kate was long gone, and Sophie moved through life like a lost soul—present but drained of vitality. Her marriage to Ricky was wonderful at first, but eventually grew cold and mechanical, filled with long silences and the occasional sharp exchange. While Ricky pursued his affairs, she often sat alone on the back patio in the late afternoons, a glass of wine in hand, staring at the red cliffs with a heaviness that never left her face. To those who saw her, she seemed withdrawn—aloof, but inside, Sophie was suffocating under the weight of her past. She hated the man she had once trusted, hated the lies they had built their lives upon, and, most of all, hated herself for the choices she had made and the lives those choices had damaged beyond repair.

And in an ironic and cruel twist of fate, she found herself living five doors away from Julia Fielding, the older sister of the college student she had killed twenty years earlier. How was it even possible? Was God punishing her? After all the prayers, there were times when Sophie questioned her faith and wondered why she had to endure this unbearable torture. She contemplated running or worse. As time passed, the hours of sitting alone in her study or garden seemed to provide more questions than answers. Could she confront Julia and ask for forgiveness for a horrible mistake? Could that work? Could she be free of this seemingly lifelong burden?

In the summer before her death, Sophie tried to regroup. Once a month, she would slip out of her house in the late afternoon, dressed with a quiet elegance that surprised anyone who caught a glimpse of her. She favored tailored slacks, silk blouses, and vintage jewelry that hinted at a more glamorous past. These evenings were reserved for the professional women's group she'd recently joined, an eclectic mix of executives, consultants, academics, and entrepreneurs who met at rotating restaurants and hotels around Denver. The meetings began with cocktails at the bar, followed by a seated dinner where topics ranged from policy and leadership to personal growth and literature. Though Sophie rarely spoke about her past, she carried herself with an authority that made others listen when she did. Her knowledge of business strategy, ethics, and pharmaceutical regulation gave her credibility, even if no one quite knew what she had done.

These gatherings became one of the few social constants in Sophie's life, and she took them seriously. She always arrived early, greeted the concierge by name, and made a point to remember the waitstaff who served their table. Over the months, she grew particularly close to a small group of women. They often lingered over a second glass of wine after the others had left. To outsiders, it might have seemed out of character—this reclusive woman from Warriors Way dressed like a diplomat, laughing softly over dinner in a downtown bistro—but for Sophie, these nights were a way to hold onto her identity, her intellect, and a world that once felt like her own. She would often think that this was the life Kate would have lived if not for the one horrible night twenty years ago.

On the day of her death, Sophie pondered the invitation from Marilyn to attend the next book club gathering on Thursday night at Julia's house. It was an impossible situation, but the idea that she could meet other women from the neighborhood warmed her soul. As often happened, her mind began to wander, and she replayed the accident for the thousandth time, wishing Julia could somehow see how deeply the guilt had settled into her bones. Maybe a simple evening discussing a novel could be the first fragile step toward forgiveness.

That afternoon, Sophie pulled into a narrow parking spot outside her favorite used bookstore. The store, tucked between a vintage clothing shop and a record store, had always been a quiet refuge for her. She headed straight for the fiction section, scanning the spines with a sense of quiet determination until she found a used copy of *The Night Watchman* by Louise Erdrich—the book Marilyn had mentioned for the book club.

As she stepped outside, Sophie felt a strange mix of satisfaction and unease. She rarely tried to involve herself in neighborhood activities and knew full well that her presence at Julia's house would be unacceptable. Still, a part of her longed for connections, something she hadn't allowed herself over the years. Maybe if she showed up with the book in hand, ready to discuss it, things would feel different. She'd be seen in a new light. She took one last look at the storefront before getting into her car, unaware that this quiet, hopeful act would be one of her final gestures—a small, poignant reach toward a community that had never quite let her in.

In a few hours, her death would be violent and sudden—the final act of a life filled with sadness and missed opportunities.

CHAPTER NINETEEN

Friday, Early Afternoon

Jake and James sat in the study as the laptop illuminated their faces. Marilyn hovered nearby, arms crossed, her expression a mix of curiosity and dread. Jake's deputy friend had sent him a copy of the zip file from Julia's flash drive, titled "Atonement." Inside there was a series of PDFs, audio files, and five video links.

James and Marilyn looked at each other in disbelief. "You just can't make this up," James said, the words heavy with the weight of the past few days. "It's all so crazy."

After a few moments of reflection, the three turned their attention back to the PDFs full of journal entries meticulously written by Julia. They chronicled years of emotional torment—grief over her sister's death, a slow-burning hatred for Kate Jennings, the shock of seeing her again on Warriors Way, and the agonizing struggle to control her desire for revenge.

One entry, dated three months earlier, read: *I see her at Safeway, grocery shopping. I want to crash into her cart and scream Angela's name. Instead, I hide in the back corner of the store until she leaves. That's what makes it worse.*

The final file included five video links from the doorbell camera showing Julia and Todd's front porch. The timestamps were a chilling narrative of the night of the murder.

8:02 p.m. Julia leaves with the dogs, a large flashlight, and a book.

8:27 p.m. She returns, crying. Something appears to be smeared on her right sleeve.

10:45 p.m. Todd arrives home and parks in the garage.

10:55 p.m. Todd leaves with the two dogs.

11:15 p.m. Todd returns and goes inside.

Jake sat back. "The timelines match what we think we know. The time of death was between 8 and 9 p.m. Julia was out walking the dogs at that time. Todd, on the other hand, was out well after the murder took place. At most, he could have tried to cover Julia's tracks, but the video evidence doesn't support that."

"But why leave all this information behind?" Marilyn asked.

Jake tapped the flash drive. "Because she wanted it to be found. She wanted to tell her story. She's not running away from what she did. She's running away from the consequences."

As they finished reviewing the files, Jake received a short text. It was a summary of the final coroner's report. The findings were grim but revealing. Sophie had suffered blunt force trauma to the side and back of the skull, consistent with a heavy object striking multiple times in quick succession. The report detailed hairline fractures, brain hemorrhaging, and patterned contusions.

Marilyn looked at James. "Julia had that metal flashlight with her Monday night. It might match that profile."

At the same time, Ricky sat alone at the kitchen table, the dim glow of his laptop casting sharp shadows across his face. An old email account pinged with a message from an unfamiliar address, but the subject line froze him: "Urgent, the police are looking for you." The sender was a former friend and colleague from his University of Chicago's PhD program; someone Ricky hadn't thought about in over a decade. The email was brief but chilling in its implications.

The Spirit County Sheriff's Department contacted our department with photos and questions about Bruce E. Bricklin. They have images of you from Michigan and Chicago and are asking about your research. They suspect you of something. I don't know what you've gotten yourself into, but it's only a matter of time before they connect the rest of it. KEEP ME OUT OF IT.

Ricky's pulse hammered in his ears as the words sank in. They had his old name. They had pictures. And worse, they were asking about his research—a past he had buried so carefully when he walked away and disappeared into a quiet life in Deer Park Ridge. He shut the laptop slowly, staring out into the yard beyond the kitchen window. For years, he had stayed under the radar, living as a ghost in plain sight. But now, with the sheriff's department pulling threads that led straight back to Michigan and Chicago. Whatever happened next, he couldn't afford to sit still. He looked around his house and back at a picture of Sophie. "These idiots are going to get me killed, too."

He was scheduled for another interview with Lieutenant Walker at the Highlands Ranch satellite office on Friday afternoon at 3 p.m. He expected them to press him hard about his whereabouts on Monday night. Ricky knew the walls were closing in. The questions about his past, the police activity in the neighborhood; he could feel the fabric of his carefully constructed life beginning to fray. It was time to find a place to think. He went out to the backyard with a shovel and dug up a sealed metal box. Inside, there were a few thousand dollars in cash, a burner phone, a laptop, and a stack of $500 gift credit cards. He'd have to be careful, but he now had money for food and gas and a way to communicate with his handlers. He switched the license plates on his SUV and headed for the mountains.

———

Kenny spotted the black SUV in his rearview mirror for the second time just after turning out of his driveway. At first, he told himself it was nothing—just another neighbor hustling about on a Friday afternoon. But as he merged onto Rampart Range Road, the SUV edged closer. Uncomfortably close.

"Back off, buddy," he muttered, gripping the steering wheel.

The SUV didn't back off. If anything, it tucked in tighter, almost matching the small corrections of Kenny's SUV.

"No, no, no . . . not today," he whispered. His pulse ticked upward, an unwelcome reminder of how fragile his cover now felt.

By the time he pulled into the lot of the indoor driving range, he was sweating. He parked, killed the engine, and glanced again at the mirror. The black SUV pulled in seconds later, slow, deliberate, settling two rows behind him.

"What do you want?" Kenny breathed.

He sat frozen for a full minute, pretending to check his phone. The driver of the SUV didn't move. Didn't leave. Didn't even try to hide that it was watching him. Finally, he stepped out, grabbed his clubs, and walked inside, forcing himself to act casual even though adrenaline charged through his body, and he felt weak-kneed. He swiped his membership card, linked up with his buddy Frank, and they hit three buckets of balls.

When he came back outside, his stomach sank. The SUV was still there. Engine running this time.

"You've gotta' be kiddin' me," he whispered.

He climbed back into his SUV and pulled out of the lot. The black SUV eased in behind him as if it had simply been waiting for its cue.

"Okay . . . okay, stay calm," Kenny said aloud.

But he knew better. Every lane change he made, the SUV mirrored. Every slowdown, the SUV matched. When he exited C-470, the SUV followed until suddenly, at a crowded intersection, it veered left and vanished into a swarm of traffic as if it had never existed.

The silence inside his own SUV felt too large. Kenny kept glancing at mirrors that reflected nothing but normal afternoon drivers.

"You're losin' it, man," he whispered, though he didn't believe it. "Somebody's checkin' on me. Or worse."

His hands trembled as he pulled back into the neighborhood. He checked the mirror one last time before turning into his driveway. His street was empty. And somehow, that made him feel even less safe.

After getting inside, Kenny paced the length of his great room, running a hand through his hair as King sat on the rug, ears perked and eyes locked on him.

"I'm tellin' you, boy," Kenny muttered, "This is bad. Real bad. That SUV followin' today scared the hell out of me."

King whined softly, leaning forward as if urging him to sit.

Kenny dropped onto the couch with a groan. "Yeah, I know. I sound crazy. But I'm not imaginin' this thing ridin' my tail."

The dog rested his chin on Kenny's knee, and he scratched behind King's ears with a trembling hand. "I swear, buddy, I can feel eyes on me. I don't know what Ricky's hidin', but someone thinks I know more than I do." Kenny's voice cracked. "And I hate that you're caught up in this with me. You didn't ask for any of this." King nudged him firmly, as if reminding him he wasn't alone.

Kenny took a shaky breath and wrapped an arm around King's neck. "What scares me most, King . . . what keeps me up at night . . . is thinkin' they'll come after me next. And if somethin' happens . . . " He swallowed hard. "Who's gonna' take care of you? You're the best thing I got in this world."

Sensing Kenny's tension, King let out a low whine.

"Yeah, I know. You'd take'em on yourself if you had to. But let's hope it doesn't come to that. We just gotta' keep our heads down, buddy. Stay sharp."

CHAPTER TWENTY

Friday Afternoon

The sheriff's department sent a car to pick up Ricky at 2 p.m. for the interview. No answer. The deputy knocked several times and then walked around the back of the house. He found a freshly dug hole, a muddy shovel, and an empty metal box. He called a report in and asked for backup.

Police activity again churned on Warriors Way. Jake, who was back at James's house, stood up, told him to stay put, and walked up to Ricky's house. A deputy was already inside near the front door.

Jake let himself in. "Why are you here? Is Ricky being investigated or charged with something?"

The deputy stopped. "Jake, you shouldn't be here, but you might as well come in. Don't touch anything. Ricky called Sheriff Carson just before 2 p.m. Said he was afraid something might happen and needed help. Carson told him to stay put, but it looks like he had other ideas. That's all I know."

The house was spotless. No dust, no clutter—as if they had never truly lived there. The living room looked staged, too perfect.

"Looks like someone has been doing some cleaning this week," Jake muttered.

In the bedroom, carefully pressed suits and other clothes lay across the bed as if Ricky had selectively picked his wardrobe before escaping to the unknown.

Jake looked at the deputy. "Is this guy actually on the run?"

The deputy's silence said everything.

The sheriff's office issued a BOLO—Be on the Lookout—alert for Ricky. A quick records check found that his bank accounts were untouched. The Delgados' home security camera didn't catch his car leaving. It was like he had vanished into thin air. About thirty minutes later, James's phone pinged with a headline and story from a local news website:

LOCAL MAN VANISHES AMID MURDER INVESTIGATION

On Tuesday morning, March 17, Deer Park Ridge resident James Brookside discovered the body of Sophie Delgado at the entrance to Warriors Way. The Spirit County Sheriff's Office launched an immediate investigation and later determined that the victim had been killed on Monday evening between 8 and 9 p.m. A BOLO was just issued by the sheriff's department for Ricky Delgado, the victim's husband. No further information is available.

Ricky was gone. James nodded. "But why vanish now?"

At about the same time that Deputy Yang saw the BOLO alert for Ricky, she received a follow-up email from the University of Michigan. Reluctant at first to share her personal impressions, Dr. Travers offered another glimpse into the life of Bruce Bricklin:

Bruce wasn't just a brilliant chemist. He had this odd mix of being a bit of a tough guy. He carried himself with quiet confidence, like he'd been through something before graduate school, but he was also an extraordinary man. Honestly, he had a way with everyone, especially the ladies. Bruce could charm the skirt off pretty much any woman he wanted, even when he didn't seem to be trying. And his memory was unreal. He could recall obscure details from lectures, papers, and even random conversations years later. Bruce was the guy everyone wanted as a partner on their research projects.

Yang reread the message, her instincts sharpening. That combination—charisma, toughness, and an encyclopedic mind—painted a picture of someone capable of reinventing himself completely and keeping secrets buried deep.

Deputy Yang spun around in her chair and read Dr. Travers' email for a third time. It was late Friday afternoon after an extraordinarily long week. She was looking forward to dinner with Ryan and a few of their friends at a wine bar in Old Littleton. And yet, she had one more search that needed her attention.

"Who was Kenny Jacobs or Fredrick R. Lee, and why was he important?"

Yang went to work. The fact that these two men had resurfaced years later under new names in the same quiet neighborhood wasn't something she could chalk up to coincidence. She sorted through online corporate filings, legal databases, and pharmaceutical research journals, looking for any overlap—shared addresses, mutual employers, financial transactions, even court records. Her gut told her that whatever bound Bricklin and Lee together after graduation held the key to Sophie's murder. Were they partners in something illicit? Rivals who turned on each other? Or fugitives from a shared secret too dangerous to leave behind? The deeper she dug, the more the lines between her professional curiosity and personal obsession blurred, each clue drawing her further into the mystery of how two brilliant men went from promising futures to hidden lives—and why that past had finally caught up to them.

After another two hours of work, Deputy Yang turned off her computer and changed into her Friday night outfit. She decided to come back in the morning and dig a little deeper. For now, she was exhausted and needed a night with her friends and Ryan, accompanied by a glass of red wine, a good dinner, and the most decadent chocolate dessert on the menu.

The bistro was buzzing with life as happy-hour customers celebrated the end of the workweek—glasses clinking, laughter bouncing off brick walls, and a jazz trio working through sultry renditions of current hits. Both feeling better after double shots of cold medicine, Yang and Ryan arrived together but pretended not to, joining their friends at a long, candle-lit table near the window.

"You two showed up at the same time again," teased Mia, swirling her cocktail with a knowing grin.

Ryan shot Yang a quick glance, his lips twitching with a smirk. "Pure coincidence," he said with a smile, raising his glass.

Yang leaned closer to Ryan, her voice playful but soft enough for only him to hear. "You might want to work on your poker face. Right now, you look like you want to take me on the dance floor for a slow and intimate tango." She winked and smiled.

Ryan offered a coy smile back and whispered. "I would love to tango with you if I knew how."

Mia was watching Yang and Ryan. "Alright you two, save the lovey-dovey stuff for later."

Plates of tapas arrived—spiced shrimp, marinated olives, and truffle fries disappeared fast. The energy around the table built as the night went on, laughter rising with every new round.

Ryan brushed his knee against Yang's under the table, testing the line of their new relationship. She rested her hand on his thigh.

"So," she said, turning to him with a sparkle in her eyes, "are you sticking around for their famous chocolate lava cake dessert?"

Ryan tilted his head, returning the look. "Only if we split it. Then maybe . . . we grab an Uber to somewhere quieter for a nightcap."

Yang smiled, "I was hoping you'd say that."

CHAPTER TWENTY-ONE

Friday, Late Afternoon

At about 5:30 p.m. on Friday, both James and Jake received a group text from Sheriff Carson. It was an invitation to dinner at his Sedalia ranch, located about fifteen miles south of James's house. The message was clear: "Attendance is mandatory." James apologized to Marilyn, and the two men headed out.

Nestled just west of the quaint mountain town of Sedalia, Colorado, lay the sprawling 300-acre ranch owned by Jason Carson. The property was a blend of rugged terrain and serene pasture: rolling meadows dotted with rabbitbrush, stands of ancient ponderosa pines, and meandering creeks that traced sparkling ribbons through the land. At its heart sat a weathered but lovingly maintained ranch house—an authentic homage to early Colorado homesteads, with timberplank walls, a wraparound porch, and a soaring stone fireplace. It was now Carson's retreat from the scrutiny of voters and an aggressive press that hounded him constantly. Jason dreamt of the day when this land and home would be his protection from an ever-more complex and challenging world.

Jake looked around and said, "Spectacular place, Sheriff."

"Not bad for a poor Black child from the ghetto."

James rolled his eyes. "Yeah, but your dad was a rich corporate lawyer, and you grew up in a big house in Cherry Creek three doors down from John Elway."

"Hey man, you're killing my street cred with Walker here," Carson growled. "He thinks I grew up on the wrong side of the tracks. But enough of that, we have serious business to discuss."

James turned to Carson as they walked inside. "Where's Trudie tonight?"

"I told her I was inviting you scoundrels over for dinner, so she headed up to Fort Collins to see the grandkids."

The four men moved to the large kitchen. Walker pulled side dishes out of the refrigerator, including a large bowl of homemade potato salad, while Carson sliced a delicious-smelling brisket. Jake mixed martinis, an essential for proper digestion. James opened two bottles of red wine.

Carson's German Shepherd was laying in the corner calmly watching the men as they prepared for their meal. The dog had a beautiful, thick coat of fur which was too much for James to ignore. He walked over and gently stroked the dog's head. Carson gave him a look as he placed the brisket on the table.

Carson said grace, and the men attacked their dinners. After fifteen minutes with little in the way of substantive discussions, James broke the ice. "Jason, great meal, but why are we here?"

Carson took a last bite of food and treated himself to a full pour of wine. "We have a problem with our murder investigation—really, two problems."

Jake smiled. "Are you talking about us, Jason?"

"The two of you are always a pain in the ass, but that's not what I'm talking about. We have a murder. The motive could be years of revenge, or an unplanned altercation that went wrong. You both have the background information on Ricky. If this is a revenge killing, Walker and I think we need to focus on Ricky and his connections. If it was an unplanned altercation, we have solid information that Julia Krantz was out on the street at the time of the murder. She has a motive based on the car accident that killed her sister. Could be her. Both Ricky and Julia are now missing. We also have this guy, Kenny Jacobs, who was possibly out on the street when Sophie was killed and who may have an old connection to Ricky. Multiple possibilities with one dead body."

James decided it was time to throw in a twist. "I think you all know that I was an intelligence officer for over forty years. I was never a spy, but I fully understand the concepts of cover, deception, and back-stopping someone's identity."

He rested his forearms on the table, his eyes scanning between Carson, Walker, and Jake. "You all know the difference between a standard law enforcement cover and what we build in the intelligence world," he said quietly. "An undercover cop might work a persona for months, but a deep-cover operative might live theirs for decades. It's not just a false name and a job, it's a fabricated life: education records, tax returns, marriages, even kids, if necessary. The key is depth and patience. Their story must withstand hostile scrutiny from a foreign counterintelligence service, not just a suspicious neighbor or a street informant. They'll have hobbies, habits, friends, and enemies—all carefully crafted to reinforce the illusion. And if they're good, they'll seem as normal as anyone else on your street. That's why someone like Ricky gives me pause."

James looked out of the window, then returned his attention to the men around the table. "The background information on Ricky has come too easily, considering we suspect he is in some type of witness protection program. Jason, your guys were able to pull this gangster storyline from accessible law enforcement databases. I'm not buying it. I think the clothes, fedora, and Sinatra act are part of a cover plan that was created for him, maybe by the Feds. First look at Ricky, and we see a guy who lives on Warriors Way. Look a little deeper, and we find a guy supposedly from Vegas who has been supporting investigations into organized crime and federal prosecutions. Maybe we need to look deeper because I think this is all a diversion, and our Ricky is far more important than we know."

Carson went to the kitchen and brought back two more bottles of wine. He looked in everyone's eyes. "I have three guest bedrooms that are made up. You're all spending the night. I don't need a bunch of DUIs attributed back to this little gathering. Understand?" Everyone reached for their phones and called their spouses with the news.

James hit the speed dial for Marilyn. "Hey, sweetheart. Just wanted you to know Carson insisted we stay over. Martinis and glasses of wine have been flowing a little heavier than they should, and he doesn't want anyone driving down those backroads tonight."

There was a pause, then Marilyn's warm but firm voice came through. "That's smart, James. I'd rather you stay put than end up wrapped around a tree, or worse."

"I'll be back in the morning, promise."

Marilyn's tone sharpened with playful warning. "And don't do anything stupid like deciding that you and the boys should go out looking for bears or mountain lions. I can imagine how slow-witted that group can get after too much alcohol."

James laughed, shaking his head. "What, you don't trust my wilderness instincts?"

She sighed with amusement. "I trust your instincts. I just don't trust them when they've been dumbed down with too many martinis and glasses of wine. Make sure you get some sleep. I'll see you in the morning." James said goodnight and returned to the others.

Carson continued the earlier conversation. "James, you make a great point. The backstory on Ricky came too easily for my guys, and we really haven't dug up enough on Sophie beyond her very boring life as your neighbor and the car accident."

"Alright, fellas, you've been patient, and I think you deserve to hear where this is headed," he said. He quickly summarized Deputy Yang's findings related to Bruce Bricklin's PhD in chemistry and Fredrick Lee's degrees in finance and law, and the potential they were linked to organized crime.

James felt his stomach tighten as Carson spoke, while Jake let out a low whistle and rubbed his chin. "So, they both come out here, change their names, and try to vanish. And now Sophie ends up murdered." Jake shook his head. "That doesn't sound like a coincidence."

Carson nodded grimly. "I agree."

He swirled his glass of wine, his voice hardening.

"Listen carefully: this isn't a game. If Bricklin and Lee were hiding from something dangerous, there's no telling who else is in the mix. And James, Yang told me about the Delgados' and Kenny's trips back to D.C. and the shell game that was played with the purchases of their homes. We don't know 100 percent what all this means, but finding our killer has gotten more complicated and probably dangerous. I need you two to promise me you'll keep your heads down. Let us do the hard police work."

James and Jake nodded.

Carson's dog moved next to James's chair after the meal. James absentmindedly had been stroking the dog's head for an hour when Carson finally chuckled and said, "You know, James, you've been petting that dog all night like it's a stress ball."

James paused, glanced down, and shrugged. "Didn't even realize I was doing it," he said quietly. "Guess it helps keep my head straight."

Carson took a sip of wine and shook his head with a grin. "That's exactly why you need a dog of your own. Cheaper than therapy and way more loyal."

James smiled faintly, his hand resting on the dog's back. "Marilyn would say getting a dog is a bad idea."

Carson laughed. "That's what everyone says, right up until the dog saves them."

Carson delayed for a moment. "Okay. Let's move on. So, what are we missing and how can we close the loop?" James, Walker, and Jake were silent.

Walker spoke up first. "We don't have access to the type of databases you're talking about, James. We'd need more help from our federal friends, and I doubt that's going to happen if Sophie's death is viewed as a neighborhood murder investigation. It might happen if we can convince them that this murder served a bigger purpose."

James chimed in. "As you know, I've been working with an old agency friend for the last day or so. He confirmed the Delgados and Kenny made not just one, but thirteen government-funded trips to D.C. between 2016 and 2023—all arranged through an official travel agent."

He let that information sink in for a moment, then continued. "Additionally, the Delgados made two more trips in the last month or so without Kenny. I'm going to make a low-confidence assessment now, so bear with me. Sophie and Kenny had a confrontation last year where threats were exchanged. Could these two trips without Kenny be a sign that their partnership or mutual dependence on one another had fractured?"

Carson's eyes narrowed as he replied. "That's a hell of a lot of smoke. I need another drink. Hell, I might need two drinks after that news."

The alcohol continued to flow for another two hours, before the men retired to their respective bedrooms.

James stood on the back deck of Carson's house, the night air cold against his bare chest and feet. Fog hung low over the expansive property, muffling every sound. Suddenly, he was back on his driveway looking at the entrance to Warriors Way. He could see the stop sign and Sophie—her silhouette jerking violently as someone attacked her.

"Sophie!" he tried to shout, but his voice snagged in his throat, swallowed by the fog. He strained to move, to run toward her, but his legs were stone, rooted to the concrete driveway.

"No . . . no, not again," he whispered, panic clawing up his spine as the scene unfolded helplessly before him.

Suddenly, the attacker vanished into the darkness, and Sophie staggered toward him. Within seconds, she was standing at the base of his driveway—blood running down her neck, her hair tangled, her blue eyes clouded with despair.

"James . . ." her voice cracked like broken glass, "why didn't you save me?" He felt his stomach drop into nothingness.

"Sophie, I didn't know," he managed, his voice shaking.

"I saw you in the window," she said, taking a step closer. "I called to you. You looked right at me. Why didn't you come?" Her accusation pierced deeper than any nightmare had yet.

His throat tightened as he tried to answer, but no sound came out. He lifted his arms, forcing himself to move toward her—but the moment he took a step, she vanished, dissolving like smoke in a gust of cold wind. The driveway, the street, the night, all of it flickered and collapsed around him. James gasped and sat upright in Carson's guest bedroom, drenched in sweat, his heart pounding so violently it hurt.

"Jesus . . . " he whispered, running a trembling hand over his face. "What the hell is happening to me?" The room spun slightly, the aftermath of too much alcohol still buzzing through his system.

He lay back down slowly, staring into the darkness. His head throbbed; his thoughts tangled like loose wires sparking against each other.

Sophie's voice—her accusation—still echoed in his ears, too sharp, too real. The vision of her bloodied face clung to him, an image he couldn't shake. He closed his eyes, trying to steady his breathing. Eventually, the fog of exhaustion pulled him under again, though a part of him feared what dreams might come next.

SATURDAY

CHAPTER TWENTY-TWO

Saturday, Early Morning

James woke up early, hungover and still a bit shaken from his dream last night. He headed to the kitchen as the first rays of sunlight began to illuminate the foothills. Coffee was made, and Carson was cooking a breakfast casserole. Fresh bread was already on the table.

"Jason, I need to ask you something straight. Do you want me to step back completely from everything related to Sophie's murder?"

Carson looked up slowly, his jaw tightening. "James, you've been in the middle of this since hour one. So, before I answer, tell me what's driving the question."

James sat down, elbows on his knees. "It's getting complicated. Julia's disappearing act, Todd's inconsistencies, Ricky's past, Kenny's misleading statements—every thread I pull leads straight through my own street. And Marilyn thinks I'm putting us in danger."

He paused, lowering his voice. "I don't want to cross a line with your deputies or compromise what you're building. If you need me out, say it."

Carson studied him for a moment. "You're not stepping on toes. This is how investigations work. You're just ... orbiting a black hole filled with unknowns. But this murder is getting messier by the hour." Carson reached for his coffee, took a sip, and grimaced. "Here's the truth," he said. "If you walk away right now, I lose the one person who can see through these people better than anyone on my payroll. But if you stay in, you're going to get pulled into whatever this really is—whether it's revenge, cover-up, something less, or something bigger."

James nodded slowly. "So, you're saying I'm damned either way."

Carson gave him a thin smile. "Pretty much. But if you want my advice? Don't step back. Not yet. We're too close to understanding what really happened to Sophie Delgado."

Jake and Walker made their way to the kitchen. Walker was holding his pounding head and regretting the extra wine and shots he did at the end of the night. Everyone grabbed cups of coffee and sat at the table. There was no conversation, just four quiet men checking their phones and texting good morning to their wives.

The Brookside house was quiet when James and Jake got back to Deer Park Ridge, except for the rhythmic hum of the refrigerator and the occasional bark of a distant dog. James started the coffee maker, and they took seats at the kitchen table.

James tapped his pen against a notepad. "Julia disappears. Ricky disappears. Connected?"

"Absolutely," Jake said. "My gut says Julia didn't just run because she was guilty. She was afraid. Afraid that Ricky might suspect her."

"You think Ricky really believes she was behind whatever happened to Sophie?"

Jake shrugged. "He probably knows she was out on the street during the murder and that she holds a grudge against Sophie because of the accident."

James walked over to the coffee pot, poured two mugs, and returned to the table. "Here's what I can't square," he said. "The information we have shows Ricky was tied to the big pharmaceutical players, helping them with research and product development through legit channels. That paints him as a corporate player, not a back-alley hustler. Yet the same files hint at him making side deals, funneling opioids straight to outfits that had nothing to do with the companies. That's not just a contradiction, it's playing both sides of the board."

"That's exactly the problem," Jake replied, taking a sip of his coffee. "If Ricky were embedded in the company's hierarchy, he would have access to the supply chain, data, and even other research labs. That's leverage you don't walk away from. But if he also dipped into black-market distribution, that means he was greedy, or desperate. One version makes him an asset that corporations would protect. The other makes him a liability that criminals would exploit. The contradiction doesn't just confuse the paper trail, James—it muddies the motive for who wanted him and Sophie gone."

Marilyn appeared from the bedroom to find James and Jake at the kitchen table. She hugged James and kissed him on the head. "Hope you guys saved me some coffee. And Jake, you're here so much I think we should give you a key and assign you a bedroom. Let me warn you, rent is expensive in this neighborhood."

James and Jake laughed.

"I'll make us a fresh pot," said James.

Later that morning, Todd showed up on James's doorstep, unannounced. "I need to talk," he said, his voice rough.

He sat at the kitchen island, hands clasped tightly as James, Marilyn, and Jake looked on. "I'm certain Julia didn't kill Sophie, but they did have a confrontation Monday night. Julia hit her with a flashlight and knocked her down, but she told me Sophie stood up immediately. Julia walked away from her and swore she was alive."

James studied him carefully. "Julia hit Sophie? Why on earth would she do that? No wonder you two have been acting so strange!"

"It just happened. It was a mistake."

Todd took a deep breath and told them about the car accident where Sophie killed Julia's sister and the boiling rage.

James, already aware of the accident, put his hand on Todd's shoulder. "This is a lot to take in, my friend. I have to ask this question; did you tamper with or move Sophie's body?"

Todd swallowed. "No. I took the dogs out when I got home after Julia told me what had happened. I walked to the entrance of Warriors Way. I didn't know what I would find. I certainly wasn't expecting to find Sophie dead and propped up against the post. When I saw her, I was shocked and left at once. I didn't touch anything."

Jake crossed his arms. "I don't know what to believe, Todd. Regardless of what you say, it's my understanding that you gave false statements to Deputy Ryan. That's not smart, and Carson knows about it." Todd buried his face in his hands.

As they were talking, Jake's phone buzzed with an incoming text. He pulled it out and announced. "The sheriff has Julia. A deputy found her parked at the county courthouse in Castle Rock this morning. Apparently, the car had been there all night. Maybe she was going to turn herself in."

Todd was relieved and panicked at the same time. "I need to let Faith know that Julia's been found. I also need to tell her there's a potential that I'll be called back in by the sheriff for further questioning and maybe even detained. We haven't been truthful with her about what happened, which is something we'll have to fix."

Marilyn looked at James and back at Todd. "We'll check on Faith and please, know that we're here for all of you, whatever it takes."

Five minutes later, James and Jake received a text message from Deputy Yang asking to do a video chat. James grabbed his laptop and positioned it between himself and Jake. Yang's face appeared, her expression sharp and focused.

"I didn't expect to find you together," she said, giving a quick nod. "I've pulled together what we have so far on Ricky and Kenny, and the Bricklin and Lee storyline. Sheriff Carson wants us to compare notes and see where this leads."

"Appreciate you looping us in," James replied. "What have you got?"

Yang, still sniffling, shared her screen, displaying academic records and internship files. "During Ricky's graduate years, he completed an internship at D.J. Singer Pharmaceuticals, a company with labs and major offices in Detroit, Dallas, and Chicago. His research focus was controlled substances and enzyme pathways, which is . . . interesting, given what comes next."

Yang paused to blow her nose. "Sorry . . . A federal drug task force's surveillance logs from Chicago show his name coming up in connection with a syndicate on the west side. Nothing direct, but he was flagged during a wiretap of a D.J. Singer employee suspected of laundering money for organized crime. No charges, but the timing is curious."

"And Kenny?" James asked.

"Kenny overlapped with Ricky at Michigan, roommates for a period of time. But he majored in business with a financial management concentration and went on to law school at Michigan. He specialized in corporate law and clerked for a firm that represented pharmaceutical companies. And here's a possible link to Sophie: while Kenny was clerking in Dallas, Sophie was living there under the name Kate Jennings. She worked in pharmaceutical sales. One of Kenny's clients was D.J. Singer Pharmaceuticals. It's possible their paths crossed."

"That's not just possible—that's likely," Jake said, frowning.

"Exactly," Yang agreed. "I'm going to send you both the files. Sheriff Carson wants us to start mapping out a timeline of where Ricky, Kenny, and Sophie overlapped. Their shared histories could explain a lot about Sophie's murder."

James nodded. "And if there are old debts or grudges buried in their past, this might be the crack in Ricky's polished façade we've been looking for."

As the conversation wound down, Deputy Yang glanced at the clock. "Alright, gentlemen, I think we've covered as much as we can for now. I'll keep digging into Ricky's and Kenny's ties to D.J. Singer and see if I can pull any additional financial records."

"Good," Jake said. "I'll reach out to a contact and see if there's anything in their archives on D.J. Singer's organized crime connections that didn't make it into the official reports."

James nodded, his face set with quiet determination. "And I'll map out a timeline based on what we know. Maybe Marilyn and I can spot patterns."

Yang glanced between the two men and added, "Let's reconvene Sunday late morning. That should give us all a chance to gather more pieces. Also, I just heard that Sheriff Carson has scheduled an update for Sunday afternoon at 4. He'll want you two to attend."

"Sunday it is," James agreed.

With that, they exchanged quick farewells and ended the call, the screen winking to black, but the weight of their task hanging heavily in the air. Jake was worn out from the evening at Carson's ranch. He decided to head home for a shower and a change of clothes. He had a feeling it was going to be a busy weekend.

CHAPTER TWENTY-THREE

Saturday, Midmorning

Julia sat across from Sheriff Carson in the sterile, windowless interview room. Her hair pulled back tight, her face pale but composed. Carson, flanked by two deputies, slid the flash drive across the table. "This is yours, right?"

Julia nodded. "I left it for you. I wanted you to understand everything. I wanted someone to know I wasn't a killer, I was grieving. But in the end, I made a mistake hitting Sophie." She shifted in her chair. "I want to cooperate, but only if you guarantee my safety."

"Safety from who?" Carson asked.

Julia hesitated. "Ricky. I'm afraid of him. Men like that are always watching. They're like a lion stalking its prey. Tense, eyes fixed, very deliberate, kind of hiding in plain sight, ready to pounce when they get the chance. I know that sounds crazy, but honestly, he gives me the creeps."

Carson and his deputies exchanged looks before he motioned for her to continue.

Julia's voice trembled now. "You have the flash drive, so you know about my sister and the accident. I didn't really know Ricky and Sophie. They've been living just a few doors away and were not very social. On occasion, I'd seen them from a distance, but we didn't cross paths often. About two years ago, my friend Allison was visiting from Dallas, and we went to the mailboxes near my house. Sophie was also there getting her mail. Suddenly, Allison freaked out and whispered to me, 'Oh my god, that's Kate Jennings – the woman who killed your sister!'"

"How was she so sure it was Kate Jennings?" Carson asked.

"She and Sophie were classmates at a private high school a few years before the accident. They even attended the same Christian summer camp in middle school."

Julia buried her face in her hands. "I remembered from the trial that Kate was a strikingly beautiful woman, but it was hard at first to make the connection. Sophie was now in her 40s, not wearing any makeup, and dressed in very plain clothes. Then something about her profile hit me hard. It *was* Kate Jennings. Sophie said hello and mentioned how nice our property always looked. I remembered that voice. How she lied at the trial. How her rich, privileged parents testified and made excuses for her being so drunk."

"What did you do?"

"I almost got sick and just walked away. I think she recognized me too, but she didn't say anything. When we got back to my house, Allison told me her parents knew Kate's family. She returned to college after the accident. Kate's parents, who were very connected, helped her get a job with one of the big pharmaceutical companies in medical research and sales." Julia paused and took a sip of water. "Apparently, Kate made big money pushing opioid painkillers and was heavily involved in assuring doctors and patients that these medications were not addictive. That's about all Allison knew. So, I did my own research. Local newspaper articles said Kate Jennings was questioned as part of a federal investigation. Even though the investigation continued, they didn't mention her again. In fact, I couldn't find anything on her after 2015.

"I stayed clear of Sophie after that until early last summer. Todd and I were out front with the dogs. Ricky and Sophie stopped in their car to ask about the new purple flowers Todd had planted earlier that week. Sophie tried to be overly friendly. My skin was crawling being that close to her. She was alive, and my sister was dead. She had a life and made lots of money. Probably the money they were living on now. I knew what she was trying to do. I walked away and let Todd answer their questions. I'm certain Ricky could see the hate in my eyes. Guys like that can read people."

Carson nodded. "Any contact after that?"

"Ricky came to me last October. I'm not sure if it was connected, but there was a rumor on the street that Sophie had gotten into a big argument with Kenny a few weeks before about his dog. Not a surprise, no one likes that dog except for James." Julia paused. "Sorry, the dog is fine. He's just a little too rambunctious and likes to jump up on people."

"Okay," Carson said, "let's get back to Ricky."

"I'm not sure why he approached me. Clearly, he had done his research on me before the discussion. He knew about my sister Angela and the crash. Bottom line, he asked me to forgive Sophie. I told him no. He looked . . . disappointed."

"Why did the confrontation with Sophie happen now?"

Julia looked straight into Carson's eyes. "Todd normally walks the dogs at night, but he was late coming home from Fort Collins. The dogs were really misbehaving, so I was already tense. The meeting on Monday night was not planned. I've never seen Sophie out walking that late, so I was surprised to see her. Shocked, honestly. Sophie was down at the mailboxes next to my house. As she walked back up the path toward her house, we came face to face. I quickly walked away, but I could hear her following."

"Did she threaten you?"

"No, she called out and asked me to stop and said something about forgiveness and the book club meeting I hosted Thursday night. I walked faster toward the entrance to Warriors Way. She caught me and touched me on the shoulder. One of the dogs playfully jumped at Sophie, which seemed to freak her out. We had a quick, heated exchange about the dog and my sister, and I hit her once across the face with the flashlight."

"So, she asked for forgiveness after more than twenty years and you attacked her. Interesting. Are you sure you hit her only once?"

"Yes. It was stupid and impulsive, but I know I didn't kill her! I read in the paper that she was beaten and leaning against the stop sign. One hit from a flashlight couldn't do that kind of damage, and Sophie was not a small woman. Our meeting was at least 20 feet from the stop sign. There's no way I could have moved her into that position."

Sheriff Carson shook his head as if he was suspicious of Julia's story. "The past is the past, and I'm sorry about what happened to your sister. But what I hear and see in your eyes is not grief, it's more like vengeance. Look, I was in the Army for twenty years, and now I'm a sheriff with lots of women on the force. I've seen them do the impossible. I think you found yourself in a stressful situation on the night of the murder and were capable of more than you're willing to admit, to include moving her body. But here's my bottom line: you were on the street with Sophie on Monday night, you attacked her with a heavy metal flashlight, and now she's dead. When I do the math, you're suspect number one."

Julia sank in her chair, looking crushed by that comment. Outside, a storm was moving in across the Rockies. And Ricky, wherever he was, hadn't left his final mark—yet.

CHAPTER TWENTY-FOUR

Saturday, Midmorning

While Sheriff Carson was interviewing Julia, Lieutenant Walker and Deputy Ryan returned to Kenny Jacobs' house for a second interview. Lieutenant Walker stepped out of the patrol SUV and glanced toward the grand home set high on a foothill in Deer Park Ridge. He turned and noticed that the sun was now illuminating the red rock formations bordering the golf course below. With resentment building inside him, he knew he would never own a home like this on a lieutenant's salary.

Walker knocked firmly on the front door. A few seconds later, it creaked open, and Kenny appeared, still wearing pajama bottoms and a long-sleeved shirt, looking slightly irritated.

"You guys again?" Kenny muttered.

"Morning, Fredrick," Walker said evenly, emphasizing the name. Kenny's eyes narrowed, but he didn't speak. "Mind if we come in? Just a few more questions, and I think we're all better off having this conversation inside."

Kenny hesitated, then stepped aside without a word. The officers entered the large great room, the scent of coffee lingering in the air. King, being unusually calm, was half asleep in a sunny spot near a sliding glass door.

Walker remained standing, his posture steady but not aggressive while the other men sat on a large leather couch. "We've verified your identity. You're not Kenny Jacobs, you're Fredrick Lee. Law degree from the University of Michigan, class of 2006. Your roommate during undergrad was Bruce Bricklin, now known as Ricky Delgado. Ring a bell?"

Kenny—Fredrick—exhaled sharply, eyes darting toward the window. "I figured this was comin' after I heard Ricky disappeared." he muttered. "You people dig deep."

Deputy Ryan flipped a page on his clipboard. "We also know the two of you collaborated with a pharmaceutical company starting in 2010, D.J. Singer. The same company that did early-stage painkiller research before the opioid boom. A few of your former colleagues have been showing up in federal investigations from back then. These weren't casual connections. We want to know what kind of work you and Bricklin were really involved in."

Kenny closed his eyes, his jaw tightening. "We were legal and research advisors, that's it. We weren't manufacturin' pills in a basement if that's what you're thinkin'. But I'll say this, things got murky. We were asked to sign off on studies we didn't fully trust. Bricklin got out before things turned ugly. I stayed longer than I should have."

He paused, then met Walker's eyes. "But whatever's goin' on now, whatever happened to Sophie, I had nothin' to do with it. And you'd better figure out who did before you waste more time on phantom storylines from fifteen years ago."

Walker didn't flinch. He studied Kenny for a moment, then said quietly, "You're right, we dig deep. And right now, we're trying to separate the bullshit from substance. But here's the problem: the murder of Sophie Delgado isn't ancient history. It happened this week. And you living here under a fake name, walking your dog multiple times per day on their street, having a confrontation with the victim last fall, and being on Warriors Way at the time of the murder —well, that makes your past very relevant."

Deputy Ryan added, "You both walked away from a company that's been tied to opioid litigation, shell corporations, and research tampering. If there's something you haven't told us, now's the time."

Kenny rubbed the back of his neck. "I kept my distance for a reason. I changed my name in 2015—after D.J. Singer collapsed and the Feds started sniffin' around." He looked up, eyes sharp. "There's more. Sophie, or rather Kate Jennings, worked for the same company. She was beautiful and brilliant as the company's point person for pharmaceutical sales. Kate and I started as colleagues. We dated briefly before she and Ricky became a thing, about 2009, I guess. I knew she was out of my league. Somehow, we stayed close friends. So, you had Ricky the chemist or researcher, me as a senior lawyer for the company, and Kate as the front person. Does that help you put things together?"

Walker didn't break eye contact. "People don't relocate to the same quiet neighborhood by accident, Fredrick."

Kenny rubbed his hands together, eyes darting between the floor and Lieutenant Walker's steady gaze. "Look, Lieutenant . . . It's not what you think," he explained with a shaky voice. "Ricky, Sophie, and I—we've known for a long time what we did, the harm we were part of. We weren't saints, but we weren't runnin' from it either. The prosecutors . . . they brought us in, gave us a chance to make things right. We've been collaboratin' with them for years—quietly—helpin' map out supply lines, fake clinics, the whole rotten pipeline feedin' the opioid mess. We were tryin' to clean up what we helped break.

"Hidin' us up in these foothills was not our choice. It was because of Ricky's stupidity and greed. He cheated some extremely dangerous people."

Walker's jaw tightened, but he didn't speak. Kenny went on, desperately. "I swear to you—we were tryin' to stop the bleedin', not make it worse."

The silence thickened for a moment before Ryan finally spoke. "We'll need a formal statement—everything you can remember about D.J. Singer Pharmaceuticals, the research, and Bricklin's role in it. If he was tied to something bigger, something dangerous, it could be the reason Sophie's dead."

After Walker and Ryan left, Kenny's mind flashed back to 2013, to the lab that reeked of disinfectants, stress, and conversations. Bricklin leaned over the conference table, reviewing the newest trial results while Fredrick sat across from him in a crisp suit, flipping through the legal summaries.

"They're pushing hard on this compound," Bricklin had said, tapping a folder labeled Trial Series 3B – Neural Suppressants. "Too hard. The margin for addiction is off the charts. Have you seen this report? This is bad science being dressed up to look clean."

Fredrick exhaled and glanced toward the frosted-glass hallway, having made sure no one was in earshot. "I flagged it in the compliance review. But if we push back, they'll just find someone who won't." He paused. "You thinkin' of walkin'?"

Bricklin had nodded, slowly. "I've seen where this ends. They're going to make billions off this drug. And then the lawsuits will follow. I'm not going to be the guy holding the bag. Neither should you."

Kenny thought back on those days, recognizing how quickly things had fallen apart. He now faced a sheriff's department asking too many questions. The press knocking on neighbors' doors and running updated stories daily. The possibility that Carson or Ricky would piece together loose ends and come after him. And a menacing black SUV that was scaring the hell out of him. Yes, it was only a matter of time before attention would turn to him, and he would be forced to move on.

CHAPTER TWENTY-FIVE

Saturday, Early Afternoon

Jake returned to James's house around 1 p.m. after a quick meeting at the sheriff's satellite office in the Deer Park Ridge shopping center. He carried a thin file folder, sealed and marked with a red stamp: Law Enforcement Sensitive. Jake quickly reviewed key points from Julia's interview with Carson.

James took a long breath, staring out at the street below. "So, we have Julia and her hate for Sophie. Then there's Ricky, Sophie, and Kenny, three old friends, hiding from past mistakes. I don't know whether the two storylines are separate or cross over. If Julia's the murderer, it's pretty straightforward. If not, it could be Ricky, Kenny, or someone from their past catching up to Sophie that night. We also need to ask why now? Maybe they crossed someone powerful on one of those recent trips to D.C."

Jake set his water bottle down with a quiet thud. "Carson's right about one thing, this isn't just about a confrontation on Warriors Way. Question is . . . how far do we dig before we're in over our heads?"

James frowned, knowing Jake was right but feeling that same restless pull he'd felt ever since he found Sophie's body.

James opened the folder Jake brought from the sheriff's office. Inside was a grainy photo of a much younger Ricky—in a tailored suit, with a cocky expression, seated beside a man whose name was blacked out. Another document revealed a laundering operation tied to unsolved disappearances in Nevada.

Jake continued, "He vanished before testifying in a second case. Then he reappeared under protection."

"If he's hiding again, it's not because of Sophie's death," James noted. "It's because the past has found him. Either his Vegas past, if it's real, or the corporate drug past, which is probably real."

"Ricky's silence means something," Jake said. "Either he's dead, or he's planning his next move."

James stared out the window. "We need to find out who else from his old life might be circling."

"This other thing with Ricky and Sophie," Jake began, tapping a finger against a DOJ report, "may go deeper than either of us imagined. I pulled federal case files from 2019 and 2020. The opioid settlements. They could be connected in ways that would explain both their money and why they've lived like shadows on Warriors Way."

"I've been researching the role pharmaceutical companies played in this crisis," James said. "Between 1999 and 2020, more than a half million people died from opioid overdoses. The federal government started realizing, far too late, that pharmaceutical companies had flooded the country with painkillers, marketing them aggressively as safe and non-addictive. OxyContin, Vicodin, hydrocodone—you name it. And the FDA approved it all." He paused to rub his temples. "By 2017, we were losing 50,000 people a year. Whole towns in West Virginia and Ohio decimated. Morgues ran out of space. And the DEA started asking why. Why were rural pharmacies ordering millions of pills? Why were distributors not reporting suspicious shipments?"

Jake frowned. "I read about those lawsuits. Didn't one family settle?"

"Yes and no. One company agreed to pay a fortune, over $6 billion in bankruptcy court. Another filed for Chapter 11 and agreed to be dissolved. The money is supposed to fund addiction treatment and education. But the families behind these companies insulated themselves. They pulled billions out before the lawsuits hit."

Jake nodded. "Let's stir the ashes. See who smells like smoke."

Sheriff Carson met with DA Allen Butler at 1 p.m. on Saturday. He pushed Butler to charge Julia with second-degree murder and obstruction of justice. The DA was not in a rush to decide. His team was reviewing evidence and would be ready when they were ready. Todd was brought back in for questioning again, and his story was cracking. Many details shifted about his actions and statements related to Monday night. He was detained as a possible accomplice. Carson was unsure whether he would be charged.

Meanwhile, Marilyn took a plate of food to Faith, who was alone, not knowing what was going on with her mom or dad. Hugs were exchanged, but few words were spoken. The normally talkative and entertaining Faith just sat there. Marilyn had decided in advance that she would not volunteer any of the new information from Julia's file or Todd's visit that morning.

Marilyn took Faith's hand. "This week has been confusing for all of us. First, the tragedy of Sophie's murder. Then, your parents haven't really spoken to us all week. Has your dad told you anything?"

"No, he's barely said a word to me since I got home on Thursday. All I know is that my mom was found this morning in the courthouse parking lot. It's all so crazy and I really don't understand why she disappeared yesterday." Faith said.

"I don't understand it either."

Faith's eyes filled with tears as the two women hugged.

"Do you want to spend the night with us?" Marilyn asked.

"No, I'm fine to stay here with the dogs."

Marilyn patted Faith on the back. "I'll check on you tomorrow. Call any time if you need anything."

One street over, Kenny was almost apoplectic after his second interview with Lieutenant Walker and Deputy Ryan. He reached out to one of his contacts and demanded an immediate meeting. Kenny now sat across from Special Agent Miller in a quiet corner booth of a diner off I-25, his hands trembling around a coffee mug.

"You don't get it," Kenny said. "Ricky, Sophie, and I were a team. We were doin' important work. All that fell apart last year. Now I don't know who I can trust. Every time Ricky smiles, I feel like there's a threat behind it. Now Sophie's dead, and I'm tellin' you, Miller, that means the list just got shorter . . . and I'm next."

"Why do you think you're next, Kenny?"

"There's been a black SUV that's been parkin' down the street from my house and followin' me around. There are people out there who want to settle a score. Some because of Ricky's greed and some because of what I did."

Miller didn't blink, just stirred his coffee slowly. "Kenny, you need to stick to facts. Paranoia doesn't help me help you."

Kenny's voice rose. "It's not paranoia if it's true. I've seen what happens when people like them decide you're a problem. Plus, now I have these clueless jerks in the sheriff's department and the press houndin' me, exposin' me."

Miller slid a legal pad across the table. "Who are these bad guys? Names, places, dates—give me something to work with."

Kenny shook his head, glancing out of the diner's sun-streaked window as if expecting someone to be there. "You don't understand the kind of people we're talkin' about," he murmured. "I found out that Ricky and Sophie went behind my back last month in D.C. Why, I don't know. But now I have to assume they put a target on me, and someone will come. They won't just knock. They'll make it look like an accident, or worse, like I was never here at all."

Miller tapped his pen. "Then help me get ahead of it. Otherwise, you're just waiting for them to find you."

Kenny met his eyes, a flicker of desperation showing. "I'm not waitin'. I made that mistake 11 years ago. I'm runnin' like Ricky. The only question is how far I'll have to go before they stop chasin'."

His voice suddenly became hoarse, the words slow, like they'd been locked away for years. In that moment, he seemed to get lost in time. "You think I don't know what happens to people who cross them?" he whispered. "In 2014, I was in Phoenix, supposed to meet another company lawyer, a friend, about a large shipment of pills and moving money. The plan was for him to pick me up in the hotel parkin' lot in the mornin'. When I found his car, the window was open. He was dead with his brains all over the windshield. We'd talked only 15 minutes earlier to discuss the plan for the day."

There was silence before Agent Miller finally spoke. "You witnessed it?"

"No." Kenny's voice cracked. "I smelled the blood and his brains. It was a warnin'." He let out a bitter laugh. "I didn't even go back into the hotel. I took my car, drove to San Diego, ditched it, and vanished. Changed my name twice, worked under the table. I didn't talk to my family, didn't see my friends. Just stayed one step ahead of the people I used to work for."

"And that's when we found you."

"Yeah, you did," Kenny said slowly, staring at the wall beyond Miller like it could open a hole to the past.

CHAPTER TWENTY-SIX

Saturday, Midafternoon

A light snow was falling in Deer Park Ridge just after 2:30. James and Jake were reviewing files and researching the federal witness protection program when a knock came at the front door. James opened it to find a man in a weathered parka, eyes hidden under a ball cap. For a moment, the shadows played tricks on him, then the man stepped forward. It was Manny, his neighbor.

James stepped aside, every instinct on alert. Manny sat in the kitchen, glancing out the windows as if expecting someone to crash through them. He looked at Jake. "James told me a few years ago that you are a retired cop."

Jake nodded.

"I need to talk," Manny said, his voice low. "I read this morning about Ricky being missing. I really don't want to get involved because the guy is in trouble, but I met Ricky in 2012 in Vegas. Look, you can use this information however you want. Share it with the sheriff or not but keep me out of it." Manny sat back, relieved to get that out.

Jake and James didn't interrupt.

"I was in Vegas for a week doing IT work with a security company," Manny continued. "Each night, I would hit a different casino. On the third night, Ricky and I were sitting together, playing blackjack at The Venetian. Ricky was dressed sharp—dark blazer, crisp white shirt, and his signature fedora tilted just so. He wasn't reckless with his chips, but he wasn't timid either. I remember how his laugh carried over the clinking of glasses and chiming slot machines. He talked non-stop about Vegas. After about an hour, a guy walked up behind us and called him Bruce. Said they needed to go. Before leaving he gave me a business card with just a phone number. Told me if I was ever back in Vegas to give him a call as if he was a longtime resident. He walked away with a tidy stack of black chips and disappeared into the crowd like he owned the place."

Manny thought for a moment then added: "One odd thing, he kept recommending places to go and restaurants I should try. It seemed weird that he acted more like a tourist than a local. Like he had been there for a week or two and wanted to share his experiences. It was 'try this place' or 'I was there last night.' Or 'the show at another hotel is great, went with a friend on Saturday night.' Look, I did theater in high school and college. Preparing for an acting part requires research. I felt like Ricky was an actor in the role of a lifetime."

"In a way, I guess he was," James said.

Manny took a breath. "Well, that was it for Vegas. A few years later, I see this guy living up the street on Warriors Way. He was wearing the same fedora, and I recognized him immediately. About four years ago, I guess in the summer of 2021, we met at a community concert down by the front entrance. He was friendly. We talked about hunting and Deer Park Ridge stuff."

"Yeah, he's a real friendly guy," Jake smirked.

Manny continued. "A couple of weeks after that concert, he knocked on my door. Asked me if I had ever been bowhunting.

I hadn't. Told me there was a class being offered in Parker and asked if I wanted to go. We took the class and bought the necessary bows and gear. We went hunting five or six times over the last few years. Again, a new thing for both of us. Normally, we'd go for a couple of days and stay in my cabin which is just west of Conifer, about a forty-minute drive. The place is basic, but in nice shape. What's funny is he would tell these wild Vegas stories about his time living there. They were all bullshit, but entertaining.

"During bowhunting season last September, I suggested to Ricky that we plan a weekend trip in October with the wives to catch the fall colors. There's plenty of room in my cabin and great food at a nearby café. I didn't mean to put any pressure on him. Just thought it would be a good chance for the wives to get to know each other and for us to spend a couple of days in the fresh air. But Ricky shut the idea down, saying Sophie wasn't very sociable and that she hated the woods. I didn't press after that.

"The next time we went up there, maybe mid-January, he showed up with a woman named Donna. Nice lady, a nurse, but it was very awkward for me. Then, the day before yesterday, he asked to use the cabin for a couple of days to get away from the press. He also asked if he could borrow my F-150. I told him yes on the cabin and no on the truck. He didn't push when I said no. He has an all-wheel drive SUV that would be fine for the trip."

Manny pulled out a folded map from his coat. It had two red X's. One was Warriors Way. The other, a cabin located thirty miles west of Deer Park Ridge. "Again, share this with the sheriff or not. Ricky is probably just lying low for a couple of days, so maybe none of this is important. I just want to keep my distance from him and the investigation."

Manny stood up and looked at them with real concern. "GPS alone won't get you to the cabin. It's off the grid. Can either one of you read a map and navigate in the woods?" Jake and James both smiled.

"We're good," James assured him.

Manny left as quietly as he arrived.

James narrowed his eyes as he looked at Jake. "Ricky skipped his second interview, and there is a BOLO out on him. That must mean something. Should we share this with Carson?"

Jake shook his head. "Let's hold off on calling the sheriff. This may be bad information. I say we go for an afternoon road trip to check it out."

James gave his friend a skeptical look. "Don't you think that a trip to the cabin is a bad idea? Carson told us to keep our heads down and to let his department do the real police work."

Jake laughed. "Hey buddy, the devil hates a coward."

James reluctantly agreed. "True, if you never take a chance, you never have a chance."

Before leaving, James grabbed his 9mm and holster. He stopped momentarily before closing the gun safe door and wondered if being armed created more or less danger when dealing with a suspected murderer. He concluded it was a 50/50 deal, so it was better to be prepared.

James was thankful Marilyn had run to the store and wasn't home to ask questions. He sent a quick text to let her know that he and Jake were checking out Manny's cabin and would be gone for a few hours—hopefully. He didn't mention why they were going or that he was taking his 9mm.

CHAPTER TWENTY-SEVEN

Saturday, Late Afternoon

About an hour later, James eased his Jeep Wrangler off the main road and onto a narrow, rutted forest service track, the kind of path where only confidence, clearance, and all-terrain tires stood between progress and a long walk back. The sun illuminated the sky, with clouds nesting low over the foothills. Ponderosa pines shadowed the trail, their trunks catching the light like cathedral columns. The light dusting of snow that had recently fallen added to the beauty.

James drove slowly but with purpose, scanning each turn, his instincts sharpened by years in intelligence work and now honed by something more personal—intuition sharpened by the lies, the disappearance, and the brutal aftermath left behind on Warriors Way. The Jeep groaned and shifted beneath him as he climbed higher, toward the old cabin.

The elevation brought a bite into the air, and James welcomed it. He lowered the window slightly, letting the chill slap him awake, his senses alert to the silence and the weight of the wilderness pressing in. He thought about Ricky's past—half-truths, the Vegas story, the fedora and the 1950s outfits—and wondered how much of it had been camouflage for something darker.

The road turned abruptly, revealing a clearing with a cabin hunched against the mountainside. There were two SUVs carefully parked behind a tangle of pine trees and bushes. A faint wisp of smoke rose from a stovepipe, barely visible against the backdrop of pines.

James killed the engine and stepped out slowly. Both men slipped on their shoulder harnesses and checked their respective weapons. Jake whispered to James not to load his clip unless things really heated up.

Jake motioned for silence as he knocked on the front door, no answer. He slowly pushed the unlocked door open. Inside, the air was warm from a smoldering fire with a pleasant smoky scent. On a wooden kitchen table sat a bottle of bourbon, two glasses, and a half-burned candle, still lit. Three bottles of red wine were on the counter. The refrigerator had two bottles of white wine and enough food for dinner.

Jake scanned the room. "Interesting, there's a woman's jacket hanging on that kitchen chair."

James noticed a purse on the counter. "I wonder if his nurse friend, Donna, is with him?"

James found a spiral notebook on the coffee table. Its pages were filled with a mix of confessions, names, and cryptic lines like "Too many debts. They'll never let me rest."

"Was he planning to end it?" James asked.

Jake shook his head as he searched the purse. "Not his style. It isn't a suicide note. It's a ledger . . . Yep, its Donna's purse."

In the primary bedroom, they found men's clothing, and a duffel bag with cash and a cheap phone with one number saved: CARSON.

Jake raised an eyebrow. "Jason?"

They exchanged a look. Jake smiled. "Could mean nothing, but it's another layer of mystery. Either Ricky was feeding

Carson information or Carson knows more about his background than he's told us."

Suddenly, a soft beep echoed in the cabin.

Motion sensor.

Jake and James moved to the opened door. Two figures stood at the edge of the tree line about forty yards away, barely visible in the shadows. Then they turned and walked into a heavily wooded area—slowly, deliberately. There they were—Ricky, dressed as if he'd stepped out of a thrift store noir film, and a woman Jake recognized from trivia night as Donna, Ricky's much younger girlfriend. The pair seemed relaxed, strolling side by side, until Ricky spotted the men. His head jerked back like he'd seen a ghost, and he bolted into the trees without a word.

As he exited the cabin, Jake reacted with pure muscle memory from his police days—he lunged forward, sprinting after them before James could say a word. Unfortunately, the uneven mountain path had other ideas. Thirty yards in, Jake caught his foot on a jagged stump and pitched forward with a grunt, rolling to a stop in a puff of pine needles and snow.

Donna froze, torn between following Ricky and helping the man groaning in the dirt. Her instincts as a nurse won out; she ran back and knelt beside Jake, checking his arm and cut hand, and muttering something about "men with more adrenaline than sense."

Jake, wincing but clearly pleased by the attention, waved James on with a quick, "Go! I'm fine!"

James charged after Ricky, dodging branches and vaulting over rocks in a pursuit that felt equal parts military training and bad slapstick. Ricky was fast, but panic made him clumsy, and James managed to close the distance right until they hit a steep embankment above a narrow stream. Ricky skidded down the snowy slope like a snowboarder, somehow staying upright, while James followed . . . less gracefully. One bad step sent him tumbling, arms windmilling, until he landed in the muddy creek with a splat loud enough to startle all the nearby creatures in the forest. He sat there, dripping, boots half-submerged, while Ricky disappeared into the trees.

A minute later, Ricky reappeared at the top of the bank, breathing hard, his eyes darting between the trees and the muddy figure below. At first, he didn't seem to realize who James was—just a stranger who had been chasing him through the woods. But as he squinted, recognition flickered across his face, quickly followed by something James couldn't quite read—wariness, maybe, or the calculation of someone deciding whether to run again. Without a word, Ricky slid partway down the slope, extended a hand, and pulled James up onto the bank. Their grip was brief and tense, each man's free hand hovering near his jacket as if both were suddenly aware the other might be armed.

Once on level ground, they instinctively stepped back, putting ten cautious feet between them. Neither spoke at first; the silence was thick with uncertainty. While the wind rustled the pines overhead, James tried to figure out whether Ricky's return had been an act of decency or a tactical choice. Both men kept their eyes locked, shoulders squared, caught in a standoff where neither wanted to make the first move—and neither yet trusted the other enough to lower his guard.

James broke the silence first, brushing a thick smear of mud from his sleeve. "Well," he said dryly, "that was probably the stupidest foot chase I've been in since college and I've been in some bad ones."

Ricky gave a short laugh, still catching his breath. "You? I thought I was about to get jumped by a lunatic in hiking boots. You looked like you were trying out for an action movie … badly."

"Yeah, well, it turns out I'm better on skis than boots. That was quite the Houdini act you pulled, disappearing down the hill."

Ricky shifted his weight, still eyeing James warily. "So, tell me, why are you and your friend sniffing around Manny's cabin? You didn't drive all the way up here just to ruin my afternoon walk with Donna."

James met his gaze evenly. "We were looking for you. Thought you might have answers to a few questions you've been avoiding back in Deer Park Ridge."

Ricky's expression hardened. "If this is about Sophie, or anything from before, you'd better be really sure you want to dig up that mess."

"That's exactly why I'm here, Ricky. I'm already in it." James took a slow step closer, his tone shifting from dry humor to something heavier. "Ricky … or should I say Bruce Bricklin? I know who you are. I know about Kate. And Fred, too."

Ricky's jaw tightened, but he didn't interrupt.

"I was the one who found Sophie Tuesday morning," James went on. "Leaning against that stop sign. I can't shake that image, and I can't let it slide. Whether I like it or not, I'm in this. I've got an obligation to figure out who did it."

Ricky's eyes narrowed, and for a long moment, he said nothing. James held his stare, then finally asked the question head-on. "Did you kill her, Ricky?"

The words hung in the cold mountain air. Ricky shook his head slowly, almost with disbelief. "You think I'd beat her to death and dump her where the neighbors could find her?"

James didn't look away. "I think people do a lot of things they swear they'd never do when the stakes get high enough."

Ricky's voice was edged with steel. "Not this. Not her. You've got the wrong guy."

CHAPTER TWENTY-EIGHT

Saturday, Early Evening

Robin Brookside rolled into the driveway at 6:30 p.m. sharp, her car a mud-splattered Subaru. The back was loaded with gear, a cooler full of drinks and protein bars, and a battered copy of *Forensic Biomechanics in High-Altitude Terrain* was wedged in the passenger footwell. She entered the house like a gust of alpine air—ponytail loose, fleece jacket half-zipped, eyes bright but questioning. She carried her overnight bag inside and exchanged a quick hug with her mother.

Robin had always been drawn to the edge of trails, of weather, of human endurance. Her PhD program in High-Altitude Exercise Science at the University of Colorado was a perfect match for both her academic curiosity and her physical drive. Focused on how the body adapts and responds to extreme elevation and oxygen deprivation, her research took her deep into the world of elite athletes, mountain rescue physiology, and even high-altitude pregnancy studies.

She split her time between the university's labs in Boulder and field stations perched above 10,000 feet, where she evaluated ultra-athletes' blood oxygen saturation levels during extreme physical activity. For Robin, science wasn't just data—it was motion, breath, and adaptation. The human body was an instrument shaped by place, and no place shaped it quite like the Colorado high country. She had plans to apply her research beyond athletics—to emergency response, military training, and even medicine. But for now, her world was high and cold, fast-moving, and utterly hers.

"Where's Dad?" Robin asked.

Marilyn gave her a sideways look. "Your Dad and Jake went to check out Manny's cabin in the middle of nowhere. That's all I know. I'm not sure what they're up to, but I'm worried, so don't ask me any more questions, or I won't be able to eat dinner."

Robin had gone backcountry skiing with friends, and suddenly, food was the priority. Trader Joe's orange chicken, a large pot of white rice, soy sauce, and ginger beer would do the trick for her and Marilyn. During dinner, Marilyn told Robin the entire story of Sophie's murder.

Robin's face changed. "That is so scary, and just fifty yards from our house."

Marilyn added. "We don't think it's random. There's too much that doesn't line up."

Robin sat back, thinking. "That stop sign. It's a funnel point. All traffic comes through there. It's visible from half the houses on the street."

Marilyn nodded. "Our kitchen window too. That's why Dad spotted Sophie in the first place on Tuesday morning."

Marilyn and Robin heard the garage door open, and the massive V-8 engine of Jake's pickup truck that had been parked in the driveway come to life. Moments later, they saw Jake pull away, and the rumble of the motor faded in the distance. James pulled his Jeep in next to the Vette and shut the door, still damp and streaked with mud from the run-in with Ricky and Donna.

He peeled off his soaked, filthy clothes, leaving a mess in a heap by the workbench, and grabbed an old, faded car towel from the back of his Jeep. Wrapping it around his waist, he slung his 9mm in its holster over his bare shoulder like an absurd action hero on laundry day. He carried a foot-long sub in one hand and a bottle of red wine in the other as he padded barefoot into the kitchen. Marilyn and Robin looked up from the counter, both caught somewhere between shock and amusement—Robin's eyes widened at the sight, Marilyn's mouth curling into a disbelieving smile.

"Hello, naked man! Rough trip? I know it's Saturday night, but isn't this a strange way to get things started?" Marilyn asked, laughing out loud.

James unwrapped his sandwich and took a large bite before answering, as if nothing at all was unusual about the scene. "Well, if it works for you, I'm game."

Marilyn gave him the once-over. "Can you imagine if Carson could see you? I'm tempted to text him a picture. Does he know you went to the cabin?"

James gave a fake smile. "No pictures, but he knows we went to the cabin. Jake and I called Carson on the way home."

"And what were you looking for at Manny's cabin?"

"We had a tip that Ricky was there."

Marilyn looked at Robin and back at James. "And was he there?"

"He was, but I'm guessing he's gone by now. Donna has an early morning shift at the hospital tomorrow, so they started packing up as we were leaving. And no, he didn't say where they were going. Ricky acknowledged it was a dumb move to miss the interview on Friday. He was going to call Carson and try to fix it."

Marilyn took on the persona of a high-stakes trial lawyer, treating him like a hostile witness. "So, what I'm hearing is that you and Jake decided to go to the cabin without the sheriff. You tipped Ricky off, and he's probably disappeared to who knows where. If you had called Carson in the first place, his team could have followed up on the BOLO and arrested him. Does that sound about right?"

James raised his eyebrows and smiled. "Aren't I handsome?"

Marilyn shook her head. "Lucky for you, yes, but that's not going to help you with Carson."

Robin looked at Marilyn and pointed at James. "Mom, am I doing a good job of acting like this isn't one of the stranger things Dad has ever done?"

Marilyn grimaced with her eyes closed. "Neither one of us is that good of an actor." Her smile faded as her eyes flicked to the holstered 9mm hanging from James's shoulder. "Would you please explain why you went to Manny's cabin with your gun, James?" she asked, her voice calm but edged with concern.

James set down his sandwich and chewed slowly before answering. "It seemed like a good idea at the time."

She studied him for a moment. "Are you insane? This whole thing has gone too far. Let me ask, did he have a gun too?"

James was tempted to say no but acknowledged that he probably did.

Marilyn looked very perturbed. "Where are your clothes?"

James sighed, rubbing a hand over his face. "In the garage. I rolled down an embankment and fell into a stream chasing Ricky."

"And did you ever actually catch him?"

James took another bite of his sub. "Not exactly. When he

realized it was me chasing him, he came back to help me up."

"What did he say after helping you?"

"He said he didn't kill Sophie. Said he's got his own mess. I don't know if I believe him, but he sure looked like a man carrying a lot of weight. I guess the press has really been hounding him this week."

Robin was still in disbelief. "Where was Jake when all this was happening?"

"He tripped in the first thirty seconds and came down hard on his hand and elbow. Ricky's girlfriend Donna was there. She's a nurse. I guess she got him into the cabin and cleaned and bandaged his arm. When Ricky and I got back, Jake was enjoying a charcuterie board and drinking bourbon."

"And then what?" Marilyn said with an 'I can't believe it' look on her face.

"Donna acknowledged to Jake that Ricky stopped at her place on Monday night around 7:45 and then they headed to Red Rocks for food just before 9, but the kitchen was closed. That all matches what Mike the bartender told Jake on Tuesday night. She could have been lying to give Ricky an alibi, but I don't think so. Jake disagrees."

Marilyn sat quietly, not knowing what to think.

Robin cocked an eyebrow, a sly grin tugging at her lips. "So . . . did you walk into Subway like that? Wearing the towel and all?"

James raised an eyebrow back, deadpan. "Oh yeah, I strutted right up to the counter, like I was a smoking hot twenty-year-old instead of being a smoking hot man who's just a little older than that."

He paused, then smirked. "But if anyone deserves credit

for bravery, it's Jake—he actually went inside to order, fully dressed, with a bandaged hand and elbow, and didn't trip over a single step."

Robin laughed, shaking her head. "Sounds like you two make quite the pair. Hopefully, no one we know saw you."

After a quick shower and feeling a bit stiff from his muddy tumble, James reappeared in the kitchen wearing pajama bottoms and a cycling T-shirt with a sketch of a bicycle that said, **On your left.**

Robin laughed at the shirt and asked, "Is that a new cycling shirt or a reference to your political leanings?"

James looked at Robin with a fond smile, grabbed the remains of his sandwich in one hand and a newly uncorked bottle of red wine and a glass in the other. Settling down at the table, he filled a large wine glass and took a long sip.

"Wait, where did you get that bottle of wine? Robin asked.

James smiled. "Ricky gave it to me. It's an expensive bottle."

"Oh, dear God. You took it from a possible murderer?" Marilyn said.

"Well, Ricky apologized to Jake and me for running and causing all the confusion. He gave us both a bottle. Don't forget that we've been neighbors for five years. Ricky and I shared that expensive bottle of red I took to Manny's for one of his holiday parties. We talked for a couple of hours that night. Guess he was just returning the favor."

Marilyn rolled her eyes. "I'm just glad he didn't want to gift you one of his ridiculous fedoras."

James smiled and finished the story with a wry grin. "So, there I was, chasing Ricky for 30-40 minutes or it could have been five minutes. You know, the heat of battle causes a great deal of uncertainty. Anyway, it was glorious until I ended up face-first in a creek." He rubbed his sore shoulder theatrically.

Marilyn took a deep breath and poured herself a glass of Ricky's wine. "Remind me again how much younger Ricky is than you?"

James sighed dramatically. "Twenty-five or so years. Apparently, age is just a number, and you know that I'm in outstanding shape."

Marilyn set her wine glass down a little too firmly, the thud echoing in the quiet kitchen. "James, explain to me again why you and Jake thought it was a brilliant idea to head up to Manny's cabin without calling Sheriff Carson first," she said, her voice tight with disbelief.

James leaned back in his chair, trying for casual but wincing at the stiffness in his shoulders. "We had a lead, and we didn't want to waste time."

Marilyn's eyes narrowed. "Waste time? You two walked into a potentially dangerous situation looking for an armed, scared person, in the middle of nowhere—and your plan was . . . what? Wing it?"

"It worked, didn't it?" James said.

Marilyn shook her head. "No, he got away, and you're both lucky it didn't end with Dr. Murphy, the coroner, zipping you two into body bags. You'd better get ready because I'm betting Carson is going to give you the ass chewing of a lifetime tomorrow."

James thought it was best not to answer.

Robin wisely changed the subject. "Mom, you told me that none of the doorbell camera videos from Monday night helped because of the distance to the corner. We should talk to John next door. He has that high deck off the top level with a view of the full length of Warriors Way. I'm sure that he has a security camera that's set back from the railing that may give us answers. He also has a strange antenna array on the roof of his house."

James and Marilyn looked at each other with complete surprise.

Robin looked both her parents in the eye and continued. "Really, I saw it last October when I rode my mountain bike up the foothill path behind Warriors Way. It's kind of hidden. You have to go halfway up the trail to see it. I still have the pictures." She pulled out her phone and scrolled back through her photo library.

James looked at the pictures. "Interesting. That type of set-up is used for secure communications by law enforcement and the military. There's a directional antenna on a telescoping mast, a VSAT dish, and a large weatherproof case with multiple cables going into the house."

Marilyn took a sip of wine and looked at James. "John is a friend. I guess it can't hurt to ask him in the morning?"

Robin nodded. "Just not without me."

James was looking out the kitchen window. "See how easy it is? One minute you're sitting here, and the next you're taking a road trip to a cabin in the woods. Or in this case, asking a slightly strange neighbor about the mysterious comms gear on his roof."

When James turned back, he found both Marilyn and Robin giving him the stink eye.

Once in bed, James reclined against the pillows, the room dim except for the soft light spilling in from the digital thermostat in the hallway.

Marilyn slid closer, resting a hand on his chest. "You've looked wired since you got home," she said. "Like you're still chasing Ricky down that hill."

James exhaled sharply. "I can't shake it. Ricky panicked the second he saw me. And then my conversation with Carson this morning . . . well, that didn't make things easier."

Marilyn raised an eyebrow. "What did Carson say?"

"I asked him if he was sure that I should continue to stay in this. His message was clear; it was a yes."

Marilyn shifted, pulling her knees under the covers. "And what did you tell him?"

"I told him I would help all I could with the investigation. But to let me know if Jake or I got out of line. I also told him I can't ignore what I saw or what I know. Ricky's hiding something, and Carson knows it, too. He just doesn't want me stirring the pot until he's ready."

Marilyn looked at James's darkened profile. "Carson's under a lot of pressure. He has to be careful not to expose himself or his department to criticism. But you're right, Ricky's behavior tonight was . . . well . . . interesting."

James nodded. "I don't think he would have run in the first place if he knew it was me. He sees something or somebody else as the threat."

For a moment, they listened to the quiet hum of the heat turning on. Marilyn reached for his hand. "So, what now? What's next?"

He squeezed her fingers. "I don't know," he admitted. "Part

of me thinks stepping back would be the smartest move. The other part thinks that if I do, something critical might slip through the cracks."

Marilyn leaned in and kissed his shoulder. "Just promise me you won't put yourself in danger again. And promise me you'll sleep tonight instead of replaying that chase on a loop."

James managed a tired smile. "I'll try. But I can't shake the feeling that tonight was a turning point."

James decided not to tell Marilyn about his nightmare last night. There was nothing she could do about it now, and he didn't want to be reminded of those feelings of terror. Best to let it go for now.

SUNDAY

CHAPTER TWENTY-NINE

Sunday Morning

Ricky rolled to a stop in front of Kenny's house just as the morning sun broke through the low clouds. He sat for a moment, gripping the steering wheel, his mind replaying the image of Sophie's body against the stop sign. When he finally stepped out, the air was sharp and cold, the quiet of Sunday morning broken only by the sound of the wind moving through the trees. His legs were sore from the crazy chase with James the night before. Wearing his pajama bottoms, Kenny was in his driveway, a golf club in one hand, and a dog leash in the other.

Ricky's voice cut through the stillness. "We need to talk, Kenny," he said, his tone edged with fury.

Kenny glanced up, his expression unreadable beneath the brim of his baseball cap. "About what?" he said, leaning the golf club against the tailgate of his SUV. "You look like hell, Ricky. Maybe you should be talkin' to the cops instead of me."

Ricky took a step closer, his eyes narrowed. "Don't play games with me. I talked to James. I know you were out there the night Sophie was killed."

Kenny's smirk flickered, but he didn't move. "So what? Doesn't mean I killed your wife. You think you're some kind of detective now? And I found out about your trips back to D.C. last month. What were you and Sophie up to?"

Ricky's voice rose. "Those trips had nothing to do with you. Look, you hated her! Everyone knew it. You called her a 'bitch' more than once. You threatened her. And now she's dead." He took another step forward, fists clenched. "I just want the truth, Kenny. Tell me what really happened that night."

Sensing Ricky's aggressive tone and movement, King began to growl and positioned himself between the two men.

Kenny's eyes hardened as he reached into his jacket pocket, his fingers curling around the handle of a gun now at his side. "Careful, Ricky," he said softly. "You're talkin' to the wrong man, and you're about to make a real bad mistake."

Ricky froze, his breath catching in his throat. The morning air suddenly felt thinner, colder. "You going to shoot me for asking a question?" he said, trying to keep his voice steady.

Kenny raised the weapon, not quite aiming it, but close enough to make his meaning clear. "You come to my house, throw around accusations, and yeah—I just might – wouldn't be the first time I killed someone. People around here should learn to keep their mouths shut. Maybe that's what Sophie should've done."

The words hit Ricky like a blow, and for a heartbeat, neither man moved.

Finally, Ricky stepped back, his pulse hammering in his temples. "You're an idiot, Kenny," he muttered. "You think you can scare me, but this isn't over."

Kenny lowered the gun just enough, smirking again. "It'd better be, Ricky. For your sake."

Ricky turned and walked quickly to his SUV. As he drove off, he could still see Kenny in the rearview mirror—standing in the driveway, calm and unmoved, the morning sun glinting off the steel of his Glock pistol.

———

It was a beautiful but chilly morning. James got up early and limped into the kitchen just ahead of Marilyn. "I know I was foolish yesterday, going to the cabin and chasing Ricky. Fortunately, no harm was done. Again, I'm sorry."

Marilyn had not slept well, and her mood had fouled since her bedtime conversation with James. "Ricky got away," she snapped. "And you could have been shot, fallen off a cliff, or attacked by a mountain lion. You and Jake were reckless."

Fortunately for James, online church was about to start. Marilyn could be heard softly praying for her foolish husband throughout most of the service.

James saw John arrive at his house next door after the Brooksides finished church at around 8:30. Still very sore from his run in the woods chasing Ricky, James stayed home and let Marilyn and Robin take the lead on questioning John, their normally friendly neighbor. John reluctantly answered the door and stepped outside to greet the mother and daughter.

It was agreed that Marilyn would start the questioning. "Hey John, do you have a minute to talk? We understand that you might have a couple of security cameras on your top deck. We were wondering, did the sheriff's office pull the video for their investigation of the murder?"

Without missing a beat, John responded. "Just one camera, and it doesn't work. I put it up there as a decoy. I'm not here at night. Figured it would scare off anyone nosing around the place. Anything else?"

Robin looked up. "We're not asking about the camera we can see, we're talking about the one on the top deck and the antenna array on the roof that is only visible from the trail behind your house."

John stepped forward. "Nothing is up there. Time for you two to go."

Looking skeptical, Robin asked again about the antenna array on the roof. "So, your setup that is designed for government-level secure communications is nothing? That is odd."

John again dismissed Robin's question. It was clear he was done talking, and he shut the door firmly. Marilyn and Robin looked at each other in surprise and walked back home.

While Marilyn and Robin spoke with John, James recorded in his journal.

March 22: Thinking back to last night and the chase. How stupid of me. Why did I run down a dark and rugged path? And no warm-up? My legs have never felt that tight and heavy. And my lungs were on fire from the thin, biting air. Surprisingly I was gaining on Ricky. His silhouette darting through the trees, desperate, clumsy, like a man who'd run out of lies and places to hide. I didn't expect him to move so fast for someone who's spent years hiding behind fedoras and half-truths. Finally, the tumble into the stream and Ricky's helping hand. How embarrassing for an old Soldier.

And Julia—God, Julia. Her being taken into custody, it was almost harder to process than Ricky's wild-eyed sprint. To think of the dinners, the laughter, the easy evenings with her and Todd. What haunts me most is how quickly the familiar was shattered. One week ago, we were just neighbors sharing a quiet street; today, the two of them sit in cells, one suspected of Sophie's brutal murder, and the other for making misleading statements. The sheriff's office may have their prime suspect, but I can't shake the feeling that threads are still dangling.

Ricky and Julia didn't move in lockstep; they each carried different motives, different fears. The truth behind Sophie's death may not be as simple as an arrest report. As I looked at Warriors Way this morning, the street looks the same—sunlight on rooftops, dogs pulling at leashes—but nothing is the same. The mountain chase was an ending of sorts, but for me, it feels more like the beginning of another layer of this story I still don't fully understand.

Marilyn and Robin returned home and found James writing in his journal in the living room. Robin informed him, "That didn't go well. He told us nothing. Said the camera doesn't work and the antenna array on the roof doesn't exist."

"Not out of the question," James mused, "but I'm guessing everything he told you was a lie."

Robin agreed as she was heading for the door with her bag. "I need to head back to school. I have a meeting this afternoon on our field test results from last week. Love you guys."

James called Jake and gave him feedback on the meeting with John. Jake was not happy that it had taken place without him.

"Yeah, it was a mistake," James admitted. "Do you know anyone who could help us figure this out?"

Jake told him about his planned meeting on Monday at the federal law enforcement field office. James was relieved to hear that news. Next up for the two men was a video chat with Deputy Yang at 12:30 to compare notes. James also reminded Jake they had an in-person meeting with Carson at 4 p.m.

As James dove into the opioid crisis, the sheer scope and deliberate obfuscation shocked even him. He started with the basics: prescription rates, overdose numbers, and the timeline of addiction waves across the U.S. What he found was chilling. The explosion began in the late 1990s when pharmaceutical companies pushed highly addictive painkillers under the guise of compassionate care. Doctors were courted with luxury trips and misleading research claiming the risk of addiction was "less than 1 percent." The FDA, either asleep at the wheel or complicit, approved labeling that downplayed the dangers.

What caught James's attention next was the financial web: the laundering of billions in profits, the shell companies, and the legal firms that quietly moved settlements behind closed doors. As drug enforcement task forces and federal prosecutors began to investigate the pill mills and overprescribing physicians, they met resistance not just from corporate legal teams but from political figures backed by pharmaceutical lobbying. One shocking thread linked executives at a now-defunct distributor to campaign donations in exchange for regulatory protection. Meanwhile, whistleblowers were silenced with payouts or smeared with character attacks. It became clear to James that this wasn't just negligence; it was an organized and sustained cover-up.

By the end of his research, James was left with a grim picture: an epidemic born of greed, protected by influence, and perpetuated by silence. It wasn't just a medical or legal crisis, it was a national betrayal. The same nation that sent soldiers overseas for less had allowed an entire generation to be consumed at home, and those who profited most were rarely held accountable. For James, it wasn't enough just to understand the facts. He needed to follow the names that kept resurfacing in lawsuits, in financial records, and, more recently, in the investigation surrounding Bruce Bricklin and Fredrick Lee. Somewhere in that tangle of data, James suspected there was a smoking gun.

With his research complete and an hour before his virtual meeting with Jake and Deputy Yang, the Brooksides decided time in the sun that had already melted yesterday's snow would help James loosen up his sore muscles and Marilyn lower her stress level. Armed with rakes, gloves, lawn bags, and a wheelbarrow, they tackled the dense layer of pine needles and windblown leaves that had settled during the winter around the rocks and gravel path near their fire pit and waterfall. The soothing sound of trickling water blended with the rhythmic scrape of metal on stone as they worked in sync, occasionally pausing to admire the mountain view or pointing out small weeds already pushing up from the earth.

James lovingly looked at Marilyn and thought about when they first met. There were many variations to the story. The version James most often told was that they met when he went to the hospital for a vasectomy consult. Marilyn came into the wrong examination room and stayed to answer all his questions. She convinced him not to have the procedure so they could have children after they got married. Marilyn never remembered the marriage and children part, but she acknowledged that she thought he was hot for an older guy. For James, the platonic flirtation during that first meeting was intoxicating.

Refocusing, James wiped his brow and leaned on his rake. "I think these damn pine needles multiply over winter just to spite me."

Marilyn grinned and tossed a bundle into the wheelbarrow. "It's not spite, it's nature's way of making sure you don't get soft in retirement."

James chuckled. "I think nature's going to have its way with me no matter what I do."

Marilyn stepped over to the waterfall and adjusted a few rocks. "Regardless, the deer, turkeys, and bunnies appreciate our efforts."

"I'm sure. Let's bag this mess and be done with it for a month or two."

After getting ice water, Marilyn sat at the kitchen counter. "Before you go into your meeting, I just want to offer my thoughts about your research. Every conference or briefing I've ever attended related to opioids was eye-opening. Patients who are given more than a three-day supply after surgery are twice as likely to still be using them a year later. It's heartbreaking how quickly dependence takes hold."

James leaned forward, brows furrowed. "So even when doctors think they're helping, they might be setting patients up for trouble down the road?"

Marilyn sighed. "That's exactly it. I've seen it in my own patients too—bright, responsible people who never thought they'd struggle with addiction. At first, it's just pain management, but then the body adapts, tolerance builds, and soon they're chasing relief that never fully comes. The experts keep stressing the same message: we have to prescribe less, monitor more closely, and offer alternatives whenever possible. Otherwise, we're not just treating pain—we're creating a whole new problem."

James went into the living room and turned on the TV. As he quickly flipped through the channels looking for today's March Madness college basketball schedule, he stopped on *Meet the Press* when he heard a familiar voice. The murder of Sophie Delgado was a lead topic for the program and the Brooksides' local congresswoman was front and center leading the charge.

Valerie Noble from their district sat tall in the *Meet the Press* studio chair, hands folded neatly as the cameras rolled.

"What happened to Sophie Delgado in Spirit County is exactly what I've been warning about," she declared, voice sharp and confident. "A woman beaten to death less than one hundred yards from her home. This is what happens when we ignore the rising crime epidemic in our country."

The host, Martin Jeffries, raised his hand gently. "Congresswoman, with respect, local investigators have said they have no evidence of broader crime trends here. This may be an isolated incident."

Noble refused to yield. "Martin, I met Sophie myself at

a Saturday morning run just last month. She told me she was worried about strangers wandering through the neighborhood—her words. This was a woman afraid in her own community."

Jeffries shook his head slightly. "But again, the sheriff has not linked her murder to an outsider, or to any trend at all. Isn't it premature to cite this tragedy as national proof?"

Noble flashed a thin smile. "Premature? Or prophetic?"

Another panelist, former prosecutor Kelly Keene, stepped in. "Valerie, you're using a woman's murder to score political points—there isn't any data backing your claim," she said firmly. "Spirit County's violent crime rate is one of the lowest in the state. You know that."

Noble countered at once, "Data lags reality, Kelly. People feel unsafe now. Look at Sophie. Look at her neighbors. They're terrified. And until we restore strong sentencing laws and stop coddling criminals, this is going to keep happening. Thank goodness we have residents stepping up to protect the neighborhood. These patriots are doing what the sheriff's department is failing to do, protect our citizens." Her tone suggested the issue was already settled.

All the panel members shook their heads, and Jefferies jumped in. "Congresswoman, those so-called patriots were arrested and charged with public intoxication and possession of a weapon while intoxicated. Both are serious offenses. Are you condoning this type of behavior?"

Noble gave him a dirty look. "You just don't get it, do you? Our communities are at war, and if breaking rules is what it takes, then so be it."

Jeffries tried once more to pivot. "Congresswoman, critics

say you're oversimplifying a complex investigation for your legislative agenda."

Noble didn't miss a beat. "If calling for law and order is an agenda, then yes, I'm proud of it. Sophie deserved better. The people of Spirit County deserve better. And I intend to make sure Washington finally listens."

She turned to the camera as if addressing the nation directly, leaving the host blinking in a brief, stunned silence before he moved to a commercial.

James and Marilyn listened in disbelief, knowing that Sophie's murder was most likely linked to a tangled web of lies and illegal activity, not whatever marginalized group Noble was implicating.

CHAPTER THIRTY

Sunday Afternoon

At exactly 12:30 p.m., James joined the virtual call with Jake and Deputy Yang, the three of them appearing in separate frames but locked into the same focus.

Yang had spent the morning digging through old court filings and whistleblower press reports. She shared her screen, pointing out anomalies in SEC disclosures and obscure pharmaceutical licensing arrangements.

James had mapped out the opioid crisis storyline and the points at which Ricky, Sophie, and Kenny's actions could have intersected.

Jake, ever the strategist, kept the conversation moving briskly, pulling together timelines, questioning assumptions, and flagging gaps that Sheriff Carson would undoubtedly press them on during the 4 p.m. meeting.

In his office since early that morning, Carson had just finished reviewing the latest forensics update when his phone buzzed with a restricted number. He answered, already bracing himself.

"Sheriff Carson?" Governor Hawthorne's voice came through hard and dry. "Sheriff, I just watched Valerie Noble on *Meet the Press*. She practically turned Spirit County into a war zone on national television. Tell me you've got real progress on the Delgado murder and not the same vague updates I've been hearing all week."

Carson exhaled slowly. "Governor, we're working the case aggressively. I've got a prime suspect. The DA is reviewing the evidence as we speak but has yet to decide whether to file formal charges. You should know there are gaps in the case. I still have deputies running down other leads, and our crime lab is pushing the evidence as quickly as possible. This isn't a political circus for us, this is a homicide investigation."

"That's not good enough," Hawthorne snapped. "I want a full update by close of business Monday—timeline, the prime suspect, forensics, every damn thing you have. And Carson … if there's something you're not telling me, now is the time."

Carson straightened up in his chair. "You'll have a complete, unvarnished report, sir. But I won't fabricate certainty to satisfy the congresswoman's talking points."

The governor grunted. "Fine. Just get me answers. And fast." The line went dead, leaving Carson staring at the phone, frustration simmering beneath his steady exterior.

Sunday afternoon at 4, James, Jake, Lieutenant Walker, Dr. Murphy, Deputy Ryan, Deputy Michaels, and Deputy Yang met in Sheriff Carson's office. Both James and Jake were limping as they entered and took their seats.

Dr. Murphy looked at James. "Hey buddy, did you fall off your bike?"

Carson laughed. "No, he's just old."

Carson opened the meeting. "I just got off the phone with Governor Hawthorne. He is really pissed about Noble's interview on *Meet the Press*. All of it was pure politics. The pressure is on, folks. We need to wrap up this case quickly. Murphy, you're up first."

Dr. Murphy nodded. "Two updates; first, the deputies went back to the Krantz house yesterday and retrieved the flashlight that Julia mentioned in her interview. Based on the testing we did in our lab, there were no blood traces at all. It makes me question whether it was the actual flashlight Julia used. Second, trace DNA was found under Sophie's fingernails. It didn't match anyone in the national databases, but the sample did come from a female. The court order to collect a DNA sample from Julia is pending."

Carson put up his hand. "Just a minute. What do we know about the flashlight we got from the Krantz's house? Was it the one she used to hit Sophie Delgado on Monday night or did they switch it out?"

No one responded to his question.

"Michaels, after this meeting you go to Julia's holding cell and ask. If she doesn't give you a straight answer, ask Todd Krantz."

Walker continued. "Even though the DNA evidence isn't a direct hit to Julia, it's damning when linked with her timeline, Marilyn Brookside's statement, and the surveillance footage. We also have statements from Julia where she acknowledged an altercation with Sophie and striking her with a heavy metal flashlight. Our problem is that the flashlight's leading edge isn't consistent with most of the injuries. That means we don't have the actual murder weapon."

Lieutenant Walker looked around the room and back at Carson. "So, we have damning evidence against Julia, but I don't think this is a done deal yet, boss. There are too many twists and turns that need to be resolved."

James and Jake glanced at each other, hoping there was other evidence to clear Julia.

"I'm distributing Kenny Jacobs' statement based on our second interview with him yesterday," Walker continued. "It highlights that Ricky, Sophie, and Kenny were supporting criminal prosecutions and that their relocation to Deer Park Ridge was not their idea. He didn't say who or how they got here. My gut tells me they probably crossed more than one person from their past so this case may be significantly more complex than initially believed, with the possibility Sophie's murder was a targeted attack. I'm not sure if it is connected, but he mentioned a black SUV that had been parking on his street and followed him to an indoor driving range last week. So, I think we need to keep the professional hit option on the table."

Carson interrupted. "Back to Julia, can we make an ID based on any of the doorbell cameras from Warriors Way?"

Walker shook his head. "No, it was drizzling so the videos are hazy. One did catch two women walking with two dogs toward the crime scene just after 8 p.m., exactly when we think Sophie was attacked. It is not clear enough to positively identify either woman. Ten minutes earlier, another camera showed a man with a large dog walking about one hundred yards from the crime scene. We assume that it was Kenny Jacobs. We also have video clips from the Krantzes' doorbell camera that show Julia and Todd leaving and returning to their home on Monday night. They confirm what Julia provided in her timeline."

Carson sighed. "Any of the cameras show someone who could have been Ricky Delgado or another possible suspect?"

Walker shook his head. "The cameras are helpful, but they are triggered by motion. Most of the houses on Warriors Way are set back far enough from the street that it's hit or miss on when they turn on."

Carson nodded. "What I'm hearing is that nothing has really changed. We have confirmation that Julia was on the street at the time of the murder. She acknowledged an altercation with Sophie and that she hit her with a heavy metal flashlight."

Walker nodded and then pointed to Deputy Yang.

"Sir, not much new since our last update," Yang reported with a raspy voice.

Carson looked at James, who spoke up. "You have a copy of the timeline I prepared. Separately, I want to offer a perspective mixed with some speculation. There are billions of dollars of company profits still missing that are believed to have been moved offshore. Civil and criminal court cases are ongoing. Per Walker's second interview with Kenny, we have to assume that Ricky and Kenny still have value to our federal partners, but the press reporting tied to Sophie's murder could put them at risk from their past lives. Assuming they're in one of the federal witness protection programs, they'll probably have to be relocated and given new identities."

Carson looked at Jake.

"My Vegas fusion center connection is ninety-five percent certain that Ricky was the 'The Chemist,'" Jake said, "meaning he was involved in developing and hiding sales to illegal markets."

Walker offered final comments. "The unknown we still have is Ricky's whereabouts on Monday night during the time of the murder and leading up to his arrival at Red Rocks around nine o'clock."

Jake reluctantly jumped in. "I had a conversation with Donna yesterday. She said Ricky came to her place on Monday night before they went to Red Rocks. That would give Ricky an alibi during the time of the murder."

Walker gave Jake a dirty look.

Sheriff Carson stood and looked around the room. "Thank you for your hard work. I'm convinced this isn't just a neighborhood dispute gone wrong. It's decades of secrets and guilt boiling over. Maybe there is a connection to the opioid crisis and federal prosecutions, maybe not. Regardless, it is our job to solve this murder based on the facts available. Julia had motive, opportunity, and now a forensic link."

He paused, letting the weight of the words settle. "It hasn't been released to the public yet, but Julia is pending criminal charges and an arraignment for Sophie's murder. I'm still waiting on the DA. If more evidence surfaces, we'll deal with that when the time comes. But for now, we're staying the course." Carson paused. "With that said, I know some of you disagree. I'm interested in getting opinions on the other suspects. Jake, you go first."

With the afternoon sunlight pouring across the room, the others fell quiet. "Jason, I think Donna was lying about Ricky being with her Monday night, and I'm convinced Ricky killed Sophie," Jake explained. "The marriage was dead and he was having an open affair with Donna. He was out most nights, drinking, flirting, and acting like a man who'd already moved on."

Carson raised an eyebrow, and Jake continued. "And Ricky's past? It's finally catching up with him. With that kind of pressure . . . secrets, lies, old debts . . . men like that crack. I think Sophie became a liability, and he snapped. Last, he's the husband. They're always my number one suspect."

Carson exhaled sharply, nodding his head. "Great points, Jake, thank you. James, you're next. Tell me what you think."

"Jason, Kenny had motive—real motive. He and Sophie had a major blow-up last fall. She blamed him for dragging Ricky into those illegal opioid sales, and Kenny knew it."

Carson frowned, arms crossed, while James continued. "Kenny's the paranoid type, and he has a bad temper. I golfed with him more than a dozen times. Even on a good day, he played angry. Honestly, it was uncomfortable to be around him until it was time for a beer after we finished the round. Kenny probably knew Ricky and Sophie went back to D.C. last month without him. If he thought they were about to turn on him, maybe cut a deal, he'd panic. And a panicked and pissed off Kenny would be dangerous. We know he was on the street around the time of the murder on Monday night."

"So, you're saying he struck first to protect himself?" Carson asked.

James nodded. "I think he saw Sophie as the weak link . . . and he silenced her."

Carson looked around the room. "I like your scenario. Anyone else have anything to add? Any other suspects or thoughts? I have a great deal of pressure on me right now, so it's time to speak up."

The room was silent.

Carson closed his eyes for a moment. "Jake, suppose it was Ricky, the husband. He could have been planning the attack for months. Hell, he may have tried ten times waiting for the perfect night where it all came together. I see it as a kind of Groundhog Day scenario."

Jake smiled, clearly liking what he was hearing.

"Somehow, he sets it up where Sophie had to get the mail," Carson went on. "He's waiting, and bam, he kills her. Think about it, the night was overcast with light rain. No one should have been out. What he didn't count on was Julia and Kenny being on the street walking their dogs. Still, he watches what happens between Sophie and Julia. Maybe Julia's story is true. Their confrontation was quick and more of a street scuffle. Ricky waits for Julia to leave, and he steps in to finish the job. We come in, and the evidence points us toward Julia. It's perfect."

Carson shook his head and laughed. "Hell, we should think about selling the book and movie rights for this one. We have Julia, Ricky, Kenny, or maybe, a professional hit man. What's crazy is they are all plausible options if we consider the emotional drivers for murder. Team, we need to keep digging, and time is not on our side."

The meeting attendees stirred in their chairs, but paused when Carson held up a hand. "Okay. One last thing, I have a meeting with our federal partners tomorrow morning. Assuming there is no new information, I'll hold a press conference later in the day. Until then, keep your mouths shut. Got it?"

Everyone in the room nodded yes except Jake. He had decided not to tell Carson that he also had a meeting with the Feds tomorrow. It might be a decision he would regret later but for now there was already enough tension between him, James, and Carson.

James and Jake asked Sheriff Carson if they could remain behind after the meeting.

James started. "We want to follow up on our trip to the cabin. We're sorry we didn't call you before we left. It was a mistake and we should have known better."

Carson's eyes were now laser focused on James, and not in a good way.

James started to summarize their trip to the cabin to include asking Carson if Ricky had called him about rescheduling the interview. After a few minutes Carson looked like he was going to explode.

"It's none of your damn business if Ricky called. I asked you to be careful and to let us take the lead on police stuff." Carson said. "You knew there was a BOLO out on Ricky! You didn't know how he was going to react when cornered. What if something stupid happened and one of you got yourselves killed? Just as bad, now the guy is on the run because of you two. I should have you arrested."

Carson stood and pointed toward the door. "Look, I know there is more to this story that you're not telling me. But I don't care. Nothing you've said changes the course of this investigation. In fact, it reinforces that Julia is our number one suspect. Last, are you really trying to convince me, James, that you chased down a man in his mid-forties? I'm going to be laughing about that one all the way home. Did you tell

Marilyn this story? Someday, over drinks, I want to hear the real deal. Now, get the hell out of here."

Once out in the parking lot, James and Jake had a tough time containing themselves. Jake was laughing so hard he doubled over. Then James noticed Carson, looking out his office window and giving them the finger. James grabbed Jake. "Let's get out of here before we end up in the cell next to Julia."

After dismissing Jake and James, Carson summoned Walker back to his office to discuss next steps in the investigation.

"James made some good points about Kenny," Carson said. "We've looked at him from a distance. Maybe it's time we got up close and personal with a search warrant for his house."

Walker nodded. "I agree, but probable cause isn't a gut feeling," he said flatly. "We need facts tying Kenny to Sophie's murder, not just his slightly odd behavior or an old argument."

Carson nodded, tapping a pen against his notebook. "What I'm struggling with is the bridge—something that puts him in motion that night."

Walker shifted forward. "It's close," he said. "There's motive, but too many inconsistencies. A judge is going to ask what we expect to find in Kenny's house—clothes, a weapon, evidence of planning. If we can articulate that clearly, we might get the warrant."

Carson closed his notebook. "Get Yang and Ryan to tighten up the timeline from Monday night, firm up the confrontation angle, and build a convincing argument about the ten-year-old connection between Sophie, Ricky, and Kenny. One more piece, and we're there."

Ten minutes into his drive home, flashing lights filled James's rearview mirror and he eased his Corvette onto the shoulder of US-85.

Deputy Ryan walked up with a half-smile, tapping on the glass. "Colonel, you were moving a little quick out here—clocked you just shy of 65 in a 55-mph zone," he said, leaning down.

James handed over his license with a polite nod. "Long meeting with Sheriff Carson, Ryan. Guess I was still running the conversation in my head."

The deputy studied him for a moment, then handed the license back, coughing hard in the process. "I'll let you off with a warning this time. Just keep it closer to the limit—we don't need any more excitement around the residents of Warriors Way."

James held his breath trying to avoid getting Ryan's germs and smiled. "Fair enough, Deputy. I'll behave."

Before moving on James emptied a small bottle of Purell into his hands and rubbed vigorously. During the rest of the drive, James felt the weight of the case pressed down on him in a way he hadn't expected. Julia's pending charges felt like a punch to the gut—despite the evidence, part of him still hoped there'd be an explanation that didn't end in a courtroom. He kept replaying their neighborhood conversations, her laughter at trivia night, the way she spoke about books and her career. It all felt surreal.

As James reached C-470, he called Marilyn. "Hey, how about if we meet in twenty minutes at Red Rocks? I need to talk, and I can't shake this horrible feeling."

Marilyn paused, then said, "Faith is here. I'll bring her too. Tell us as much as you want, but I can't leave her."

At the restaurant, the three of them found a booth away from other customers. The clink of silverware and low hum of conversation filled the tavern. As they dug into their dinners, James carefully and gently laid it all out—female DNA under Sophie's nails, the doorbell cameras, the blood trail, the connection to Sophie, and his growing certainty about Ricky, Kenny, and Sophie's ties to the opioid industry and federal investigations.

Faith sat silently, listening intently, while Marilyn slowly shook her head. "Faith, I know this is all hard to believe. It is for us too. We need to stay positive and hope it is all resolved quickly," she murmured.

James nodded, staring into his beer. "I agree. Also, Jake is meeting with the Feds tomorrow. I have a good feeling for some reason."

"I hope you're right," Marilyn said.

Faith looked at the couple helplessly. "So . . . Mom's in jail with charges pending for Sophie's murder? And Dad's sitting in a cell for lying to the sheriff. What happens now?"

Marilyn sighed, setting down her glass of beer. "It's not over, Faith. The DA still has to build a case, and we all know there are pieces missing. Your mom being held doesn't mean we've got the whole truth."

James's gaze went momentarily to a 1967 Shelby GT 500 Mustang parked outside the window. Then he looked back at Faith. "Exactly. Your mom might have hit Sophie in a moment of frustration or rage, but there's a bigger story here and too many connections that don't line up. I think your dad's misstatements are more tied to confusion and disbelief than anything else. It's common when people find themselves in stressful situations like these. The brain often mixes reality with wishful thinking. The result can be answers or statements that may be taken out of context."

Faith started to look more hopeful.

James continued. "Look, you need to be stronger than you've ever been in your life. We'll be here for you and your parents no matter what happens. Can you stay here for at least this week and work remotely?"

Faith nodded. "I already cleared it with my boss. Not a problem."

When James and Marilyn got home, they hugged for a long time. Neither knew what the coming days and weeks would bring. James had the same positive feeling he mentioned earlier. Could the meetings with the Feds tomorrow be a breakthrough?

At the Carson ranch on Sunday night, Jason sat with his wife, Trudie, at their kitchen table.

"Every road I walk down has too many unknowns," he said quietly. "Nothing feels solid."

Trudie nodded her head in support.

He looked up at her. "On paper, Julia's our prime suspect. The proximity, the confrontation, the odd behavior, the inconsistencies—it all points her way. But I can't shake it, Trudie. She just doesn't fit. Not for something this brutal."

"So, who does?" she asked gently.

Carson sighed. "Ricky Delgado, for one. A marriage rotting

from the inside and too many secrets and lies. And then there's Kenny—anger issues, history with Sophie, real motive if you scratch the surface. Either of them makes more sense than Julia ever will. There also may be people from their past who wanted to send a message." His jaw tightened. "Meanwhile the press wants a headline, the governor and county leadership want closure, a congresswoman wants a false narrative, and they all want it yesterday. They don't care if it's right, just that it's done."

Trudie stood and wrapped her arms around him, resting her cheek against his shoulder. "I know that look," she said softly. "It's the one you get when the noise is loud, but your gut is louder."

Carson exhaled, the tension leaving him. "I just don't want to get this wrong," he said.

Trudie squeezed him a little tighter. "You won't. You never take the easy path, Jason. You'll do what's right—and you'll make sure Sophie gets real justice."

Carson poured himself a glass of wine and took a sip. "I have an early morning meeting with the Feds tomorrow. I think they'll help me with the unknowns on this case. At least, I hope so."

MONDAY

CHAPTER THIRTY-ONE

Monday Morning

At precisely 8 a.m., the front doors of the funeral home in Centennial swung open to reveal an elderly couple stepping slowly inside. They moved with the heavy stillness of grief, their expressions worn and vacant, the weight of the past week etched deeply into their faces. The staff greeted them with quiet reverence and led them to a private room where, after signing the final documents, they were handed the remains of their daughter, legally listed as Katherine L. Jennings. Her mother took the small, ceramic container with trembling hands and instinctively wrapped it in a pale, handmade baby blanket she had kept since Kate's childhood. It was faded pink with delicate stitching, and for a moment, the mother simply held it in her lap, rocking slightly, as if trying to comfort what was no longer there. Her father looked on, beyond all hope, expecting to see the beautiful face and rich blue eyes of his beloved daughter safely captured in his wife's arms. It was not to be, and once again, he wondered why a life filled with so much promise had ended so violently on a quiet neighborhood street in Colorado.

Across the road, sitting behind the tinted glass of his dusty SUV, Ricky watched from the driver's seat, a weathered hunting jacket pulled around him and a Broncos cap shading his eyes. He hadn't moved in an hour, but when he saw them walk out, their pain unmistakable, a fresh wave of guilt tightened in his chest. Kate's mother slid into the passenger seat of the car, cradling the urn in the baby blanket like something fragile and sacred. Her father circled around to the driver's side, pausing for a moment before climbing in, his hand wiping at tears he no longer had the strength to hide. As they drove away, Ricky watched their car disappear in the morning traffic. He stayed frozen in place, watching the last thread of his old life unravel and vanish, leaving only the questions, the silence, and the ache of everything that had gone so terribly wrong.

Minutes later, Ricky got out of his SUV and stood in the shadow of a hardware store across from the funeral home, hands shoved deep into his coat pockets, the ball cap pulled low. One of his handlers, Agent Morales, approached with another agent trailing a few steps behind. "You saw them take her?" Morales asked quietly.

Ricky nodded, eyes still fixed on the morning traffic. "Yeah," he muttered. "Kate's parents looked like ghosts. I shouldn't have been here … but I had to see it."

Morales exhaled slowly. "You were told to maintain distance."

Ricky snapped his gaze up. "I kept my distance. After everything I did for you people. That girl deserved someone here. I was a jerk to her at the end, but she was my wife, and a part of me still loves her."

Agent Dwyer stepped closer, voice firm. "Ricky, we need to talk about next steps. Things are too hot for you with press reporting and that black SUV circling. We're not sure who they are, but it's not us. We need to get you out of here. What about your stuff at the Warriors Way property?"

"I'm not going back there," Ricky asserted. "Not for a night. Not for an hour. Not for a damn toothbrush." He stepped back, breath ragged. "Sophie's murder changed everything. The whole street is crawling with tension, neighbors looking at each other sideways. It's only a matter of time before someone connects dots they shouldn't."

Morales held up a calming hand. "We understand. But relocation protocols aren't simple. You don't just get to pick up and vanish."

Ricky jabbed a finger at her. "I earned a little leeway. I want out of Colorado. Get me to California—northern coast, quiet town, something off the map. I know you have private jets sitting on the tarmac at Centennial Airport. Get me out of here today."

Dwyer frowned. "That's not exactly how this works."

"Then make it work. You know the threats on me aren't dying down, and after Kate . . . I can't breathe in this state anymore."

Morales exchanged a look with Dwyer, then sighed. "Fine. We'll initiate the request. But Ricky . . . you need to come with us now and stay quiet until we give the word. Oh, and what about Donna?"

Ricky adjusted his hat and handed Dwyer his car keys. "Staying quiet is the only damned thing I've got left. And there are plenty of Donnas in California, but I'm going to ask for your help with something. I've got money set aside to fund her kids' college. I just need a legal way to funnel the money into some type of 529 plan. I'm sure that won't be too difficult for one of your resourceful colleagues to figure out."

Morales nodded her approval.

Three miles away, Jake did a quick morning workout and dressed in his best blue suit. He was on the road by 10 a.m., heading to the Denver field office. Jake was good friends with the Special Agent In-Charge. They had worked side by side for three years on an organized crime task force. When Jake arrived, he found a spot in the visitors' parking lot and headed to the front entrance. The guard at the reception desk had a visitor's badge waiting.

Moments later, a young agent arrived and escorted Jake to a windowless room on the fourth floor. Two agents were waiting. Another young agent had a folder filled with forms. Jake was asked to sign a non-disclosure statement and a temporary read-on for law-enforcement-sensitive information. Once done, the agent left, and another agent entered the room. It was John the builder, James's next-door neighbor, but that was not the name on his credentials. The badge read Agent Steve Gilbert. Gilbert and Jake looked at each other and smiled.

Jake finally laughed. "I knew there was something going on with you. Remind me to never let you do work on my house."

Gilbert smiled. "Agreed. I'm the Denver senior handler for six people in the witness protection program," he explained. "All are providing valuable services in addressing cases tied to the opioid crisis and organized crime in Nevada, Colorado, and other western states. And Ricky is the most important. Another Deer Park Ridge resident is almost as important; you know him as Kenny, from one street over. He was a lawyer and financial manager and knew how the bad guys moved and protected their money. And the house on Warriors Way is a place we've had for years. It's been a good place to meet different clients."

"I know all about Kenny. By the way, I'll tell James not to expect any real progress with your home renovations."

Gilbert continued. "Early last fall, there was an altercation between Sophie and Kenny about his dog and other things. Apparently, the dog had gotten into her prized rose bushes. It was the end of the season, so I'm not sure why it was so important, but it was. Sophie lost control. She even tried to kick the dog a couple of times. Kenny went to hit her, but Ricky came out just in time and pushed him away. Sophie threatened to call an old friend and have him killed. Kenny was shocked, scared, and angry. Sophie even mentioned that she knew people were looking for him."

Jake interrupted. "How did you get all these details?"

"Kenny talked to Ricky and me after the incident. We thought it all was taken care of until Monday night. Kenny was walking his dog and apparently saw the altercation between Julia and Sophie. After Julia walked away, he followed Sophie to the end of the street. They started to argue, she pushed him, and he hit her with his golf club. The dog jumped up at her, and she kicked it in the ribs. Then Kenny lost it and beat her to death. He leaned her body on the post, which we think was a message to Ricky."

"How do you know all this detail?" Jake asked.

The agent smiled. "Everything was captured on the hidden high-resolution security camera from my top deck on Monday night. James's daughter, Robin, had it right."

Jake was flabbergasted. "Why is this information just coming out now? Did Carson know you might have video?"

Agent Gilbert nodded. "Carson knew about it, but we had a technical delay downloading the video. We weren't sure if we had anything. One of my tech guys figured it out yesterday. We could have saved Todd and Julia Krantz a lot of heartache otherwise. But rest assured that new information will reach the Spirit County Sheriff's Department in the next few hours, exonerating them. They'll be released early this evening."

Jake was relieved. "What about Kenny? What happens to him?"

"That's a more complicated question," Gilbert explained. "I'm not 100 percent sure about the timing. He'll be arrested and prosecuted. We'll have to work out the details with Carson because we still need Kenny for our investigations. We're sure Ricky knows what happened between Sophie and Kenny, and we assume he'll lie low for now. That's about all I can tell you. Let me remind you that you've signed a non-disclosure agreement. If you reveal or repeat anything from this meeting, you will be prosecuted. That includes your friend, James. Understand?"

"Not so fast," Jake protested. "So, let's talk about what's really driving this case and the connection with Big Pharma and the illegal sale of prescription drugs. You know that I know that Ricky, Sophie, and Kenny were involved in big cases related to the opioid crisis."

Agent Gilbert nodded.

"I need clarity here," Jake said. "You've known Ricky, aka Bruce Bricklin, and Kenny, aka Fredrick Lee, were both tied into the pill network, but what's their role going forward? If

I'm going to make a difference in protecting the good people of Warriors Way, I need to know whether these two are assets or a threat, because right now, they're acting like both."

The agent looked hard into Jake's eyes. "Your interest in this case has been about a woman murdered on Warriors Way last Monday night. That case is solved. Ricky and Kenny's value to federal law enforcement on several complex criminal and civil cases is out of your lane. Yes, there is a real connection between the Vegas storyline and the opioid cases. Leave it alone."

"Look, it's my understanding that you and James have been extremely helpful to Sheriff Carson. Again, that case is about Sophie's murder. Take the win, Jake. I strongly suggest you leave everything else up to us, or you two knuckleheads will find your nice retirements suddenly get complicated. IRS audits, disruptions to your pensions or social security, or Medicare claims being denied or taking a long time to resolve. Are you starting to understand me, my friend?"

Jake looked at Gilbert and nodded in frustration.

Gilbert went on. "Sheriff Carson was fully briefed this morning on everything I just told you. The arrest warrant for Kenny is being finalized as we speak. Carson understands the importance of backing off on the larger factors surrounding this case, and he has agreed to move on. Again, you and James had better do the same. And don't think your friendship with my boss will save you if you don't."

Jake took a deep breath and nodded in agreement. He was handed another form to sign that revoked his temporary access to law enforcement-sensitive information. It was almost 2 p.m. when Jake finished his meeting. As he drove home, Gilbert's one-way conversation, or, more accurately, outright threat, played repeatedly in his mind. After about twenty minutes, he relaxed. Carson and his federal buddies would do the right thing, and justice would be served. Time to move on.

Shortly after Jake left for home, Kenny made a phone call, his voice shaky and breathless when the line connected to Gilbert's office. "I'm in trouble. You and Agent Miller don't get it, man—they know where I am. I saw a black SUV parked across from my house all night. Same one from last week."

There was a pause before Gilbert spoke in a low, steady tone. "Kenny, slow down. You've called us three times in twenty-four hours. You're safe. No one's coming after you."

Kenny's words tumbled over each other. "Safe? Sophie's dead, Ricky was here yesterday mornin' threatenin' me, and I'm next. I can feel it."

"Kenny, listen to me," Gilbert said firmly, his voice clipped but calm. "If there was a credible threat, I'd have a team at your door right now. You need to stick to the plan, stay where you are, and stop drawing attention to yourself."

Kenny's breathing came fast through the phone. "Stay put? You're askin' me to sit here and wait for a bullet in the head."

Gilbert sighed. "I'm asking you to trust the process. If you run, you'll be alone and vulnerable. If you stay, I can protect you."

Kenny was quiet for a moment, then muttered, "Yeah . . . I've heard that before." Then Kenny's voice became gravelly and uneven. "Gilbert . . . I took care of Sophie that night, one less threat."

Gilbert was careful with his words, not wanting to let Kenny know there was a warrant for his arrest pending. "You're telling me you killed her?"

Kenny exhaled shakily and blurted out everything he was thinking, barely taking time to breathe. "She turned on me. Said she was goin' to spill everythin'—names, dates, the whole operation. You see, we were partners, and I made us all rich by embezzlin' from the fraudsters for almost seven years. I figured out how to skim over $47 million from offshore account transactions, and the idiot bosses, families, and drug corporations were clueless. But suddenly bein' rich wasn't good enough for Sophie. She was sick of livin' in Colorado and sick of Ricky. Especially after she found out he took Donna to their Vail condo in December. Honestly, it broke her heart."

"What does Ricky's affair have to do with you, Kenny?"

"She blamed me for everythin' wrong in her life just because I started the money thing. She claimed I was the one who pulled Ricky into black-market sales, which was bullshit. That was all Ricky's doin'. Suddenly, Sophie wanted to move back to Dallas and reclaim her life as Kate Jennings. That would have been a death sentence for all of us. When I saw her arguin' and fightin' with Julia that night, I knew it was my chance. She was distracted . . . vulnerable. I figured Julia would take the blame."

"You need to understand what you're saying right now," Gilbert said. "You're confessing to murder."

Kenny's words spilled out faster, and he became even more frantic. "It wasn't planned! After Julia walked away, Sophie saw me standin' there. She started yellin' and laughin' at me. I walked over and hit her hard with my golf club. Then she saw

James and Marilyn in their kitchen window and screamed for James to come save her. What a joke. I would have killed that pathetic jerk, too. He accused me of cheatin' during a local golf tournament a couple years ago and we were teammates. His stupidity cost us second place. Plus, it was embarrassin'."

Gilbert was fidgeting and seemingly getting a little bored. "Did you cheat?"

"Hell, yes, I cheated. So what? It wasn't the Masters."

"Kenny, please continue."

"After I finished Sophie off, I put her up against the post. It was a message to all the clowns on Warriors Way who gave me a hard time about my pajamas and not always cleanin' up after King." Kenny paused and took a deep breath. "Listen to me, Gilbert. If she had talked, I'd be dead within a week. I didn't have a choice."

Gilbert's reply was cold and deliberate. "You always have a choice, Kenny. And you made one that's going to end everything for you."

The wind off the Pacific carried the smell of salt and kelp as the two people walked the wet, packed sand near the bluffs. Ricky, now Dave Canyon, kept his hands in the pockets of his light jacket, sunglasses on despite the fading sun.

"I landed two hours ago, and I'm already a new man," he said, a crooked smile tugging at his mouth. "Private jets are hell on the environment, but they're efficient."

Agent Morales didn't smile back. "Efficiency is why you're still breathing," she said evenly. "But don't confuse speed with safety. The next six months are going to be hard—pretrial motions, sealed testimony, names you thought were buried coming back up. You keep your head down; you keep your mouth shut."

Dave glanced toward the horizon, the sun sliding toward the water. "I can do quiet," he said. "I've been practicing it for the last ten years."

They turned toward the path that led up from the beach, Morales's shoes crunching against the gravel. "Quiet means boring," she continued. "No old habits. No reconnecting. No curiosity about who's asking questions back in Deer Park Ridge. No Donna. You're Dave Canyon now—freelance consultant, a widower who likes long walks and bad coffee."

Dave laughed softly. "You forgot the part where I'm haunted and remorseful."

Morales stopped and faced him. "I didn't forget," she said. "I just don't care. Trials are coming, Dave. You're a witness, not a spectator. One slip—one drink too many, one conversation with the wrong person—and the protection goes away."

He raised his hands in mock surrender. "Message received."

As they headed back toward town and the agents' car, the lights of Half Moon Bay, California, flickered on, bars already filling with the Monday after-work crowd. Dave's gaze lingered on a place with open windows and music spilling out onto the street. He saw at least three women go in that piqued his interest.

"Low profile doesn't mean monastic, right?" he said.

Morales followed his eyes, then shook her head. "It means you blend in, not stand out," she replied. "One beer. Early nights. And remember, you don't exist to anyone who asks. Oh, and the fedora is out, and casual beach attire is your new thing."

Dave nodded, already calculating, already drifting. "Understood. I'll be invisible."

After the agents drove away, he walked over to the doorway of the lively bar. He felt a soft ribbon of Pacific air curl around his ankles. He smiled as a jolt of energy coursed through his body, a feeling he thought had died long ago.

After a few moments Dave walked back toward his new apartment. Across the parking lot he could hear the muted crash of waves and, somewhere beyond the low fog laid the promise of wide fairways and greens cut clean against the coast. Golf clubs, he thought—real ones this time, not the battered set he'd borrowed years ago, something high quality and professionally fitted to give his days shape and hours a reason to move forward. Two local courses, both perched on cliffs like they had nothing to fear, seemed to offer exactly what he needed: long walks, quiet concentration, and the comforting illusion that a man could still improve his swing even if the rest of his life had gone irrevocably off course.

This was a new beginning for him. No more Sophie or Kenny or smoking or drinking at that depressing tavern. He vowed to get himself back in shape and to start living life in the light and not the dark.

After the call with Agent Gilbert, Kenny sat alone with the confession still hanging in the air. He became emotional thinking about Sophie and what he had done to a friend and former lover; it was almost too much to bear. For a few reckless months last summer, she had made him feel seen again, not as a neighbor or a nuisance, but as a man whose attention still mattered. He replayed her laughter, the way she'd touched him as if it meant something permanent, even though he knew, even then, it didn't. Sophie wanted to move on from Ricky, Colorado, her secret life, and yes, him. When she ended it on Labor Day weekend, calmly and without drama, he told himself he understood. He said it was for the best. But what he felt was humiliation, not acceptance, and that feeling calcified into something darker as the months passed.

The argument in October came back to him with cruel clarity. It hadn't just been about King trampling her garden, that was the story he let everyone believe. He'd gone to her house that afternoon because he couldn't stand the finality of her silence, because he wanted her to reconsider, to admit that what they'd had hadn't been a mistake. Sophie hadn't yelled; that was the worst part. She'd been firm, controlled, and unmoved, telling him it was over and that he needed to leave her alone. She also told him she was thinking about moving back to Texas to be close to her family and old friends. At that moment, he knew she was a vulnerability he might have to address. In the end, Sophie said she was sorry and hoped he would forgive her.

It was Kenny who momentarily lost control and escalated the conversation to a confrontation that required Ricky's intervention. He understood the truth he had refused to see then: it wasn't love that drove him back to her door that day, and it wasn't love that fueled his rage. It was the terror of being erased, and Sophie, by choosing to walk away, had done exactly that.

Kenny now moved through his house in a frenzy, muttering to himself. His hands shook as he double-checked every lock on the doors and windows, glancing through the blinds at the street below. The black SUV wasn't there anymore, but in his mind, its shadow still lingered.

In his bedroom, Kenny pulled a duffel bag from the closet and began filling it with clothes, a small first-aid kit, and a worn leather pouch holding neat stacks of hundred-dollar bills. Next came the $500 gift cards, three fake IDs with his face and different names, and two sleek black credit cards tied to untraceable offshore accounts. He zipped the bag tight and carried it to his car, tossing it onto the passenger seat beside a backpack with bottled water and protein bars.

After loading King into the back seat of his BMW SUV, he slid behind the wheel, fired up the engine and sat for a moment, staring at his beautiful home and thinking about his late wife. With tears streaming down his face, he left. There would be no coming back.

Kenny slowed as he neared the entrance to Warriors Way. James and Marilyn were on their front deck with another couple. Kenny knew his hate for James was irrational, but so what? Not much in his life these days was rational. For an instant, he contemplated turning. How satisfying it would be to smash James's skull as he had Sophie's. But time was not on his side, so he drove on and left the neighborhood.

Kenny's early evening departure from Deer Park Ridge coincided with the Spirit County court issuing a warrant for his arrest. A BOLO to all law enforcement agencies in Colorado followed moments later. Kenny's timing to go on the run could not have been worse as he gripped the steering wheel, sweat rolling down his temples as the speedometer pushed past ninety heading down I-25. His car was spotted almost immediately by the state patrol and the pursuit began.

Carson was leaving his office near I-25 with his driver when an alert was issued, and he joined the chase.

Suddenly the black SUV appeared behind Kenny. It shadowed his every move as if their actions were perfectly choreographed.

"Come on, come on." he muttered under his breath, weaving between cars as the wail of sirens grew louder.

Kenny looked in the rear-view mirror and laughed momentarily at the irony of being chased by both the cops and the sinister black SUV.

Sheriff Carson's voice crackled over the radio to the lead Spirit County Sheriff's cruiser. "Keep him boxed in when we hit the next stretch."

The dispatcher's voice came back, calm but urgent: "Copy that. We've got units setting up just north of Colorado Springs."

As the sheriff and state patrol vehicles moved into position, the black SUV peeled away and fell behind slower moving traffic.

By the time Kenny roared past the Air Force Academy, two state patrol SUVs slid into position ahead of him, their light bars flashing like beacons in the early evening glare. Carson's SUV raced up behind Kenny. Using the integrated loudspeaker, Carson issued a loud and clear warning. "Kenny, pull over before someone gets hurt!"

But Kenny just clenched his jaw and pressed harder on the gas—until a sudden PIT maneuver from a trailing patrol unit sent the BMW skidding sideways. Tires screeched, the smell of burning rubber filled the air, and the car spun onto the shoulder, dust billowing.

Kenny sat trembling in the driver's seat, cruiser lights strobing across the inside of the cab as King barked frantically from the back seat. "King ... buddy, hey—easy, boy," Kenny said, voice cracking as he wiped at the wetness on his face.

But King only barked louder, pacing in the narrow space, nails clicking on the plastic protective mat. "I know, I know," Kenny whispered, clutching the steering wheel. "They're just here to talk. They're not gonna' hurt you."

Outside, deputies shouted orders he barely heard because King's frantic yelps drowned everything else out.

"King, please," Kenny begged, twisting in his seat to look at him. "I'm sorry, boy. I'm so sorry about everythin'."

The dog whimpered now, confused and frightened, still watching the shapes moving outside the windows.

Kenny choked on his own breath. "I messed up. I told them ... I told them what happened. They ... they're comin' because of me, not you."

King barked again, sharp and worried, and Kenny closed his eyes. "You're my only friend left, King," he said softly. "Just ... just stay calm, okay? Let's get through this."

Carson jumped out of his SUV before it fully stopped, weapon drawn. "Hands where I can see them!"

Kenny, still in his vehicle, was breathing hard as he yelled out the window. "Carson ... you don't understand—they're gonna' kill me!"

Carson's expression stayed flat. "You'd better get your hands up, or we're going to kill you. Now shut up, you're going to jail."

Kenny's SUV sat idling on the shoulder of I-25, steam curling from the grill. Deputies crouched behind their vehicles, rifles aimed, while the whine of the loudspeaker cut through the wind. Kenny sat in his vehicle and suddenly put a handgun to his head.

"Kenny! Put the gun down!" Carson's voice boomed across the asphalt.

The driver's door creaked open, and Kenny stumbled out, his face slick with sweat. He raised a trembling hand, pressing the barrel of a Glock 19 to his temple. "Don't come any closer!" he shouted hoarsely. "I'm done . . . I can't go back!"

Carson took a careful step forward, his hands out. "You don't have to do this, Kenny. We can fix this, just drop the gun."

Kenny's voice cracked as tears streaked down his cheeks. "Fix it? My wife's dead . . . and now I've gone and ruined everythin', I didn't mean to kill her. Sophie wasn't supposed to die. She just—she threatened me and wouldn't stop screamin'."

The deputies exchanged looks but held their ground. Carson's voice softened, breaking through the sirens and static. "It's over, Kenny. Let us help you."

Kenny shook his head, sobbing. "I'm sorry . . . please find someone to take care of King."

Then he pulled the trigger.

The scene was momentarily silent until King started barking and howling from the back of Kenny's SUV. Slowly the sheriff and state patrol officers holstered their weapons and secured the crime scene. It was an ending to the pursuit that no one wanted.

Returning to his SUV, Carson knelt and said an emotional prayer. He then called Walker and told him what happened.

When he stood and turned around, there was a flurry of activity around the crime scene and on his radio.

The occupants of the black SUV eventually worked their way through traffic and continued south on I-25. The chaotic scene around Kenny's vehicle sent a clear message that their job was done. After a couple of quick phone calls, they headed to the airport in Colorado Springs, turned in their rental, and booked outbound flights.

CHAPTER THIRTY-TWO

Monday Evening

While Kenny's escape from Deer Park Ridge was ongoing, Jake and his wife were enjoying drinks and dinner at the Brooksides' house. They sat on the front deck on an unusually warm March evening with a seemingly bottomless supply of dirty martinis with blue cheese olives. The view stretched east toward Denver, sparkling under the darkening spring sky. Marilyn and Dee excused themselves to make a salad.

Jake raised his glass. "To one bizarre week. We've done our duty. It's time to get back to our normal lives." Since the Brooksides knew where he had spent the afternoon, a key question for Jake to consider was what to tell them.

James wondered about the curious toast, but it was time to fire up the grill and cook four beautiful steaks. After James finished his magic, the two couples sat down to eat.

Jake smiled and opened the conversation. "Are you ready for one hell of a story?"

He told them almost everything. The hidden high-resolution camera on John's top deck. The confrontation between Julia and Sophie. Kenny stepping in later and killing Sophie. The pending warrant for Kenny's arrest. Sophie's game. Kenny's game. Ricky's game. How the federal law enforcement agencies were still running with both the organized crime and opioid crisis cases. How Todd and Julia would be exonerated and released. The threat that he and James better backoff from their investigation or face repercussions from the Feds. He didn't tell them about John the builder's real identity. That was a detail he would keep to himself.

At one point James let out an involuntary gasp as he took in the information. He had suspected Kenny was the killer, but hearing it confirmed was almost overwhelming. After Jake finished, the four agreed to save further discussions and questions for another day.

After a great meal and too many martinis, they enjoyed dessert. James reminded Jake that they had committed to a gig at Red Rocks on Thursday night. Jake reminded James, "Keep your mouth shut, or we'll both end up in trouble."

Dee escorted Jake to the car and helped him into the passenger seat. "No driving for you tonight."

As Dee drove home, Jake leaned back, watching the dark ribbon of road unspool in the headlights.

"I hate to admit it," he said, a crooked smile tugging at his mouth, "but this past week lit me up. Talking through Sophie's murder with James—timelines, motives, the little things that didn't quite line up—it felt like slipping back into an old uniform. I didn't realize how much I missed the work until my brain started firing again."

Dee smiled without taking her eyes off the road, her fingers relaxed on the steering wheel. "I could tell," she said gently. "You've got that look—half excited, half dangerous. Just remember, you also had three bucket-sized martinis. So, let's agree it's a mix of fond memories and good gin talking. Tomorrow you can go back to being happily retired."

As things settled at the crash site, Deputy Michaels walked up to Carson with King on a leash. "Boss, any thoughts on what we should do with the dog?"

Carson smiled. "I have a plan."

Carson picked up his phone and dialed James's number. His voice was strained, but steady. "James, it's Carson. We had a wild one this evening. Kenny led a host of deputies on a car chase down I-25. Tried to lose us near the Air Force Academy, but he lost control and ended up boxed in. It didn't end well. He committed suicide before we could get to him. It was a bad scene."

James was already fully aware from Jake that Kenny would be arrested, but this was a horrible ending to an already bad week. Lives had been turned upside down on Warriors Way, and now two neighbors were dead.

"Thank you, Jason. I know your department did their best. I keep thinking about Todd and Julia. They've been through so much this week. What will happen to them?"

"I'm sure things will work out fine. And James, please give Jake a call and let him know what happened. I have to update the governor, a congresswoman, and hold a press conference to put this shitstorm to rest." He paused, then added, "And there's something else. Deputy Michaels will be swinging by your house in the morning with important paperwork for you to sign. It's tied to the investigation. Nothing to worry about. Just routine. Later, my friend."

Faith was 25 miles away, waiting at the courthouse to pick up her parents. It had been a long and miserable week. Neither Todd nor Julia knew all the details, other than that another suspect had been named, and their nightmare was over. As they walked toward the entrance, Julia saw one of the deputies who questioned her. He was talking to another person who appeared to be a lawyer. It was hard to hear, but she was certain he said an arrest warrant was issued for Kenny or something. Kenny Jacobs? She now knew who had been hiding in the shadows. It all made sense.

James talked to Todd after he got home and told him about Kenny. Finally, the craziness had ended, and the friends could get back to normal. They agreed to meet in the morning to talk in more detail.

After James's call with Todd, Marilyn rested her hand gently on his arm, her voice soft but steady. "I know, James. The suspicion and pointed questions could poison our friendship with Todd and Julia. But with the truth coming out, it will give everyone a chance to breathe again."

James smiled. "I just want our friendship with them back the way it was. They're like family."

She paused, meeting his eyes. "They may need some time, but I know we'll find our way."

Julia, Todd, and Faith sat around their dining room table in a heavy, unfamiliar quiet, the house feeling smaller than it had been a week ago.

"I keep replaying it," Todd said. "Every call, every decision. So many bad turns. We thought we were managing things, controlling the damage—but we were just digging ourselves in deeper."

Julia nodded, her eyes rimmed red. "We told ourselves it was temporary," she said. "That if we just held on a little longer, it would sort itself out. Instead, we made everything worse." She took a breath and looked at her daughter. "I need to say this out loud," she ventured unsteadily. "I'm sorry. For what I did. For what I didn't say. I thought I was protecting everyone, but I was really protecting myself."

Todd swallowed hard. "Me too," he added. "I should have stopped it. I should have told the truth sooner. I was afraid— afraid of what we'd lose, afraid of what it would mean." He exhaled slowly. "Now we don't even know what comes next. Charges, no charges . . . that's for our lawyer, the DA, and Carson's team to sort out in the coming days."

Faith reached across the table and took both of their hands, her grip firm, grounding. "I don't care about any of that tonight," she said softly. "All I know is that you're home. I was terrified I'd walk out of that courthouse alone."

Her eyes filled, but she smiled through it. "I'm just . . . relieved. Relieved we're sitting here, telling the truth to each other, breathing the same air. Not tonight, but at some point, Mom, I'd like you to tell me more about Angela. I know she was very special to you."

Julia smiled.

"And whatever happens next, we'll face it together," Faith said. "But there is one more thing. James and Marilyn were wonderful to me these past few days even though you both were lying to them. I hope you'll make amends and help them understand what you were going through. Otherwise, it will be hard to ever reclaim your friendship."

Down the street, Marilyn sat curled in her recliner, the lamp throwing a soft amber circle across the living room. James was in his spot on the couch, his hands folded the way they were when his mind refused to rest. Her thoughts drifted back to the discussion she had with her Chief Medical Officer, Greg Litton, on Thursday—his voice steady, almost gentle. You think you're fine because you've seen worse, he'd said, but trauma has a way of sinking in when you least expect it. At the time, she'd nodded, professional and composed, but now the words pressed against her chest with uncomfortable accuracy.

She studied James in the half-light, the lines in his face deeper than they had been a week ago. He hadn't said much since Carson's call and their brief discussion about Todd and Julia. Now he sat there with a distant stare toward the darkened windows. Marilyn knew that look too well—the old instinct to analyze, to reconstruct every moment, to find the thread that would make sense of the chaos. Her CMOs warning echoed again: unresolved trauma doesn't just haunt victims, it attaches itself to the people who try to understand it. James had always believed that if you pulled hard enough on the truth, order would follow. Tonight, she wasn't so sure that belief was protecting him anymore.

She moved to the couch, close enough to feel his warmth, and rested her head lightly on his shoulder. What worried her most wasn't fear, but his need to make things right—to fix what couldn't be fixed, to answer a call that no longer had a living voice on the other end. She understood it; she even admired it. But as the house settled into its familiar nighttime creaks, Marilyn wondered how much weight a person could carry before the past stopped being a problem to solve and became something that quietly reshaped who they were.

She'd watch him closely for the next few months to make sure he didn't try to take ownership of this past week's tragic events. Greg had mentioned strength and stewardship, something they both needed. Marilyn was now truly grateful that she had the week off so they could be there for one another and for their neighbors on Warriors Way.

She smiled at James and thought. "Maybe a few rides in the Corvette over the next weeks would also help."

———————

Later that evening, James took time to capture his last thoughts on Sophie's murder and Kenny's death.

March 23: Hearing Kenny's name officially tied to Sophie's murder feels both shocking and inevitable. I keep remembering his nervousness, the way his eyes flicked around as if danger lurked in every shadow. Turns out, maybe it did. Whether he lashed out in desperation or cold calculation, Sophie must have become a liability he couldn't manage. What unsettles me most is how long he lived among us, quiet, unremarkable, blending in, while carrying that kind of violence inside. It makes me wonder how many more masks are being worn on Warriors Way.

Julia and Todd's return to the very same street where their lives unraveled—it's surreal, almost unnatural in its normalcy. Still, there's a difference between legal guilt and moral innocence. Kenny may have murdered Sophie, but I can't help thinking that Julia still carries part of the blame. She attacked Sophie, a neighbor, a wife, and a lonely woman who had made a mistake more than twenty years ago and was seeking forgiveness.

On this Monday evening, I hope a sense of peace will return to Warriors Way in the coming days and weeks. The lights on the horizon expand my perspective and reassure me that the world continues to spin and life goes on. Still, I cannot forget the horror of last Tuesday morning. The vision of Sophie at the end of the street will be with me forever . . .

James stopped writing and looked at Marilyn. He wondered whether he could have done anything more to change the tragic outcomes. There was no right answer to this question.

Perhaps all could have been avoided if we'd all embodied Ephesians 4:32: "Be kind and compassionate to one another, forgiving each other, just as in Christ God forgave you." But that was so often easier said than done.

He reflected on the words offered years ago by the pastor of his Virginia church. "We are all flawed, we are all imperfect." And this past week proved it.

EPILOGUE

On a beautiful Tuesday morning in mid-June with a mug of freshly brewed coffee, James was looking out of his kitchen window at the Warriors Way stop sign and reflecting on Sophie's death. It was a quiet time at Deer Park Ridge. Spring rains had turned everything green, providing nourishment for the local mule deer, wild turkeys, and other creatures. No one had seen or heard anything about Ricky since he disappeared in March. The Delgado and Jacobs homes were sold at auction for full market value, which made the neighbors happy that Sophie's murder hadn't hurt their precious property values. Charges were dropped against Julia and Todd in exchange for community service.

Suddenly, a flash of red streaked over Warriors Way and landed with an audible thud in the Deer Park Ridge Drive median, sixty yards from James's house. He realized it was a canopy with the cords tangled around what looked like a man. James quickly put a leash on King, his recently adopted Irish Wolfhound.

He headed out of his house past the stop sign and saw a man lying face up in the grass.

At the same time, Todd came running with his dogs. "Did you see him come down? He came from behind the foothills and went right over your house. A paraglider!"

Both men inched closer and suspected that the man was

dead as he wasn't moving. Still wearing his helmet and goggles, the harness clung to him. Lines tangled in the nearby pine tree and rabbitbrush. Next came the shocking observation. The victim was covered in blood, and the handle of a dagger was protruding from his chest.

James looked at Todd. "Somebody stabbed him before he hit the ground."

Cars slowed, drivers staring at the scene.

Todd swallowed hard. "It's only been three months since Sophie, James . . . and now we've got another body practically at the entrance to Warriors Way. What the hell is happening to this neighborhood?"

James pondered the irony of Todd's comment, hoping Julia didn't have a drawer full of daggers and hadn't been paragliding over their neighborhood today.

James turned, scanning the ridge line above his house. He saw Marilyn standing at the kitchen window, her hand covering her mouth. He looked back at the stranger and closed his eyes. Maybe Julia was right, it was time for him to start writing that murder mystery, maybe two.

ACKNOWLEDGEMENTS

First, I want to thank my wife, Michelle, for her unwavering love, patience, and wise counsel throughout the long journey of bringing *Death on Warriors Way* to life. Her sharp insights and honest advice made the story stronger, the characters more vivid, and the writing process far more enjoyable. She has been my sounding board, my fiercest critic, and my greatest champion, often all in the same conversation. I'm endlessly grateful for her presence through every step of this project.

To Russ, Christopher, Matthew, Wren, and Grace—thank you for serving as inspiration for five of the supporting characters. Matthew, thank you for your input on characters and writing, and for your painting on the back cover which provides a glimpse of the peaceful glory of life in Colorado.

To Jana, Tim, Barb, and Bill, I extend my heartfelt thanks for their support and constant encouragement. Their belief in my ability to finish this book, even during the moments when I doubted myself, meant more than I can put into words. Whether it was sharing a laugh, offering thoughtful feedback, or simply reminding me to keep going, their support gave me the energy and courage I needed to bring this story home.

To Betsy and Maggie, thank you for providing your expert advice on editing, formatting, uploading, and a dozen other critical tasks that were required to deliver *Death on Warriors Way* to readers, who will hopefully enjoy a fun and suspenseful murder mystery. To Jennie, thank you for recommending Betsy and Maggie, they have been wonderful.

To the book club women, thank you for taking time to read and comment on my draft novel. The roundtable discussions were informative and helped me refine key plotlines which improved the flow of the story. Also, it was the first time I've participated in a book club event. It was fun and I enjoyed being challenged by your thoughtful comments.

Finally, to all the friends, readers, and fellow storytellers who joined me on this journey, thank you for lending me your time, curiosity, and imagination. Writing *Death on Warriors Way* has been both a creative adventure and a labor of love, and it would not have been possible without you.

ABOUT THE AUTHOR

Death on Warriors Way is Dave Pyle's first novel. He lives in Colorado with his wife, Michelle, where the wide-open skies and rugged foothills of the Rockies provide daily inspiration for his writing. Dave enjoys spending time outdoors, embracing the Colorado lifestyle, and sharing life's adventures with Michelle.